A Certain
Slant
of Light

Also by Cynthia Thayer

Strong for Potatoes

A Certain Slant of Light

Cynthia Thayer

St. Martin's Griffin ❧ New York

www.stmartins.com

Library of Congress Cataloging-in-Publication Data
Thayer, Cynthia A.
    A certain slant of light / Cynthia Thayer.—1st ed.
        p.   cm.
    ISBN 0-312-26132-2 (hc)
    ISBN 0-312-27564-1 (pbk)
    1. Pregnant woman—Fiction. 2. Runaway wives—Fiction.
    Friendship—Fiction. 4. Widowers—Fiction. 5. Maine—Fiction.
    I. Title.
    PS3570.H344 C47   2000
    813'.54—dc21   00-028148

First St. Martin's Griffin Edition: July 2001

10 9 8 7 6 5 4 3 2 1

To the memory of my father,

Charles Underwood,

who surrounded my childhood with music

Acknowledgments

Many thanks to many people. First and formost, to members of my writing group: Peggy Bryant, Robert Taylor, Mick Mickelson, Thelma White, Paul Markosian, Bettina Dudley, and David Fickett, who listened, agreed, disagreed, suggested, supported, and without whom this book would not exist. To members of the medical community—Wendy Zimmer Gignoux, Doug Trenkle, Chuck Hodge, Paul Halvachs, Curtis Russett, and Susan Charles. To Pam Stewart, midwife, for her technical advice on the book and her competent, confident, and loving assistance at my grandchildren's births. To the Steuben Jehovah's Witness Community, especially Ann Seyfer and William Parr, who opened up their world to me in a kind and loving way; to Donna Kausen, Geri Valentine, and the late but ever present Brad Kausen, shepherds, shearers, spinners, and keepers of the islands, and to Susan Merrill for sharing her songs. To Barbara Sinclair for giving me her husband's bagpipe music, to Bob Worrall, bagpiper, composer, judge, for his gracious help with many of the bagpiping aspects of this book, to Andy Rogers, bagpiper, friend, for playing "Azelin's Lullaby" and for generously reading and commenting on the manuscript.

To the following composers of the chapter-heading tunes—Bob Worrall, "The Three Divorcées," "Thieves, Vagabonds, and Cowboys," and "Big Luke"; Angus Lawrie, "The Transfusion"; and Terry Tully,

"The Water Babies." The other tunes are traditional, except for "Azelin's Lullaby," by Cynthia Thayer.

To Sheila Unvala Saad, Virginia Stern, Molly Birdsall, Wendy Gignoux, Peter Underwood, Mary Jane McGinty, Fraser Campbell, Bob Underwood, and David Darmstaedter for reading the manuscript and sharing their comments; to my good friend and fellow writer, Todd Brown, for his honesty; to my husband, Bill Thayer, for his patience and understanding. To Professor Joe deRocco for, thirty years ago, allowing me to see my strengths and pointing out my weaknesses. To my friends Derek and Jennifer Grout, Mary Fraser, Candace Malcolm, and all the other folks at Melmerby Beach, Nova Scotia, for providing ideas and ambience; to my dear friend and neighbor Douglas Trumbull for his insightful comments. To my agent, Sandy Choron, for her sense of humor, encouragement, and faith, and to my editor, Kelley Ragland, for her astute editing suggestions.

THERE'S A CERTAIN SLANT OF LIGHT

There's a certain Slant of light,
Winter Afternoons—
That oppresses, like the Heft
Of Cathedral Tunes—

Heavenly Hurt, it gives us—
We can find no scar,
But internal difference,
Where the Meanings, are—

None may teach it—Any—
'Tis the Seal Despair—
An imperial affliction
Sent us of the Air—

When it comes, the Landscape listens—
Shadows—hold their breath—
When it goes, 'tis like the Distance
On the look of Death—

—EMILY DICKINSON

A Certain
Slant
of Light

C H A P T E R   1

*P*eter hears the freezing rain pelting onto the cabin roof. He knows it is dripping down the shingles, icing the windows shut, covering the trees. He hears the snap, loud like a rifle shot, a snap from deep in the woods, the snap of tree limbs laden with ice. The birches will be the first to go, then the maples, then the evergreens. He pulls the blanket up to his mouth, heaves it around his shoulders, brings his legs up to his belly, shoves his hands between his knees, squeezes his eyes shut at every cracking noise. Each time he opens his eyes, the room is still there around him, his clothes still draped on nails pounded into the wall, windows intact but iced on the outside allowing only slanted dawn light through, onto the bare wooden floor.

His arm struggles to untangle itself from his legs, from the blankets, to reach for the floor beside the bed. The tips of his fingers wave back and forth until they catch in the matted fur. "Dog," he says softly. "Dog, almost daylight." That is the rule. No dog in bed until the light comes. "Dog." His eyes close again as he waits to feel the pressure on his feet, the jostling of the bed, wet tongue on his face. Dog takes longer today than yesterday to climb onto the bunk and whines as he crawls up to lick.

Peter doesn't mind the ice. If he falls on the way to the outhouse, breaks his leg or his hip, death will be easy. His body temperature will go down down down until he is euphoric, until he doesn't even care that it is too easy, that he isn't suffering enough. But Dog is scared of sliding, of losing purchase.

Peter allows the licking to continue for a few minutes while he contemplates the day. Splitting wood. Spreading sand on the paths. Maybe a walk to observe the damage in the woods. Cut up the downed birch and maple branches for firewood. End of March is late in the year for the ice, which usually comes in February. Another sharp volley outside causes Dog to stop the licking, drop his head on Peter's face, resume the whining.

"Come on, Dog. Time to get going."

Peter pulls himself out of the warm covers and slides his legs into the dungarees on the floor by the bed. He hasn't worn underwear since the fire, a small sacrifice he's gotten used to. His red waffle-knit shirt will have to be replaced soon. That means a trip to town. He's patched the holes more times than he can even remember but now the patches have nothing to adhere to. The plaid flannel shirt is in better shape and he buttons up the front, hiding the frayed holes in the undershirt. It's time for fresh socks and he pads barefoot over to the wooden chest in the corner. The socks are right on top. Hand-knit wool. His sister has sent them every year for over twenty years at Christmas. She says you have to wear real wool socks to stave off Maine winters.

His boots stand by the cold iron stove, frost covering the outside of the frozen leather. He yanks the birch bark into thin strips, piling them loosely in the firebox, and makes a small tent of kindling over them. The bark catches quickly under the kindling. Dog sits in front of him, head cocked, waiting for the command. Peter knows not to wait too long because Dog absolutely will not get the log until he hears the command. Once Peter was in a rush and threw the first log in himself. The howling that he heard from the outhouse would have awakened the dead. No, he doesn't want to experience that scene again. "Dog. Bring the wood." This is Dog's favorite part of the day, the time when he can do something, feel competent, and Peter never forgets to give the command, even in the summer when there is no fire. Then Peter brings the wood back to the spot beside the door when Dog isn't watching, ready for the next morning. It is Dog's only trick.

Dog trots as quickly as he can over to the pile of wood by the door. The maple log he chooses is thick and heavy. He drops it before he even gets turned toward Peter but then muscles his mouth around the wood until he has a tight grip. He is not going to drop it again. His gait is slower now, his left leg dragging a bit. Peter waits patiently by the frigid stove, breathing his white breath into the space in front of him. He hopes Dog delivers the log before the kindling is burned up but refrains from encouraging him. Peter knows Dog will bring it as quickly as he is able. Dog looks up at Peter before he lowers the log. Peter jabs at the kindling and places the maple on top of the popping and flaming cedar sticks. One log is all Dog needs to bring. Peter always keeps an adequate stack of wood right beside the stove but Dog never seems to notice that. He only sees his own logs, the small heap of logs beside the front door. Peter sometimes teases Dog and makes him wait for a long time before he gives the command. The old dog would never get the wood without the command. Peter thinks he might die first.

He lowers two pieces of birch from his stack by the woodstove onto the flame and lingers his hand over the fire until he feels it, hot against his index finger. He doesn't allow himself to shove his whole hand directly into the flames. Just enough to be too hot for a moment, to know what it feels like. When the logs catch he shuts the round iron cover, closes the damper, and heads for the door. Give the stove a chance to warm the place up. After the ice melts in the coming days, there will be trees to cut up, plenty of firewood for the next three years. At the front door, he shoves his wool-covered feet into an old pair of rubber boots and pulls open the inside door. The storm door doesn't open at first.

Iced over. Peter leans into it with his shoulder. Imagine, being locked in his cabin. Unable to get out. That would be fine, something he might look forward to except for the animals. Nobody there to feed them. But he leans into the door again, feeling it give with his body weight.

Ice covers everything like shellac poured over the world, flash-frozen the instant it hits the surface. Dog whimpers, straddling the threshold but Peter gently pushes his rear end and shuts the door.

"Time to pee," he says.

The sky is grey but Peter knows that when the sun comes out, the whole Maine coast is going to sparkle like millions of earth stars. The radio said it might clear by this afternoon. Before the fire, twenty years ago, they all might have come up to see the ice, and he would have put new film in his camera, strapped on his ice-cleats, and photographed the whole area, maybe even walked down the road, taken pictures of downed trees, ice-covered telephone wires, frosted fences. But now it is just Peter. Just one man living alone. No need for pictures. His rubber boots plant themselves on a solid plateau while he urinates away from the path.

"Come on, you too," he says to Dog, who doesn't move.

Peter maneuvers his way along the short path to the outhouse where the ice has settled like a dome over the roof and walls. He kicks the door. *Bam.* Cracks the ice enough for the door to move. He wonders if he could suffocate inside if the door ices over after he enters. Probably not unless it rains and refreezes.

Inside it is dark except for a piercing slant of light squeezing through the cut-out half-moon in the top of the door. The ice over the moon becomes a prism which throws dancing reds and yellows and blues onto the wall. His fingers are stiff with the cold as he unsnaps his dungarees and lowers them to his ankles. The wooden rim around the hole is cold but dry. It makes him glad he reroofed the outhouse the previous fall. Dog's whimpering moves closer until it comes from directly outside the door. "Go on," Peter says. "Let me be." The reading material is old. Nothing but a few tool catalogs and a *Newsweek* from January. Peter settles into the reading position, holding a Johnny's Seed catalog in front of him. It's difficult to see the words because of the dark but the pictures of radishes and corn and delphiniums are clear. He flips the pages, blowing white breath over the vegetables and flowers, blotting out the continuing sounds from the other side of the door.

A rush of cold air hits his ass. He wonders how the wind could permeate the wall of ice covering the outhouse. He loves this time of day, the visceral act of depositing his waste in the ground, the cold, the anticipation of a cup of coffee. The ice covering everything enhances the excitement, except for Dog's fear of slipping. He mustn't stay too long. Things to do. Almost out of toilet paper. That means a trip to the store. A new undershirt and a bunch of toilet paper. Perhaps tomorrow when the ice loses its slickness he'll try that new country store out on the highway. He drops the seed catalog and folds the remaining toilet paper in half, in half again, and again. Every day at the same time. Like clock-work.

The dungarees are cold and rough. He tucks his shirts into the pants and snaps them, lowers the lid onto the wooden seat, presses outward on the door. The ice hasn't frozen it shut and it pops open easily. From the doorway of the outhouse, he watches the smoke curling toward the sky from the brick chimney top. Good, he thinks. The cabin will be warm when he gets back. Dog, as if he has been waiting for Peter, lifts his leg at nothing and empties a stream of yellow which freezes instantly on the shimmering ice at the side of the path. Peter waits for him to finish, allows him to go first up the slippery path toward the cabin. He hopes the ice melts soon because it is almost time to plant the peas and he remembers the smell of fresh parsnips pulled from the cold earth. The garden off to the right resembles the smooth skating rink on the front lawn of the old house, before the fire, except for the Brussels sprouts stems and corn stalks jutting up like frosted soldiers caught in attack mode. If he had pulled those old plants in the fall, he could put on his skates and try it. But the skates are gone. They, too, in the fire.

No skates for years and years and years. He would never skate again. He's too old now, anyway. He should have had grandchildren. They would skate in the garden, glide around the dead stalks in S turns, stop at the edge of the path, their blades shooting up a spray of frost. But he doesn't have grandchildren. He doesn't have children.

Dog's rear legs slip out from under him and he whines again. "Come on, Dog," Peter says, "keep going. Almost there." He tries to place his rubber boots in spots near rocks or between plant stalks to keep from sliding backward while his hands hover, ready to touch ground if he needs to break a fall. Dog reaches the door first, wagging with relief and anticipation of oatmeal. A firm tug pulls the door open and Dog falls off the stoop into the garden in the scramble to enter the cabin. Peter has to pull him up by the collar, guide him into the warm room. Standing on the floor feels good, safe, as Peter yanks his feet out of the cumbersome rubber boots and ambles to the stove to make the coffee.

He always grinds the coffee beans, puts the coffee in the percolator, places it over the hottest part of the wood stove before he allows himself to set up the dollhouse. It used to be the most difficult part of the day, waiting. But he makes himself do it. Now it is the routine. First the outhouse, then the coffee, then the dolls. He closes the lid on the stove before he approaches the small colonial house open in the front like a movie set.

He's been meaning to put another window in the back because the bookshelf is shadowed by the woodstove and the stone chimney. Sometimes even during the day, he uses his flashlight to find his Chekhov or his worn leather volume with WILLIAM BUTLER YEATS imprinted across the front cover. From the back wall of his cabin, he can see almost everything he owns. His bed, the table, his green rocker, the chest, his dishes. That's the way he likes it. Simple.

He pulls the stool up to the open front of the dollhouse, a tall stool so that he can be at eye level with the bedrooms. Leslie is the first to come down for breakfast. He used to change her clothes from nightgown to jeans and a hand-knit sweater he found in a bunch of doll clothes at a yard sale, but now he leaves the clothes on all night. He gently bends the knees and sits her at the table in the kitchen. She always got up first, made coffee, scrambled eggs, then called, "Peter, coffee's ready. Sarah, Nathaniel, time to get up. Time for school." She had sung out *school* until it became "schoooooowelll."

Sarah's room was at the back of the house, a small room with stuffed cats on the bed, on the desk, on the floor. She wanted a cat. "Please, Daddy, it's a little black kitten and he purrs and purrs and won't be any trouble."

"Nathaniel is allergic," he had said to her again on the last morning before he left. "You know Nathaniel is allergic."

"But I'll keep it away from him. Please. Not fair. He has a dog. I have nothing."

He had kissed her anyway as she struggled against him, stamping her foot. Peter knew Nathaniel had grinned at her, happy to get the better of an older sister.

Peter's hand stretches through the hallway between their bedroom and the children's, back until he is able to reach into Sarah's bedroom, reach to the bed for the girl doll already dressed for school. The roof is removable but usually he leaves it on unless he has to do some work in the back rooms. He sets Sarah in the chair opposite Leslie, slouches her leg up around the arm of the chair, places a miniature glass in her outstretched hand.

Nathaniel's bed is just inside the opening of the house. The boydoll has only one sneaker. It isn't really a sneaker because Peter has never been able to find one to fit the doll, but he colored a doll shoe with a magic marker to look like a sneaker. Only one sneaker because Nathaniel was constantly losing his sneakers. "Look under the bed," Leslie always said to him. Almost every morning. Peter stands him at the counter, red lunchbox nearby, baseball hat tilted to the side.

There. Done. The whole ritual is a little crazy, Peter knows, but it's something he has done every day for years and it is comforting. He built the house for Sarah's fourth birthday, a place to put her dolls, to place them on furniture, move them around. It was not for a grown man. He sits on the stool for five or ten minutes every morning just thinking about them, watches the dolls have their breakfast. Sometimes he moves them during the day, to the living room, to the side porch, always back to bed after supper. In the early days, right after the fire, he cried when he touched the dolls, when he placed them in the kitchen, when he changed their clothes, but now something inside him feels comforted. He can even recall the children without taking a great gasping breath.

Leslie's sweater looks dingy. And he has lost her coffee mug. Must have fallen out of her hand when Dog banged into the shelf earlier in the week. He runs his hand over the smooth wood floor feeling for the tiny mug, which has nestled itself by the newspaper basket. He doesn't like to see the dolls looking ragged. He'll start looking for another sweater. He pours himself a mug full of coffee before he settles in his rocking chair with the small volume and flips through onion skin pages to "Among School Children," moves his mouth to the words on the page until he finishes. *How can we know the dancer from the dance?*

From his place at the stove, he thinks he sees the flash of a white tail. No. Nothing. Just ice. No deer would be out in this ice. He'll have to wait until tomorrow to check on Dora, the old Indian woman next door, to see if his rowboat weathered the storm. Black Harbor is a good town. Far enough away from centers like Ellsworth and Machias and Bangor. Folks help you out if you are in trouble. In the twenty years he's lived here he's never heard of any crime worse than public drinking or dog stealing, but go south to Ellsworth or north to Machias, well, then, things were different.

Even with ice-cleats it would be a job slogging through the woods today. He pours more coffee into his mug and calls Dog over. They sit looking out the window every morning before chores start. Chores might be late this morning. The chickens wouldn't even notice but Alice's kicking should start any moment. One minute late and the old horse blasts the side of her stall. The ice is much too slippery for her to go out today anyway. Alice is close to twenty and that's getting old for a horse but she seems to be agile enough to haul some wood and harrow his garden. She has sharp caulks on her hooves but he isn't going to chance a fall on that ice.

Dog's head rests on Peter's lap. Peter sips his black coffee as the first blast of the horse feet against the side wall transcends the now-distant sound of tree limbs breaking. "Damn," he says aloud, determined to finish his coffee. As he takes a bigger sip, trying to finish quickly for Alice, he sees the woman. She leans on an ice encrusted birch. She looks like the birch, white, tall, but with a full belly. Who the hell is that? No one comes to this house. "Damn," he says once more, for a different reason. Alice blasts a second round, causing the woman to jerk her head in the direction of the barn. She is very pale and wears no gloves. Straight and stark against the glare of the ice, she is the color of white. Almost as if she is part of it all; the ice, the birches. But she isn't. She has no right. What the hell is a pregnant woman doing in his yard? His yard.

"Come on, Dog. Looks like we have some company," he says.

CHAPTER 2

The woman stands motionless as Peter approaches her, skin stark white against the red plaid of her jacket; she leans on the side of the birch tree, still, though Peter slips and falls on his way to her. He thinks she might be a mirage. Too much white light reflecting from the ice, making him see things. It seems strange that she just watches him slide until he's on his ass, watches as he scrambles on all fours to regain his footing. It's not as easy to get up as it used to be and his hip throbs from the impact, but mostly he is embarrassed to fall while someone is watching. *Damn her,* he mouths into his scarf. Should have ignored her, just gone about his business. He thinks about clapping his hands to see if she disappears, but instead, brushes off his pants as he advances toward her, this time holding onto the ice banks along the path. He is sure Alice will kick the wall of her stall again and that makes him hurry, to deal with the woman quickly and get to his animals before they destroy the barn. She is wearing a dress. Denim, like jeans, but a dress nonetheless. There is a rip near the bottom exposing a torn stocking and a big piece of the denim drags almost to the ground. The woman continues to stare past him to the window of his cabin up until the moment he touches her arm, just lightly to get her attention.

Her arms hug her chest, her pale eyes quiver below colorless lashes and brows, her pinched lips are a line of blue against the chalky skin of her face. Under her right eye, the skin surface of her cheek is blue like her lips, a faded blue.

She isn't dressed for the cold. Her gloveless hand rests on his arm. Fingers, stark white against the black of his sweater, curl around the material until they clutch the folds of wool tight. Her knuckles are scraped as if she has fallen on the ice. Peter feels the tension in her hand. He isn't used to women touching him and wishes she had chosen someone else's cabin to stand in front of.

"What are you doing here?" he asks.

"Please. I don't want to bother you. I'm lost." That's all she says. They wait there beside the birch, her fingers digging into his clothes, her chin shivering against the cold. He doesn't want a strange woman in his cabin.

"How did you get here?"

"My car. It slid right off the road into the ditch. I don't usually drive." The words come out of her stiff mouth like bullets.

"My God, you shouldn't be driving on this ice. Where's your car?"

"Must be a mile or two down the road. I followed your driveway. Thought someone must live down here because there were tire marks at the turnoff." Her voice softens a bit and the words flow together in normal speech as her jaw seems to warm up.

A crash comes from the barn. Alice busting through her hayrack. Christ. Alice will break up the whole barn if he doesn't get to her soon but he can't just pry the woman's hand off him and leave her alone in the ice. Peter hasn't had anyone in the cabin for twenty years except for the old Indian woman next door, his sister a few times, and an occasional neighbor wanting to borrow something.

The dollhouse. Jesus. It is there on the shelf, the dolls just sitting there having their breakfast, the front of the room open for anyone to see. Surely the woman doesn't need to come inside the cabin.

"I don't have a phone," he says, half expecting her to say, *Fine, thanks, I'll amble on along to the next house then.*

The woman continues to grip his sweater, fingers tightening around the wool. "Oh," is all she says. "Oh."

"Never seen such ice."

"No, never. Please, I can't walk out. I'm afraid of falling. I'm pregnant, you know."

Does she think I'm blind? How did she get in here? Walk along the center of the driveway? He looks back. No. Couldn't have. Sheer ice. She must have walked along the side amongst the trees. What the hell is he going to do with her?

"I guess you'll have to come into the cabin until I can get you out with the truck. I'll take you to town. You can call someone from there. They got a phone at the general store. Ice is pretty bad. Unusual for this late in the season, even in Maine, but shouldn't last long."

Something in him expects her to insist on walking out herself, now. He waits, feeling her shiver. He is too close to her. Breathing the same air.

"Is that a horse?" she says after a particularly loud crash from the horse barn.

"Yes," he says. "Alice. She always kicks if I don't give her hay first thing."

She finally releases her fingers from his sweater. "You'd better go feed her then. If you don't mind, I'll just go into the cabin."

If he doesn't mind? What the hell does she think? How can he tell her that he minds and that he has a dollhouse he doesn't want her to see. But if he leads her to the cabin before he feeds Alice, there might be no barn left. Christ.

"Please, just stand by the stove. I have things I don't want touched," he says, trying to keep his voice even. "Just stand inside the door. I won't be long."

As he turns away from her, he feels relief. He makes his way toward the wooden barn out on the far side of the outhouse and looks back to watch the woman make her way up the path, balancing herself on the mounds of ice-covered snow along the way. Her cap falls off behind her and she just leaves it in the path. Heaps of ghost hair cascade down her back, rest on the plaid shoulders. It is almost white like paper, like snow, like washed wool. Not white like his father's hair was, or even the old Indian woman's. Not old-age white. Hair that has never been another color before.

Peter feeds Alice, Ruby, and the chickens. "Cut that out," he says to Alice because she tosses her head from side to side and almost catches his shoulder. "Stop it." He wants to kick at her, push her muzzle away from his pockets because he is in a hurry today. The side of Alice's stall isn't too bad, just one board popped out, time to fix it later after he sorts through this woman problem.

The orange watchcap is the only sign of her in the path as he approaches the door, so at least she hasn't fallen. What is he going to do with her? She is probably hungry and cold and why is she out here by herself in this ice so early in the morning? It isn't even eight o'clock. Last night the radio warned everyone to stay off the roads until the crews had a chance to sand. And besides, there are downed electrical lines all over the place. The solar cells on the cabin roof power his radio and sometimes a single light if the sun has been shining for a while but the folks around him have certainly lost their electricity. He'd better go and check on Dora, the old Passamaquoddy. See if she needs anything. Of course, Dora has the woodstove and doesn't need electricity. She is better off than most. The radio reported stores sold out of batteries and candles, old people without heat. If you're used to something, it's hard to do without.

Through the window he catches a glimpse of the white hair. She is standing at the woodstove, warming her fingers and turns toward him as he enters.

"Warming up?" he asks.

What else is there to say? He messes with the stove lids and sets another log in the firebox. Away from the glare of the ice, her face appears translucent against the wooden walls of the cabin. He rubs his hands together over the tilted stove lid to keep her company. He doesn't think the truck will make it all the way up the slick driveway and searches his mind for an alternative. Alice? No. He doesn't want her slipping and breaking a leg. If he gives the woman the ice-grips she can walk out herself. Or can she? No. There is nothing to do but wait.

He notices she is not shivering anymore but there is a small chunk of ice stuck to the back of her hair. Before he realizes what he has done, he reaches over and tugs the chunk, which falls into his hand. He tosses it behind the stove. Plenty of ice and snow drip there from his gloves and hats and boots.

"Thank you," she says to him, her lips still bluish. *Thank you.* That's all. No explanation of why she is out by herself on such a dangerous day, why she has a fading blue bruise over the bone of her right cheek. Peter stuffs another log into the stove. "Nice dog. What's his name?"

Peter is embarrassed that he calls his dog *Dog.*

"Seamus," he says to her, hoping she believes him. What kind of man would call his dog *Dog*? "Look, I don't want to throw you out in the cold but I only have one room here. Not used to having company."

She bites her lower lip. Peter thinks she might cry. Jesus. For the first time in twenty years he wishes he had a phone. "I can't leave now," she says, studying him. "Not yet."

Peter glances over to the dollhouse. He's got to do something about it. "Excuse me," he says. He feels her stare as he does what he must do. Shakes out the old towel, drapes it over the front of the dollhouse, tucks the edges in around the top, tight so the towel won't fall. His cheeks feel hot. He thinks about the trap door in the floor, just under her feet; he's seen it in movies, just press a button and down she goes. Out of sight. He likes living by himself. Alone. Quiet. And now this.

She doesn't ask about the towel. It's as if she doesn't see him hang it there and he's grateful for that. "I'm sorry for the intrusion," she says. He barely hears her voice. "I'm cold. Do you have some tea?"

That is the least he can do. Make some tea. He nods to her, stokes the fire, places the kettle over the back lid, the hottest spot. "I've got tea but I usually drink coffee," he says, to fill in the time. "Would you rather that?"

"No. Tea. Thank you."

The day is filled with fog. Peter makes her tea. She prefers raspberry to the other offers. He feels uncomfortable leaving her in the cabin while he goes about his chores, but he can't ask her to join him. Not with all the ice. He fears she will pick up the corner of the towel and see what is behind it. Her name is Elaine. She doesn't volunteer her last name and he feels that she might not tell him even if he asks. She says nothing about the bruise, even when she sees him staring at it. They talk about nothing. Tea. Ice. Lunch. She hovers by the stove and offers to stoke it when he is outside cutting some fallen limbs. "Be careful," she says to him as he goes out the door with the chain saw. Be careful? What does she know about saws? Or men who use them?

He is careful. When he returns, she is sitting in his rocking chair, arms surrounding her belly, directly over the trap door. Her feet perch on the rail around the bottom of the woodstove, her red socks matching her sweater, her alabaster skin stark against the warm of her clothes. In her hands is his slim leather book.

"I read something by Yeats in high school," she says.

"I'll cook us a supper and fix up a bed after I light the lamps," he says, taking the proffered book from her hand. "I like to keep my books on the shelf." He places the volume under his *E. B. White Collected Essays.*

He knows it will be tomorrow before the truck can get up the driveway, even with chains. One night might be bearable. "I'll have to move you for a minute. Root cellar." He points to the trap door under the rocking chair.

"Oh, sorry."

His index finger digs at the brass ring and hauls the door up and over. He climbs down the ladder, thinking for a crazy moment that if he shuts the trap door above him, she might go away. Potatoes, carrots, a jar of pickled beets. Cabbage is done. Finished. Most have been eaten but a few rotted ones adhere to the stones on the floor. Potatoes and carrots. That's enough with the ham. He tells her to move the chair back after he lowers the trap door and she does.

"Raise my own food here. Not much variety this time of year." He plops the chunk of ham, which he has had soaking since yesterday, into the pot of hot water and moves it to the back of the stove.

"I'll peel the potatoes," she says.

"No." He slams the cutting board onto the kitchen table.

"Please. I want to help."

Christ. She'll probably cut the ends of her fingers off. Blood all over the place. What the hell can he have her do? "Two glasses over there in the cupboard. You can pour us some of that wine in the jug. Rhubarb. Not too sweet." He swipes the peeler over the potatoes and a couple of fat carrots. She pours him a glass and stands in front of him holding up her empty glass. "Don't like rhubarb?" he asks.

"Yes, I do. But—The baby. Do you have something else?"

"Water," he says, gesturing to the hand pump by the sink. He feels her presence behind him, hears her push the pump handle up and down, hears the water gushing into the sink, into the wineglass. She knows how to pump water. That's something.

"I don't have a car," he hears her behind him. "I lied about the car."

Peter swigs the tart wine around his mouth and gulps it down. He doesn't want to look at her. A liar. He knows she is waiting for him to speak, to make judgment on her.

"I took the bus to Ellsworth. Been walking. Got a ride from a fish truck the last bit. But I walked and walked. No ice then. It was before the ice storm."

Shit. No car. No money. Great. Now what? He tried looking after people before. He is in no state to look after anyone, especially a pregnant person.

"I stayed in that big house down by the water for three nights. One of the windows opened. The second day I lit a fire in the fireplace with some logs I found. I was going to stay there, have the baby there, but then the ice came and I was scared I wouldn't be able to get out if I needed to. Their phone isn't even hooked up. I neatened the place before I left, put all the blankets back, wiped the dishes with some paper towels. I didn't eat much. Just a few crackers and a couple of cans of stew. I left money and a note." Her voice rises and speeds up incrementally as she speaks and Peter is afraid she will become hysterical and won't ever stop talking. All he needs is a hysterical woman with a baby on the way. He wipes the counter, lines up the potatoes ready for cutting while he thinks of what to do with her. From deep inside his gut he feels the growing heat of his own anger and he is afraid of what that means.

She has moved so he can see her now and sips her water out of the wineglass. "This morning, I saw the smoke from your chimney and walked toward it. It's not far but the walk wasn't easy. I held onto branches and walked next to trees where the ice was broken up. I only fell once. I slid down the little incline behind your barn on my backside. I think I startled your horse. You can almost see the house from here." That explains the rip in her dress and the hole in her black stocking.

The old Farley place. Joe Farley had been dead for twenty-five years and it took ten years after that for his house to fall down. Someone named Underwood built a fancy place on part of the old foundation. Summer folks with lots of money from Connecticut. Come for two weeks at the end of August. Their place is bigger than any other house around. "Yes," he says.

He is curious about the woman but doesn't want to ask why she lied about the car or why she is hiding from someone or who that someone is. If he knows these things, he will be responsible for her in some way. He raises the knife over the end of the first potato and brings it down hard. The first slice falls away. Again, until the potatoes are sliced. The same with the carrots. She pours him another glass of rhubarb wine without asking and he lets it sit there until she goes back to the rocking chair.

Supper is strange. He eats supper alone every night, except for Dog, but tonight he cooks twice as much, puts two plates on the table, two forks, two napkins. There is little left of the chunk of salty ham, actually, the last piece from the previous summer's pig. There goes the plan to have creamed ham and hardboiled eggs for the next two nights. "Give this to the dog, I guess," he says, too loud. He scrapes the few bits of ham into Dog's dish on top of the dry food he gets from the feed store. She washes the dishes because she insists and he doesn't want to discuss it with her. The towel still hangs over the entrance to the dollhouse. When he passes by on the way to get spare bedding, he resists the urge to pick up the corner. His hand lingers on the towel but she watches him, at least she faces his way, and he is afraid that she will know about the dolls. It's none of her business. No reason she should see them.

The sleeping bag and pad under the bed smell musty but he drags them over to the opposite corner of the room and puts clean sheets from the cupboard on his own bed. "You will sleep in the bed. I'll take the sleeping bag. It's comfortable enough."

"Thank you," she says. He wills her to say, *Oh, I couldn't take your bed. I don't mind sleeping on the floor,* but all the willing doesn't work. She is, after all, pregnant. When Leslie was pregnant, she could never get comfortable, even in the bed. She turned back and forth from side to side, hung over the edge of the bed, then back to get close to him. At night in his bed he sometimes tries to bring back that warmth on his back, the warmth of her belly pressing against the small of his back, her hand sliding across his bare chest, fingers catching in the sparse hair.

Once he shoved her belly in the night when he was dreaming, and she cried out. After that, until Nathaniel was born, she slept far over on her side of the bed facing away from him, but only until the baby came. Leslie. Her body was comfortable. He knew every bit of her skin, her dips and valleys, the openings, the mole low on her back. Gone. Gone.

Elaine uses the bucket while he is at the outhouse. It is his idea because of the ice. "The path is kind of slick," he says. "I'll be gone for a bit. Just put the cover on the bucket when you're through." He rifles through his top drawer to find a clean shirt and an old pair of long underwear that he is pretty sure is clean and tosses it to her along with a flashlight. "Use this if you need to get up. No need to light the lamps just for a pee." As soon as he says it he wishes he hadn't. *Pee* is one of those words you don't say to strangers, kind of an intimate word. When he comes back in, she is in his bed facing the wall, quiet, maybe even asleep. All he sees is the hair like fallen wheat lying on the blanket. He struggles with the idea of lifting the towel, at least just putting the dolls back into their beds, but Elaine could turn around any time. "Come on, Dog," he says. "We sleep over here tonight. Come on, boy," he whispers from the corner of the room. But Dog doesn't budge. He has slept there beside the bed for a long time and isn't about to change now.

Peter crawls into his sleeping bag and for the first time in years, curls up with no dog beside him. And for the first time ever, the dolls in Sarah's dollhouse still sit at the breakfast table holding their orange juice and talking about morning things when the air is dark around them.

C H A P T E R 3

"Come here, Dog," he whispers in the early morning hours, before there is much light in the cabin, before he hears any stirring from his bed. He strains to see the dog but the cabin is dark and all he detects is a shadowy lump on the floor beside the bed. "Come on," he says again. The lump shifts. He hears the toenails tapping on the hackmatack floorboards as the shape moves across the room toward him. The woman, Elaine, moves in his bed and clears her throat. They have survived the night. Nothing terrible has happened but she is still there in his bed.

This morning is different from other mornings. He will have to make tea, set two places for breakfast, and there is the matter of putting on clothes. She will probably want to use his outhouse. He dresses quickly. The same clothes as yesterday. Usually he jumps out of bed, naked, and dresses by the cold stove, imagining warmth, but he doesn't want her to witness that so he struggles with his jeans in the sleeping bag before he crawls out, zipping them over his holey red undershirt. His routine is upset. He suddenly feels like crying, something he hasn't done in years, and looks over to make sure she is still facing the wall. Dog tugs at his pants leg all the way over to the woodstove.

There are still some embers left in the firebox and starting the morn-

ing fire is easy. The kindling bursts into flame after sizzling for a minute
and Peter reaches for a log. Dog begins with a barely audible howl but
when Peter stuffs a second log on top of the flaming cedar sticks the
howling escalates slowly and with no signs of abatement. Oh, God. He
forgot about that. He can't speak the words in front of the woman, yet
Dog will howl until he does. He knows that Dog will absolutely not get
the wood without the command. Fuck her.

"Shut up, Dog," he says.

Her head rises from the bed at the incessant noise.

"Hush," he says, close to the dog's ear. "Stop it."

Dog is frantic, frantic for an old dog, anyway, and the noise is almost
deafening.

"Is something wrong with the dog?" she asks from the bed, between
the last howl and the next.

"No," he says but isn't sure she can hear him. He can't imagine
another day with the woman in his house. After chores he plans to go
to the road and check the conditions. Flag down the police if he has to.
This is an emergency. "Hush," he says as loud as he can, trying to out-
shout the howling. Dog isn't going to stop. Peter knows that. "Bring the
wood," he says finally. The noise stops for a moment, then begins in a
soft and intermittent growl. "Bring the wood," he tries again, quietly so
that the woman won't hear. All the way over to the woodpile, the dog
turns to look back at Peter. Dog chooses a small piece of birch, easy to
pick up, light to carry, and brings it back to the stove. Dog is pleased
but now Peter is the one who wants to howl so loud that it will force
her out, her ears pulsing with the noise so disturbing that she will never
come back to his cabin again.

Peter hurries with the stove, sets the teakettle on the back lid,
brushes his teeth in the basin, slips his feet into his frozen boots, glad
to get out of there but afraid to leave her with his things. His head
pounds hard from somewhere inside his brain. There is now enough
light in the cabin for him to see the towel covering his dollhouse but

what good is that? "Come on," he says in as normal a voice as he can muster, and slaps the side of his thigh.

The world outside hasn't changed except that this time he pees on the other side of the snowbank away from the path. Dog cocks his head back and forth as he emits a short whine. The outhouse door isn't stuck and Dog doesn't fall on the way back. The sound of a sharp kick from the barn surprises him because Alice usually doesn't start up until after Peter pours his coffee. His hand holds the doorlatch for a long time before he opens it and goes back into the cabin. Elaine stands by the table dressed in the same blue denim dress she had on the day before. She must have found his scissors because the torn dragging piece is gone from her dress, leaving a long tear up the front exposing her thigh. The faint darkening blue of her cheek is now but a trace of tinted yellow-indigo. The tea water simmers on the back of the stove and he notices that his bed is neat, blankets folded, pillow smoothed out, as if no one had slept there at all. Jesus. Her lashes and brows are as light as the rest of her. Must be Norwegian or something.

Her hands cup in front of her holding the steaming mug with "I love you, Dad" printed on the side. Didn't she read it, for Christ's sake? Didn't she read the goddamn printing on the side of the mug? What if she drops it on the floor or nicks the rim on the edge of the woodstove?

Peter never never drinks out of that mug because it might break and he would have nothing from the boy who died in the fire. His boy. Not one solitary thing except for broken shards. Peter and his mother found the mug in the garage beside Sarah's outgrown dollhouse, wrapped in a paper bag covered with Celtic knots drawn in red magic marker. The card said, "Happy Birthday to the world's greatest dad." He opened it right then and there, before his birthday, and the pain was beyond tears, beyond anything. His mother cried but Peter just held the mug under his shirt to get it as close to his heart as possible for hours, until the doctor came with a shot. They carried him away from the charred remains of the house to Port Chester Hospital and kept him sedated for a week. Every †

stuck a needle in his arm. ˈ

"Please. Here's anoth

to her. Their hands tou

pours the hot tea into ʒ

white letters. "This ˊ

and he cradles the ˈ

into it. He imagin

dries the inside with a ɑ..

shelf where it has sat for years, ...

dollhouse, way in back behind his bagpi⸺

she watches him but he has no choice. What else ᴜ.

leaves he will bring it out and put it back on the shelf.

Breakfast is bearable. He allows Elaine to scramble the eggs and ⸺

the table. After they finish, she takes the plates to the sink, pumps the

water for rinsing, washes the dishes in hot water from the kettle.

"I'll be back soon as I do the chores and check the main road," he

says to her after he straps on his ice-cleats. "The dog will stay here. Too

icy for him. You might give him a bowl of water."

The cleats keep him from falling on his ass but still he feels uneasy,

off balance. The cracking from the woods is replaced with chimes, tin-

kling from pieces of ice-covered branches touching each other in the

wind. The sound of cleats crunching into the surface mingled with the

ice music fills the air around him, follows him past the outhouse and on

up the driveway toward the road. There are no animals or birds visible,

as if they are all frozen in their homes. No scat, no tracks in the ice.

On a short incline, his cold hands in leather mittens hold onto slip-

pery branches, pull him forward toward the road. Maybe he can get that

young Bryant boy to sand the driveway. Hates to pay anyone to do that

kind of thing. Cash money isn't easy to come by. He cuts a little pulp

wood and sells the fleece from the island to local handspinners. The life

insurance money grows in the bank, builds every year, but it is tainted

ing it for his own comfort is inconceivable. It
ergencies, like breaking a leg or some kind of
hat's the only reason he would ever go to a doctor.
t. In a little over five years he'll be old enough to be
rolls and then he'll get sewn up for nothing.

way levels off, allowing him to see the opening of the main
A raven squawks from the crooked pine, pitch-black against
ring white of the ice covered trees. It looks hungry. There is
squashed on the road to eat. No carrion left by eagles or hawks
ucky coyotes. The light dances prisms off branches onto his gloves.
he tinkling of the branches is now drowned out by rumbling of trucks.
That's a good sign. Bangor Hydro trucks are parked on both sides of
the road, the first outdoor thing he has seen since the storm that is not
slick with ice. The blacktop barely shows through the rutted layers of
frozen slush. Power lines droop from cracked poles and he knows he
won't get rid of her today.

"Excuse me," he says to the first guy he approaches. "I've got kind
of an emergency on my hands. This pregnant woman showed up in my
doorway. I need to get her out, get her to a phone."

"Hey, fella, we got our own emergency here. How far along is she?
We'll call for a cruiser if she's in labor."

"No. I don't think she is. Soon, though. If I get my truck up here,
can we drive down the road? I've got chains."

"No way, man, live wires all over the place. This road's closed."

"Shit. When do you think it'll be open?"

"No way to tell. Maybe tomorrow. Maybe next week."

Christ. Next week? He'll carry her out if he has to. "You got one
of those cell phones?"

"Yeah, but is this an emergency? Who do you want to call?"

Who to call? What an asshole. Why didn't he ask her? She must
have family or someone to call. Someone made that mark on her cheek.

Call the police? No. Not yet. "Thanks, anyway. I'll be back. Going to be here for a while?"

"What do you think, mister? Look around you." The man barely glances down from his work to answer, hovers over a batch of ripped wires with tools in both hands. Peter looks up and down the road. Maybe if he gets her out this far, the repair guys will take her into town with them. Then she can use the phone at Tuttle's store.

The way back down the driveway is easier, quieter. The wind has died and trees emit only an occasional clang from an errant gust. He is glad to see a glimpse of the cabin until he visualizes the reality of the woman and the dollhouse together in the same room. He pictures her lifting the corner of the towel, carefully tucked in around the books on the shelf, and thinking he is a foolish child. He imagines her laugh. A big laugh with full open mouth. He stops abruptly, his ice-cleats skidding down the drive, digging their spikes into the solid ice, making a trail of shaved snow along the side. He grabs at a spruce branch but even his leather mitten can't hold on although it is enough to break a hard fall. He slides onto a mound to the left of the drive, not able to hold back the crying. His cabin is barely visible through the spruce branches and he's glad she can't see him like this, face all red, sniveling like a baby.

Hands in mittens can't manipulate anything worth a damn. His mittens pull off easily. His hat is askew. He fixes it and wipes his beard with the sleeve of his jacket. Life was bearable before this. He has his horse, his goat, his dog, his chickens. A cabin all paid for. An island. Everything he needs. *Goddamn woman.* With a relief he feels the package of Lucky Strikes in his breast pocket. He taps out a couple of "strike anywhere" matches and a cigarette. Good a time as any to smoke. He straightens himself out, makes himself comfortable against the butt of the tree, crosses his legs in front of him, lights the match on the zipper of his fly.

The first one sputters and dies. The second one blazes long enough

to get an ember going at the end of the cigarette. He pulls the smoke
into his lungs, leans his head back to the trunk, and it's all right for
now. All right that there is a strange woman in his house. All right that
he feels naked, exposed to someone he doesn't know, but the mood
doesn't last long. The third drag doesn't have the same effect on his
mind and the image of the white woman, Elaine, lifting the corner of
the blue towel creeps back in.

"What the hell do you think you're doing?" he says aloud to the
lone crow pecking at the ice. "You'll never get through all that. And
besides, there's nothing under it to eat." The crow flaps away through
the birches. Since there is nothing else to talk to, Peter grinds the butt
into the frozen tree behind him and struggles to his feet. "Might as well
go back," he says, to no one.

The air is warming up rapidly. He shoves his mittens up under his
black sweater and crunches toward the cabin. At the door, he holds the
latch until it feels warm in his hand. Through the door he hears her
voice, barely audible at first, just like the wind howling under the door,
but then the words come. *"I gave my love a cherry without a stone, I
gave my love a chicken that had no bone,"* in a voice high and sure, a
voice that makes him cover his ears with his hands to keep its power
out. Power like bagpipes. He realizes he hasn't heard anyone sing since
the funeral, except on the radio. Never a lone voice singing pure and
clean like this one. He turns and slides his back down the door until he
sits on the stoop, head turned toward the sound and he can't stop the
tears flowing from rusted ducts, flowing again like a break in a dam.

"Leslie," he says aloud. "Leslie."

The silence after the singing seems long as Peter sits with his back
to the door, holding his head close to the wood, eyes looking up toward
the grey sky, waiting for another song. It begins, lower this time, tranquil,
a song to her unborn, and he feels like an eavesdropper unable to pull
his ear from the door. *"Hush little baby don't say a word, Mama's gonna
buy you a mockingbird,"* a voice coming not merely from her mouth but

from the back of her throat, a private song to part of her own body. He
hears the rockers of her chair creak in rhythm to the lullaby, back and
forth, the first beat of each measure, rock, rock, rock, rock. *"And if that
diamond ring turns brass, Mama's gonna buy you a looking glass."* He
brings his knees up to his chest and holds them hard against his body.
How to intrude? How to intrude on her private song? He feels the
pressure of his knees on the spot where he held the mug against his
chest, the mug that says *I Love You, Dad* on the side. A lullaby for a
baby. He hates lullabies.

The sound of the rocking ceases and he is aware of movement behind him. She is trying to open the door and he is sitting in front of it,
blocking her attempt. He swipes his face with a small chunk of ice, dabs
at his cheeks, dries them with the sleeve of his shirt.

"Trying to clear the landing of ice," he yells through the crack in
the door. "Just a minute. Let me get up. Damn ice is dangerous."

The whole thing is a little awkward since none of the ice is missing
from the porch floor but she doesn't seem to notice. Once he is inside
he lifts the lid of the stove to feed in another log and sees that the firebox
is full.

"I put some wood in," she says. "What's the instrument? The one
on the shelf, looks like a recorder or a flute or something?"

"My practice chanter. I don't play much anymore. It's a practice
instrument for bagpipes."

"Wow. Do you play bagpipes?"

"No." They needed to talk about real things, like getting her out,
not pussyfoot around, talking about musical instruments and putting
wood on the fire. "Not anymore."

"I'd love to hear it."

"No. It's not something you play for people."

"May I try it?"

"No." He is surprised how loud his voice is, surprised that he even
said the word *bagpipes*, something that had been part of his old life. She

knows too much now, too much about him. It's an invasion of his privacy. "We've got a problem," he says. He fiddles with the lids of the stove, not wanting to look at the woman. "Driveway's a sheet of ice. I don't think we can get up there yet, even with chains."

"I'm not much trouble."

"Electric company men trying to fix the lines. Live wires all over the road. Guy said the road's closed."

"I have nowhere to go." She sits back in the chair and resumes rocking, which seems to soothe her. He continues to tend to the stove, putting in another small split maple log, jabbing at it with the lid lifter.

"Well, it may be a few hours wait but I certainly can't accommodate a person in this cabin for another night." He paces back and forth in front of the stove, his back to the rocking chair. One more night and she'll be lifting the towel, gawking at the dolls. "The repairman offered to call your family. I need to get the number."

"I have no family." He knows again she is lying.

"They have a shelter in town. Read about it in the paper." He thinks that if she sings again he won't be able to send her to a shelter but she just sits and rocks. The singing makes him weak, makes him think about painful times. He wants to be quiet, not listen to jabbering all the time, not hear music in his head. "It's not a bad place. Nice folks. They'll take care of you." He wants to know about her, about the bruise, but once he asks, things will become different. Has she seen a doctor? Leslie went to the doctor every month before the babies were born. More often toward the end. What if she went into labor now, in the cabin, with just the two of them, no doctor? He knows about birthing sheep and goats but not human babies. Then he would really have trouble. "Do you have a number to call or should I call the shelter?"

"Please," she says right into his ear. Peter jumps because he didn't hear her leave the rocking chair and is surprised she is almost touching him.

"I mean it. I can't have you staying here. There's no room."

"I can help you. I'm a good cook." He can smell her breath, sweet from the raspberry tea. She is too close.

"No," he says, turning to face her. "No." He's heard about cases like this. Folks just show up, move in, never get them out. "No, I'm going to call the shelter. They'll come get you at the top of the driveway as soon as the road opens."

Her mouth gapes wide but no words come out. She sways from one foot to the other. Her hands move as if trying to speak for her. *Don't give in,* Peter says to himself. Two people cannot live in this little cabin. And the dollhouse is still closed up.

"I only have fifty dollars. Please. You can't throw me out in the ice." Her speaking voice doesn't have the power of the singing one and he continues to watch the dancing with his arms folded across his chest, silent.

"This cabin's too small."

"One more night." Her hands stop the dance and she folds her arms into the valley between her breasts and her belly, grips her dress tight at the sides. They stand, mirrors of each other's posture until the corners of her mouth turn upward in a half-smile. "One more night?"

"Oh, fuck it all," he says, grabbing his jacket on the way out. "Come on, Dog."

C H A P T E R 4

The trek through the woods is slow even with the ice-cleats but if he follows the trees, the ground underneath is less slick. He welcomes the silence that covers him, settles around his skin like fog, letting through only the sound of the cleats digging into the melting ice. Dora's cabin is past the Underwood house and Peter marvels that Elaine was able to navigate her way without more damage to herself. The summer house is visible if he looks through the trees although there is no path except down the driveway from the main road. Summer folks didn't mix much with the people who lived here year 'round. In the summer the trees covered any sign of a house and Peter was always glad when the leaves opened, allowing him to walk to Dora's and the boat without seeing a sign of anyone.

Dora is out spreading sand on the path to the outhouse when Peter arrives at the crest in the hill. "Dora," he yells. "It's me, Peter."

"Who else would skid through the woods on a day like this?" she says.

"Come on, old thing," he says to Dog, who is yards behind and having a hard time scrambling up the hillock. "Waiting for the dog," he calls down to her.

The sea is choppy beyond the log cabin, bouncing his small white skiff up and down, each rise catching the glint of the sun's reflection on the iced gunwales. Not enough chop to keep him out of his boat. For a moment he thinks that perhaps he could go tomorrow instead but he's been out in much worse and besides, it's only a short row to Perry's island. The ewes could be in trouble with this ice. He holds the small binoculars up to his eyes for a look. Nothing on this side of the island. Must be taking cover on the lee. His flock is down to about thirty now, having gone through a rigorous culling the previous fall. He traded his cotswald ram for a registered black romney to add some softness to the flock. Last time he was out he couldn't feel any swollen udders but this time some of the older ewes should be bagging up, getting ready to lamb. It is already late March and lambs are expected around the second week of April.

"Ain't you the brave one, coming out in all this hellish ice," Dora says. "I see you have the old dog with you. Figured he might not come again, especially with this terrible greasy weather."

Dora must be over eighty herself but lived alone here in the log cabin on the shore since her husband, Mitchell, died. Mitchell was Mi'kmaq, and Dora, Passamaquoddy, but neither wanted to live in the close confines of the reservation so Mitchell built the cabin when they first got married and they'd lived there ever since. As a teenager, Peter rowed old Joe Farley across to the island to tend his sheep from this same spot. They didn't have a haul-off line then and had to carry the heavy wooden rowboat to the water's edge each time and Dora had milk and chocolate chip cookies for them after the long row back. Once he even stayed with Dora and Mitchell for two weeks when his parents went to Europe because he'd begged, threatened to run away if he had to stay with Aunt Alison. Dora told his mother later she needed a vacation to recover from all that baking.

By car it is about ten minutes to the reservation and by boat, maybe fifteen on a good day, so Dora keeps in close touch with family and friends.

Since Mitchell died, Peter has looked in on Dora, not that she needs checking on. The previous fall he'd offered her a lamb and some of his pork but she said, no, she'd get her deer, she was sure of it. Twelve-point buck first day of hunting season. She salted and dried most of it but they had a couple of big feasts of fresh venison haunch in November with a bunch of folks from the reservation and some old fishermen from across the road. Dora and Mitchell were Peter's only friends when he first came to his family's summer camp after the fire, the only people he let through the door. They brought deer meat, clams, strawberries and mayflowers when spring came. They asked no questions, never said "if there's anything we can do." . . . Never made small talk.

"Seen any activity over at the island?" he asks her.

"The other day I thought I saw that new ram you got but he's so dark I wasn't sure. Something dark moving over on those rocks."

"I'm going out today just to check. I don't want them stuck on the ice so close to lambing."

"Come on in and have coffee. I got it all made." Dora is the only person he knows who loves coffee as much as he does. He follows her, Dog at his heels, up onto the porch and into the cabin. Almost forgets to remove his cleats but Dora doesn't seem to mind when he walks a couple of steps on her wooden floor. "Don't worry about them," she says, as he slips off the cleats and tucks them into his pocket.

She pours thick black coffee out of an old aluminum percolator into his cup and into her own. "There," she says, plopping down on the ladder-back chair. "Sit," she says.

Her cabin is warm, messier than his but with curtains on the windows and pictures of their daughter, Margaret, and her children clustered on the log walls. He used to play with Margaret in the summers when his family made the long trek from Connecticut to the cabin. His parents thought that too much time with the little Indian child might lead to something they never verbalized. Something bad. Actually, he'd touched her bare breasts once on the path from his cabin to her house. She'd slapped him, said he was like all the other white boys trying to get into her pants. She is a corporate lawyer now and rarely comes to Maine anymore. Once a year, usually at Christmastime, for a day or two.

Dora has two bedrooms off to the side and a bathroom where you could sit in the bathtub and take a bath in privacy. She even has a flush toilet but reserves it for company. Says she loves sitting in the quiet outhouse reading her magazines. No water pipes humming or refrigerator rattling or phone ringing. Peter has used her outhouse a couple of times and has gotten caught up in the stories about women finding their natural mothers and wives who had affairs with their husband's brother and men who beat their girlfriends. Can't help it. He'll start reading and next thing he knows it is a half-hour later.

They sit sipping the hot coffee listening to Dog scratch under the table. "You lose the juice?" he says.

"Only a couple hours at the height of it. Still had the woodstove."

"I figured you'd do okay," he says.

"How'd you make out? Animals probably don't like that ice much."

"Alice has been stuck in the barn. Ugly as sin. I've been trying to get the truck out. Too much ice."

"What you need to get out for? You got all you need."

"Something happened. Need to get out." Peter gulps his coffee, leaving a half inch at the bottom. He knows she won't push him too hard. She sits back, sighs, looks out the window. *She's dying to know,* Peter thinks, *just dying to find out.*

"Well," she says, hedging. "Ain't that something."

"Strangest thing."

"What's that?" Dora asks. She just can't stand not knowing.

"Oh, nothing much, some lost woman. Saw the smoke from my cabin and figured she'd get some shelter."

"And?"

"Shit. I can't put her out in this godawful mess, now, can I?"

"How long she been there?"

"Since yesterday."

"Yesterday?"

Peter nods.

"Oh, got yourself a live one, did you?"

"No, no, nothing like that. No. She's pregnant and seems to be on the run. She's half my age anyway."

Dora throws her head back and laughs loud. "She still there, you say?"

"I left her there. I don't think she's going anywhere." He pours another cup of coffee from the percolator. "I think I'm going to have a hard time getting rid of her."

"Pregnant, you said?"

"Almost due. I can't have anyone living with me in that cabin. Much too small. It was okay for the four of us as a summer place but too small in the winter. You know I can't stand people around all the time. She ought to be seeing a doctor or something. You've done some birthing. Maybe you should take a look."

"I've birthed lots of babies, you know. Been doing it for years."

Dora births three or four babies at the reservation every year. He remembers when the doctors at the clinic tried to stop her but the Indian women put up such a fuss they backed off.

"When I was young, I birthed most of the babies around here. Not just the Indian babies. You know Kenny Watson and Jared Fosterton? I birthed them."

"Kenny just retired. Sold his boat to his grandson."

They are fisherman who lived down the road and are at least Peter's age. It surprises him that he wouldn't have known that Dora birthed them, but it isn't something they talk about much.

"I'll take a look at her if you want me to. Bring her over. Probably easier for her to walk in this mess than for my old bag of bones." Dora

reaches across him to a shelf by the window and pulls out a strip of deer
jerky. "Here, old dog, something for them old teeth." Dog loves Dora's
jerky and mouths it politely before he takes it under the table and begins
to chew.

"She'll probably be gone by tomorrow, but . . . I'm going to leave
the old dog with you this time. Too icy out there on the rocks for the
likes of him." He drains the coffee cup, making a face at the last dredge;
cause your hair to stand on end, that coffee does. "You know, that
woman. She sings. Just out of the blue. Kind of strange."

"Oh, I don't know about that."

"Why? Are you a closet singer yourself? I don't remember ever
hearing you sing."

"Sing? Lord, yes. Only when no one is listening. I got a voice that'd
make a crow crap in midair. You don't want to hear it. Do you?"

"No. I used to teach music, remember. No. But the woman, Elaine,
she sings. I just wondered about other people, if they sing when they're
alone."

"Don't you sing? When you take a bath in that outdoor tub?"

"I guess I hum a bit," he says.

"I'll keep an eye on the boat," she says. "Making a stew if you have
time for lunch." Peter loves Dora and would even hug her but their
relationship isn't like that.

"I won't be long. Just a quick row out and back. Want to check if
any of them are frozen to the rocks. I'll bring the shears. Glad I stuck
the oars in the shed. Would've been covered with that damn ice." He
also has his knife in case one has to be put down. He's afraid of seeing
broken bones, cracked skulls. "Keep the coffee going."

Pulling the slippery haul-off line is tricky because each times he
hauls on it, the ice-cleats skid, throwing up shaved snow and inching
him closer to the edge of the rock. It reminds him of tugging on his
mother's clothesline out the second-story window, the pulleys stiff with
rust, afraid he would fall onto the driveway beneath. The pulleys on the

haul-off line are stiff with ice and barely move. With each tug, shards
of ice fly off the rope into the sea and the skiff bobs toward him. When
it is close enough to leap, he does, grasping at the slick seat to avoid
cracking his own skull. A few good bangs with the oars break up most
of the ice. It falls like diamonds onto the bottom of the boat. One more
bang on the seat and he positions himself for the row. His feet kick at
the shattered ice fragments, scattering them into the stern. After he unties the painter and knocks the ice off the gunwales, he plops the oar-
locks into the holes and pulls on the oars hard before the wind and tide
bring him too close to the ragged shore. He loves the ocean this time
of year, before the summer people claim it, when the fishermen are the
only ones out there and even they are rare so close inshore this time of
year. The water looks churned up but it's clear enough to see bottom
when there is a calm spot. The gulls hover overhead in masses, driven
inshore for the storm, they haven't yet gone back out. *Stroke, stroke,* he
thinks.

Back at school he crewed on a team and he still hears the coxswain's
stroke, stroke, stroke each time the oars dip into the water. *I gave my
love a cherry without a stone,* he thinks, stroke on the first beat of the
measure, *I gave my love a chicken that had no bone,* not out loud, just
inside his head, to himself. He flips a piece of rockweed off the oar,
breaking the rhythm. Then just behind him is the island shore, just a
few strokes away.

He loves that island, loved it since before he could remember anything else in his life. His mother always said it wasn't possible but he
remembers the first time he went to the island with Old Man Farley
who seemed old even then. Peter was a crawling baby and sat in his
father's lap as Farley rowed out on a sea smooth as a tabletop. He
remembers lots of leaping white sheep, puffed up with wool like marshmallows, funneling into the shearing chute. He never missed a year
shearing until he went away to college. When Old Man Farley left him

the island with seventeen decrepit white sheep that weren't even bred, Peter sold them all for meat at the Corinna auction. He was teaching then, and playing pipes professionally and engaged to the exquisite Leslie Flannigan and certainly not interested in sheep.

Peter's hands are cold. Never could row with the damn mittens on, gloves either, something about needing to touch flesh to wood to get the power and rhythm going. He pulls as hard as he is able, pushing the boat up onto the pebble beach, and jumps to shore before the tide takes it back out. It is light and easy to pull up. No ice on the tidal part of the beach but a glance up to dry land scares him, even with the ice-cleats clamped onto his boots.

He grabs the bag of tools from the bow of the boat. Hand shears, knives, even a prolapse retainer in case that old ewe drops her vagina again. Probably should have put her down last fall but he wanted one more lamb out of her, especially with that new romney ram. He hadn't had a ewe lamb out of her for years and this was the last chance. Way too old to be breeding. Probably should have put her into sausage but she was his first sheep. He'd tried those retainers you can buy at the feed store but found the one he fashioned out of a clothes hanger better, stronger, more comfortable for the ewe.

He stops at the edge of the beach and picks up a dead cane-length branch of apple wood for a walking stick that might help in moving the sheep if he has to. No sign of anything yet. It is a small island with only a few trees, a ramshackle cottage they use at shearing time, and an old cellar hole up on the rise where Joe Farley had a cabin to stay in when it got too hot or crowded on the mainland in August. He took Peter out overnight once as a special treat. Peter expects that they might be taking cover in that old cellar hole. The wind picks up, stings his face, makes him hurry even on the slippery rocks. The walking stick is a good idea, helping him keep his balance. The low bushes provide better traction and their hip-high branches protect him from falling.

The cellar hole is empty but just over the knoll he sees the flock, pawing the beach for rockweed and eelgrass and kelp. "Sheep," he calls, but there is no response. They know he never brings food. That's all right. It will be easier to check them on the beach where the ice has been washed away by the tides. They look up at him as he approaches but go quickly back to their seaweed browsing. He doesn't go too close. Doesn't want them to scatter. Just close enough to see if any are bagged up. They look healthy, some obviously full of lambs. He counts heads. Twenty-six. Four are missing. He always loses a couple over the winter to predators or old age or once in a while a ewe will cast herself on her back by slipping on a rock or falling over a small cliff. Once they are cast they might as well be dead. Damn fool things just lie there upside down and wait to die. And the black-back gulls sometimes get a lamb. Peck their eyes out. Occasionally they'll get a weak ewe. One year a coyote swam right out and took his young ram. Dora saw it swimming back.

He counts again. The new black ram is missing, along with a few ewes. He expects to find the old ewe in the center of the flock but he sees no sign of her. He lies down on the pebbles. Doesn't move. In a few minutes they follow their seaweed feeding closer to him and he can observe the udders of the closest ones. Looks like one is bagged up. No, three. Good. Ram must be fertile. He hopes to see some black romney ewe lambs out of these girls.

When he rises, the flock, suddenly aware of his presence, scatters up into the high ground, a few slipping on a particularly icy spot. He follows at a distance, looking to the sides, behind stumps and rocks, for signs of the missing sheep. Ahead he sees black. And two white. They are on the most exposed part of the island. When he is within rock-throwing distance, he sees the ram lift his head, shake it, struggle to get on his feet. Frozen, Peter thinks. The others are alive, too. He slides the last few feet and kneels down to them, feeling around the base of their wool to find where it is stuck. They struggle against him. "Keep still, you asshole," he says to the ram, whose eyes scream fear and legs lash out. The shears are sharp and he maneuvers them carefully to cut the wool free from the ice-covered knoll. The ram is first because he is the most obstreperous.

When Peter is sure the animal is freed, he pushes against the soft romney wool. "Go on, then, get up." The ram kicks and thrashes against the slickness of the ground. "Come on. Do I have to lift you up?" Peter straddles him and lifts the woolly shoulders, then the hips, until the ram is standing on all fours. He stares at Peter, shakes his head, and staggers off to find the flock.

The ewes are a little weaker but Peter thinks they will be fine. Thaw is coming. Maybe tomorrow, and the grass is right behind the ice, pushing at it. One ewe has an almost-full udder already and the other, a yearling, has a bit of a bag. It will be a few weeks.

The old ewe isn't there. He looks around the bare area. Off to the side there is the remnant of a firepit, blackened logs glistening from the frozen covering. He kicks at the logs. Someone has been out here. Not too long ago, either. Just before the ice storm. Time for a cigarette. He pulls off his mittens and stuffs them back into his sweater. The smoke warms him. He only smokes a couple a day, some days none. Only when he has done something and it is finished. Sit down and have a smoke. Leslie used to complain when he lit up right after sex. He'd sit in the bed, light the match, take one or two drags, and crush it out. "Do you have to, Peter?" she would say. Why the fuck did he do that when he knew she didn't like it? The other times he smoked outside, but he didn't want to go outside in the middle of the night just for a drag or two. But why did he insist on aggravating her? Afterwards he'd cuddle her tight to him while she went to sleep, pull her ass close, rest his hand on her soft belly, bury his nose in the back of her hair.

Then he sees her, the old ewe. Not far from the firepit, covered in a sparkling sheet of ice as if a natural part of the terrain. "Zelda?" He's had her for thirteen years. His first lamb. Raised her on a bottle when her mother got mastitis. Put her on the island with some new ewe lambs he bought the following spring. He peers through the ice to the ewe underneath. Her eyes are open, staring up at the sky as if caught in the act of worship. Poor old thing. He shouldn't have kept her but he couldn't bear to turn her into sausage. Not his first lamb. He runs his hand down the frozen mass until he gets to her hips. There are no rear legs, only the ragged remnants of hanging bits of meat where someone's knife hacked at her flesh. Then he notices the top of her head. A twenty-two hole right behind her left ear.

The firepit. He kicks through the charred remains again until he comes to the leg bones, mostly burned, but still recognizable. "Zelda," he says to the bones. "Should never have left you out here." He wants to hit something but there is nothing around him except for the ground. He kicks the logs again, hard so they fly out of the pit and scatter around on the hill. "Goddamn poachers," he screams to the open ocean, flips his glowing butt out hard as if to sear the eyes of the men with guns, so hungry that they would kill an old ewe by the name of Zelda just for her haunches.

He's got to concentrate on the good things. The good things. The udders filling with milk, the lambs coming in a few weeks, the clean wool clip that he can sell for five dollars a pound to handspinners because it has no hay chaff. There are many good things in his life, even the ice, the cold of the winters, the old dog, the wet earth that hides spring parsnips, early asparagus, new potatoes. Then he remembers the woman in the cabin.

The row back to Dora's is easier because the wind is onshore and it helps push him along. His fingers tingle with the cold and he pulls the earflaps of his wool hat down. The next time he comes out will be to castrate and cut the tails off some beautiful white or black half-romney spring lambs. "Stroke. Good things. Stroke. Good things. Stroke. Good things." He says the words half aloud, half to himself since there is no one to hear. One last stroke to bring him up to the haul-off line. He ties the painter tight before he sends the skiff back into the choppy sea. He can almost smell Dora's second pot of coffee. Doesn't even bother putting his mittens back on, just shoves his hands up the sleeves of his sweater and heads for the cabin.

C H A P T E R 5

*H*e does the evening chores before he approaches the cabin because it is late when he gets back from Dora's. Alice snorts on his neck while he dumps the grain into her feed trough. Her muzzle rubs his ear until he pushes her away. "Go on, Alice, eat your food." She'll have to go out tomorrow. She has been in her stall since the ice storm and is restless. Her breath steams up the air, smells like molasses. His hand slides hard down her piebald neck ending in a firm slap on her shoulder. "Tomorrow you'll go out, you old nag. Lots of things change tomorrow." He is glad he left the ice-caulks on her shoes but until the weather warms up a bit, this ice will be too slick even with caulks.

Dog laps at the mouth of the water pump while Peter fills buckets for Alice and the goat, Ruby. He'll put Ruby out tomorrow, too. She'll be careful, probably just stand in the corner on spilled hay until it is time to come in. She is due in about four weeks but her bag is already firm. Probably has triplets in there. He has missed the milk. Nothing like it in his coffee brandy. Store-bought just isn't the same.

Alice and Ruby are friends. Strange kind of bedfellows, a horse and a goat, but both are apoplectic if separated for any length of time. When he comes home from yarding wood with Alice, Ruby is always standing up on her hind legs, front feet looped over the top of the page wire fence, screaming at them.

He smells dinner before he even opens the door. Hungry from the long day rowing and navigating the icy island, he finds it strange to smell food coming from his own cabin when he hasn't cooked it himself. One more night. That is it, no more.

Elaine stands at the woodstove as if it were her own, pokes at the food in pots, stirs something with the long wooden spoon he whittled for rendering the lard.

"Hello," he says.

"I cooked dinner," she says. Her belly is larger than he remembers, pressing against the chrome rail of the woodstove as she works. Her half-smile is back but at least she isn't singing. The air in the cabin is full of bread smells and there are three pots on the surface of the stove. He rarely uses more than one pot at a time, just throws everything in together.

"That's nice," he says as he flicks on the radio, turned down low.

"I didn't touch anything. Just the cooking pots and the food." Her voice is soft and small, not like her singing voice at all, but he feels that somewhere inside her is a bigger voice hiding out. "Soup first. Sit down."

The table is set with salt and pepper and glasses, even folded cloth napkins she must have found in the back of the drawer and a chunk of butter in the crockery bowl. Dog whines for his dinner and Peter scoops out a quart of special food for fat old dogs into the dish. "There's your dinner," he says quietly, and takes his seat at the table. It's warm in the cabin, much warmer than usual, and he takes off his sweater. The soup steams from the bowl she places in front of him. As she goes back for her own, he notices her hair is wound into a tight roll at the back of her head but he can't see any barrette or clip holding it together. Looks like it is tied in a knot. "Try it," she says as she joins him. Her face appears whiter with the hair pulled back away from it and he strains to see the bruise in the half light.

Chicken soup with rice. Tastes like she might have found the bottle of vermouth. Green flakes of dried parsley and cilantro float on the top of the broth. Chunks of his canned chicken cover the bottom of the bowl. When he makes soup, that is the meal. Soup. Sometimes bread, too. But never soup and other things afterward. "Good soup," he says. Might as well be pleasant. He might have to get tough with her in the morning. He wishes he hadn't been so abrupt earlier when he left the cabin. He wishes he hadn't sworn at her. That was mean. He wants to be tough, not mean. "I'll have a little more," he says.

After his second bowl, she clears the dirty dishes from the table and brings clean plates. "Carrots with maple syrup," she says as she sets down a platter heaped with shining carrot coins. Mashed potatoes overflow another small bowl and a blob drops off onto the cloth. He scoops it up with the serving spoon before he fills his plate. "I found the pickled beans and canned chicken in the basement. I hope it's okay. There were quite a few jars left." He tries to picture her pulling up the trap door and maneuvering her bulky body down the steep ladder into the root cellar. "This bread's my grandmother's recipe. You don't even have to knead it. Porridge bread with molasses. I couldn't find molasses so I used maple syrup." He thinks of the hours of sitting outside watching the sap boil down to just the precisely perfect moment when it is concentrated enough but not burned, just so he'd have enough for a few mornings of pancakes. His precious syrup made in February and stored for the whole year, half used up for one meal. Christ, she put the stuff in everything except the potatoes. He heaps his plate with the vegetables anyway. The trip out to the island made him hungry. She has put something in the potatoes. Garlic, he thinks. He serves himself another spoonful.

The bread is delicious. He slathers butter all over the top of the still-warm bread and watches it melt down into the holes. She is proud of herself, he can see that. "That's not all," she says when he finishes everything on his plate. "There's more." She sits, silent, waiting for him to respond. "I've made something else."

What is this? A guessing game? "Oh," he says. "Something more. What could that be?"

"Pie," she says. "Lemon pie. There was a jar of lemon curd up on the shelf with dust all over the cover. Lemon meringue pie." He stands, picks up his plate to bring to the sink. "No. Sit down. I'll do it." She takes his plate and her own, clears off the butter, the bread, the pickles, and brings more clean plates. The pie is behind the water pump just as she says. Meringue, lightly browned on top, just the way Leslie made it.

His sister sent the lemon curd soon after the fire, so it has been there for almost twenty years. No wonder the top was covered with dust. It's a wonder she even got the top off the jar. And used it without asking. She appears at the table holding her creation looking like a goddamn magazine ad for Little Miss Housewife except for the white of everything—hair, skin, lashes, brows. "Small or large piece?" she says. Lemon meringue pie. Used to be his favorite. Leslie always made it on Sunday if his father was coming for dinner and that was often. After his father died, Leslie made it at least once a month, just to remember him by, and always at Easter.

He feels like there is no way out. He looks around the room, away from the pie, over to the towel. It is askew. The corner no longer tucked into the bookshelf. "Well, small or large?" she asks again, placing the pie in front of him. "Do you like lemon pie?" She is too close again. He smells her skin, like lemons, feels her warm breath on his face. "Cat got your tongue?"

"I hate lemon pie." Peter is surprised at his response. "You don't live here. What right do you think you have taking over everything?" He feels trapped in his chair, no way to get out of it because she is there, so close to him, he will have to touch her to move. "Tomorrow we'll get you out of here. You can go home, wherever that is." He is afraid to look up at her. She doesn't move, continues to lean on the table above the pie. He wants to push her back, away from him, but he sits on his hands, shoves them far under his legs, lowers his head more. Why doesn't she back up, move away from the pie and the table and him? But she leans like a statue.

The first sign he has that she is crying is the tear which falls onto the top of the perfectly browned meringue. It hesitates, then slides down the peak and nestles itself into the white of the valley. One tear. He waits for another and wishes he has pushed her back, just enough so the tear had fallen onto the floor or onto her dress.

"If you loan me some money, I will leave right now," she says. "I will pay you back. If you don't loan me money, I will need to stay here."

She straightens herself and stands holding her belly. Idle threats. What right does she have to demand money? Extortion, he calls it. He pulls his hands out from under him and pushes the pie into the center of the table. Her face is flushed but her mouth is firm. Set. Not quivering.

It's dark outside. Pitch black now. It would be hard to get up that driveway even with a flashlight and ice-cleats on her boots. They are statues again but are staring at each other this time. When he was a child he was always the best at that game, could stand for ages without even blinking or twitching. It is harder to do that now and he has a sudden desire to laugh. The back of his neck tenses up as he holds back the urge and scrambles for his next move.

"Sit down," he says. "The news will be on any minute. We'll see what's happening with the roads." She's not leaving tonight anyway, that's obvious. "I have no money to give you."

She sits at the table, hands folded on the surface in front of her, those eyes looking directly at him. She doesn't speak.

"I can give you a hundred dollars and you can spend one more night."

Her lips part for a brief moment, then close. Silence.

He pulls the package of Luckies out of his shirt pocket and taps one out. Just as he lights the end, she speaks.

"Please don't smoke."

That's all. *Please don't smoke.* Well. It's his house and he will smoke if he wants to. He pushes his chair back from the table and takes a big drag from the cigarette, blows the smoke away from her toward the door. Dog ambles over to him and touches Peter's leg with his nose.

"Please. It's not good for the baby and it's not good for you."

Peter takes another drag and exhales fast, blowing smoke over the table, and grinds the butt out on the plate that was to be for his pie. He rubs Dog behind the ears. "Look, tomorrow, you go somewhere. I don't really give a shit where that is as long as it is out of here. I'm sorry you have problems, but everybody has problems." He thinks of Leslie behind the towel and the dollchildren frozen in their own two-day game of statues. "I'm not going to throw you out in the cold but you can't stay here. The radio will give us some news."

He moves the dial back and forth, past country music and Mozart, until he hears ice storm news.

"Power companies have been working through the night to restore power to coastal communities hardest hit by the storm. Some roads are still closed but most should be opened by tomorrow morning." He gestures with his eyes to the radio, nods his head toward her. "People are requested to check on their neighbors, especially ones who may be housebound, elderly, sick. Melanie and Richard Dalton, an elderly couple from Franklin, were found dead in their living room, apparently victims of hypothermia. They had no heat or telephone." Peter and Elaine watch each other across the table as the topic on the radio shifts.

"And finally on the storm news tonight, Elaine Sinclair, thirty, from Bedford, Maine, has been reported missing from her home and is believed to be down east in the vicinity of Black Harbor." Elaine glances out the darkened window toward the Underwood cottage. "No foul play is suspected but the woman may be confused. She is fair-haired, five-foot-five, almost eight months pregnant. If you have any knowledge of her whereabouts, please call the station."

"Confused?" she says. "Confused?"

He doesn't want to know any more about her. He doesn't even want to know why she has a fading yellow bruise under her right eye. He knows enough. The place will be crawling with husbands and police if she stays much longer. That's all he needs, a bunch of strangers snooping around the place.

"Are you going to call?"

"I don't know."

"I'm not confused. Well, maybe I am confused. There's no need to call the station. Besides, you don't have a phone, do you?"

"No."

"I feel safe here. I have some thinking to do. I have to think about the baby. It seems like God is here in this place."

"God? No God here," he says.

"Yes, there is."

"Fine. Let's get some rest and tomorrow I'll take you to a safe place where they'll take care of you."

"I have some decisions to make."

The radio plays Bob Dylan singing "Blowing in the Wind," and Peter turns it down low enough that he can barely hear if news comes on again while he helps her clean up the dishes. He isn't worried about batteries. Just bought a bunch before the ice storm in case the solar cells didn't have enough sun. The lemon pie sits undisturbed in the middle of the table, the tear now undiscernible amongst the weepings of the meringue.

"I might take a small piece of that pie now," he says, as quietly as he can. No point in upsetting her any more. "But I can cut it myself."

CHAPTER 6

*T*he night is longer than usual because Peter's hip bone pushes against the hard hackmatack in every position he chooses. This is the last night he will spend on the floor in an old sleeping bag, breathing air that smells like someone else's old shoes and stagnant turtle water. He hears Elaine making night noises, snuffling, scratching, turning from one side to the other. As he adjusts his body so that his hip is away from the hard wood, he hears her rise and thump around the cabin. He turns slowly in his sleeping bag toward the sound, hides his face, watches her move. She limps, favoring her right leg, leans down to grab her calf. "Drats," he hears her whisper, and then he hears something else outside. Drips. Slow drips. Not streams of melting ice, but small drops falling from the cabin roof, falling from trees in the woods, hundreds of trees each releasing a drop of melted ice.

Elaine sits on the edge of the bed, her wheat-colored hair resting on her shoulders. In the dark of the cabin he sees only outlines except for the hair. She clears her throat and lowers herself into his soft comfortable bed next to his old dog and pulls the covers over her head. She shifts back and forth from side to side for a long time and then there is nothing but the sound of breathing and the shapes of familiar furniture.

He lies on his back so he won't have to smell the staleness of the sleeping bag while he waits for the light. After chores he will attach the chains to the truck tires and get her out of here. Get his home back.

Even his breathing feels forced, afraid he will wake her up if it is too irregular. He tries to see the dollhouse, see if they are still having breakfast, tries to tell if the towel still hides the rooms, the dolls, his family. The shelf looks dark, without pattern, the towel blending in with the greyness of the books beside it. When he first moved to the cabin the nights were long because he was lonely, not used to being by himself in the dark, not used to waking up and making his own coffee, until he brought Sarah's old dollhouse in from the barn and placed it on the shelf where he could see it from his bed. Now the idea of waking up with another person in the cabin unnerves him. Breathing the same air as a woman for the whole night frightens his body into tensing the muscles of his legs until he isn't sure he will be able to move them if there is a flood.

He begins to discern the sounds of the drips, the different musical notes they make as they hit the ice covering the driveway, the earth of the kitchen garden, stone, trees, the hood of his truck. His arms are stiff at his sides and his neck aches from holding his head still. When he thinks he cannot stand the rigidity even one more minute, he detects the day, just a faint glow of light through the front window. His hand follows his groin, fingers the pubic hair, touches his flaccid penis with the edge of his hand. The only thing on his body not stiff. He rarely masturbates anymore, another sign of growing old, he suspects. Perhaps he ought to make more of an effort. He lies his flat palm over the limp and slightly damp lump waiting for movement. Anything. The sound of the drips begins to take on a pattern which he tries to interrupt. An old tune. It's like counting cracks on the ceiling of the dentist's office or obsessively counting steps as you mount stairs. The more you try to stop, the stronger the pattern becomes. A strathspey. Common time. Four-four time. The drips fit exactly into the measures. Four drips per measure. Four measures per part. Repeat on part one, repeat part two.

His penis moves a bit, like a small mouse, terrified to really go anywhere, caught between two cats, flinching. And then nothing. No stiff hard thing. The flesh all around it is harder. He laughs almost aloud. The softest part of his body is his dick. He pulls his hand away, back to his side like a wooden soldier and begins to move his toes, to get himself ready to get up and make her goddamn tea and pull the frozen chains around the rear tires of the old truck and get things back to normal.

The light in the window brightens and the old dog sniffs and flops onto his other side. "Come here," Peter whispers to him. "Come on," he says as he taps the floor with the back of his hand. He sees the eyes as they open, hears the padding of the old feet on the wood, watches the form sway and lurch, until he feels the cold moistness on his thumb, his hand, up his arm. Peter turns his face so it will be easier for the old dog to reach.

He will be pleasant to her this morning. Last night worked out all right. He ate the pie, over half the pie at two pieces each. His mother's was better but Elaine's crust was passable and the meringue high and light with brown tips and white hollow spots where the meringue dipped toward the lemon.

He reaches for his old jeans, last time he'd be putting them on inside the damn sleeping bag. He brings them in through the unzippered side and struggles to push his feet through the legs. Dog licks at him, making it even more difficult. "Go on," he whispers so the woman doesn't hear. The shirt he doesn't mind putting on where she will see him. He hasn't seen her move under the blanket. Dog is already at the woodstove waiting for his command as Peter pulls on his wool socks and shoves his feet into the workboots beside his sleeping spot. He can see now that the towel is hanging exactly the way he adjusted it the previous night and he tries to throw a message of apology through the towel into the doll bedrooms.

"Get the wood," he says quietly but audibly to Dog. "Go on, get the wood."

Dog settles his sagging mouth around two small birch logs and brings both together while Peter tears birch bark into strips and lights them with a match before he places them into the firebox, shoving a few cedar sticks on top as kindling. The cabin feels warm this morning but perhaps it is only because of the noise of the dripping water all around him, the top layer of ice covering his truck, the outhouse, the Brussels sprouts in the garden, all turning back to water at once. He thinks the sun will shine today.

He flicks on the radio. Power lines fixed, it says. He looks out the window to the truck, to the driveway up to the road. Sheer ice. But with chains, it will be possible. She stirs but he doesn't look around. Before he leaves the cabin he checks the stove dampers, makes sure the lids are settled into their recesses. Dog slips once on the walk down the path toward the truck but recovers easily. The ice is melting but not as fast as he imagines from the sound of the dripping. The trees are still covered with a thick layer and he notices the broken branches that have given up to the weight of the frozen shell around them. Peter thinks fleetingly of putting on the chains and throwing the woman into the truck wrapped in his blankets before she has a chance to wake up and whine more, but he knows his animals will not stand for that.

He hears the kick just as he opens the barn door. Blam. He throws grain into Alice's trough and gives the goat her allotment. They are both eating the same sweet feed and they will have to put up with that until he can get to the feed store. He cuts the twine from the hay bale and tosses them each a couple of leaves. Water can wait.

The chains feel cold and heavy in his hands, as if his fingers might lose their blood and turn white if he holds the links long enough. In order to put the chains around the tires he lies down on the ice-covered gravel and spreads them out behind the wheels. Easiest way is to back onto the chains and then connect them but he isn't sure the truck will back up over them on this slickness. His skin feels cold, the cold from ice melting on the surface invades the back of his jacket rising through his sweater, through his holey red undershirt into his chest cavity.

After a brief spin in front of the chains, the truck consents to his pressure. Two feet. That's all it takes to center the tires directly on the chains. He leaves the engine running just in case he needs to make an adjustment, forward or back, and lights a cigarette. When he goes out to Perry's island, he rarely brings his cigarettes. Dora can smell it on him. "Get them goddamn things outta here," she rails at him. "I know you been doing that weed. I smell it on you." God, couldn't she be a pain in the ass. But that woman, Elaine, of all the goddamn nerve to tell him to not smoke in his own cabin, for Christ's sake. He flicks the ashes onto the floor on the passenger side and takes another long drag. They all smoked in the bagpipe circle when he was into that. All the judges, the pipers, even the open pipers, professionals like he was, smoked like steam engines. Onlookers used to wonder how they could blow up those bags and keep the air coming with lungs like tar. *Talent,* he'd say. *Raw talent.* There was a real tight group of pipers, all knew each other, competed fiercely during the day, drank beer together at night.

He stubs the butt out into the ashtray and gets out to check the chains. Perfect. Right over the center of the links. He snaps them into place, tugs to make sure they are tight, firm, then turns the engine off. He doesn't want anything else to go wrong with this woman thing. It has to be today. First he'll get her out of here. Somewhere in town. The shelter, or the bus stop, or even some church. They're equipped to handle these things. Then he'll go see Dora.

Elaine is up when he gets back to the cabin, up and making her infernal tea. "Good morning," she says.

"Good morning," he says.

They nod to each other, avert their eyes as if no one has anything to say. But they have everything to say and no way to say it. Peter opens the lid of the stove to shove in a piece of maple. The stovebox is already full with birch on top of a stick of oak. He searches for his jar of coffee beans on the shelf. He usually makes it after he goes outside, after the outhouse trip.

"The coffee's made," she says. "There on the stove. It's finished perking. I moved it to the side."

Christ, she knows woodstoves, what kind of wood to put in, how to make coffee in a percolator, stuff most women don't even know how to do anymore. He and Leslie used to have one of those Mr. Coffee machines where you just pour the cold water in one hole and the hot coffee came out the other hole. *Peter,* Leslie'd say, *the coffee's made,* and she'd kiss him lightly on the cheekbone. He always poured his own.

Peter cuts a large piece of lemon meringue pie, over half of what's left, and sits down at the table, Dog at his foot waiting for bits of pastry to drop onto the floor. Elaine brings her steaming cup of tea to the spot opposite him and sits down.

"Well, I guess I owe you something. Some explanation of why I'm here."

"Nope. You don't owe me. Soon as we finish breakfast, I'll drive you to town. As I see it, you have choices."

"No, I want to be honest with you."

"There's a new shelter, built last year to help women like you, and I heard they take any folks in trouble. The bus stops at Jordan's Market at ten, headed for Bangor and points south, or I can drop you at the general store where they have a pay phone. Those are the choices. Three of them. One. Two. Three."

"Please, won't you listen—I appreciate being able to stay here. I want to tell you why I'm out here in the middle of a storm, why I happened on your place, why I can't go home."

Jesus. He almost said it outloud. Jesus. Almost like a prayer to a

God. Please God. She can't stay here any longer. "I don't care where you go but you can't stay here."

"Can you loan me some money?"

"Two hundred. Will that do it? I'll give it to you. I never loan money."

She sits quietly watching him. She expects him to give it to her right now. He glances over to the coffee can on the shelf by the water pump and she follows his gaze but doesn't speak. Finally he goes to it, shoves his hand into the can and comes up with a fistful of twenties. He counts them out. Ten twenty-dollar bills, most ragged and wrinkled except for three brand-new from the bank.

"Two hundred dollars," he says. He places them on the table in front of her, half expecting her to say, *No thank you. I don't need any money.*

"Thank you," she says, before she carefully folds the bills and places them in her pocket. "Thank you."

"Don't worry about paying me back. Should cover a bus ticket and hotel if you need an overnight."

"I can't pay you back. I've prayed hard. Every night of this pregnancy. I prayed all last night."

That's all he needs is some religious fanatic, praying all over the place. Peter knows there's no God, knows there's no point in praying to something that doesn't exist. When Leslie and the children died, he tried to pray. He got down on his knees beside his hospital bed like Grandmother taught him and stayed there until his legs were numb, until his knees ached, waiting for comfort, a sign from God that everything would work out. And all he got was sore knees. It's not like he tried it only once. Must have been every night for a week. That's the last time he'd ever prayed. Fucking waste of time. And now he is expected to ask her why she prayed. He can't even say the words.

She sips her tea, her hair catching the light of the rising sun. "I want to tell you why. I want you to understand why I showed up at your door and why I can't leave."

"Can't leave?" he says. "Can't leave?" He can't help it that he says it twice. He wants to say it again but he keeps his teeth clenched tight. No point in it. "I can take you to a friend's house where there's a phone. You can call from there. That's it. Don't argue." He swirls his fork around the plate, scooping up the last bits of lemon curd and crust and the now sticky meringue. He can't remember speaking so firmly to any-one since his own kids. Not even often to them. Just before the fire, Nathaniel left his new purple bicycle out in the rain. "You don't have any respect for your belongings. See if I get you anything else new. Don't argue," Peter'd said. He remembered the exact words and how they rattled around in his head for months after the fire. The last words he ever spoke to his own son. He left for a competition before Nathaniel came home from school. He wanted to wait, to kiss him, tell him he was sorry, that he had been in a bad mood, but it got too late, he couldn't chance missing his plane. The words ricocheted off the rind of his skull. *No respect. No respect. Don't deserve anything new. Don't argue. Don't argue.* At first the words grew louder each time they hit something, bounced, swelled, hit again, bounced, swelled. But after a while some of the words just stuck to the sides of his skull, broke off, softened, until he could stand it, until he could drink his coffee without vomiting. And now he has spoken like that to the woman, Elaine. *Don't argue.*

She doesn't flinch. Sips her tea again, slowly, watching him the whole time, waiting for him to back down, he knows that. He wishes he weren't afraid to let her stay with him but that is absurd. No one who lives in this small a cabin would be able to have another person move in, at least not in winter. Absurd.

"I am desperate. I need help. I chose you because your cabin was the first one I found that had a person in it."

He considers having a cigarette right there in his own kitchen across the table from her, considers flicking the ashes into the sticky trace of lemon meringue pie, considers grinding out the butt into the middle of the white china plate, just because it is his cabin, his table, his plate and she needs to know that. "Come on. Get your things together. If you're not warm enough, take that sweatshirt from the peg. You can keep it."

"I'm going to need a lot of help. Please. You can't throw me out."

"I can't?" he asks. He leans forward on his elbow, combs his fingers through his beard, raises his eyebrows at her. "I can't? What the hell do you think the two hundred dollars was for? To buy curtains for my cabin?" She sits quietly, hands folded behind her steaming tea. "Let's get going." It's her lack of reaction that finally makes him sit back, try another tactic. "The radio said that the lines are fixed. The ice is melting. Listen."

They sit like statues, ears cocked to the front of the cabin as if somehow they can hear better through the door. The drips are muffled now, as if the drops of water are larger, softer. As long as Peter can get the truck up the driveway, everything will be fine. He worries a little about her state of pregnancy but remembers that fetuses are tougher than one might think and a little jolting in the truck, bouncing around, won't be a problem.

"My baby is coming soon. It will need a transfusion." She bites her lower lip and he thinks he detects fear beyond the filmy surface of her eyes. She places her hand over her mouth and he wonders if she is practicing her next speech with her lips. Her fingers have freckles on them and her nails are like workingmen's nails, short, ragged around the edges, but clean, clean like a piper's nails. Just as he is ready to get up, start the truck, urge her toward the door, she lowers her hand to her lap.

Transfusion? Why the hell would a little baby need a blood transfusion? Maybe Elaine's a bleeder. Maybe that's why she's so white.

"I am terrified. I thought it would be easy. I thought it would be easy to trust in Jehovah and let Him help the baby. But I sing to it. Talk to it. It isn't easy at all."

Peter doesn't want to hear another lullaby or any talk about fetuses and babies. He doesn't want to encourage a discussion that might slow down the movement toward the truck but it is hard to just ignore what she is saying. Is she crazy? A fanatic, perhaps. He really doesn't want to know anything more about her. He stares past her, focuses on the sound of the thaw. He needs to think about the rest of the chores, try to get some of the ice chipped out of the paths, take care of fallen branches that might be dangerous. The woods will need days of work, especially the birches which seem hardest hit.

"Peter," she says, patting the table in front of him as if he couldn't hear her voice. "Will you listen to me?"

The loud blast of a car horn cuts her off and Peter jumps to his feet and bolts for the door. It is rare that anyone comes to see Peter unless there's a problem somewhere, an accident, but never to just chat about everyday things. He almost loses his footing by the front door because Dog pushes him from behind and it takes him by surprise. Peter grabs the doorjamb and steadies himself. It's Brendan in his four-wheel-drive truck. Not even any chains. That's a good sign.

"Hey, Pete," Brendan calls from his truck. Some of the local fishermen call him Pete and he never corrects them. Most of the locals never shorten their names. Robert and Thomas and William. But out-of-staters' names always get shortened.

Peter cautiously steps his way down the path to the turnaround at the bottom of the driveway. "Brendan, what's up?" Peter says as he slaps the hood of the new red truck hard enough to hurt his fingers. He pulls a Lucky Strike out of his pocket and taps the end on the top of the side mirror as Brendan rolls his window all the way down. "How's that boy of yours?"

"Can't do nothing with him. Warren hauled him in last week for drinkin' and drivin'. Trying to get him to come in with me. Lobstering. Bitch to get a license if you ain't related. Thought it would be a good chance for him. I dunno."

"Oh, he'll come around. What brings you down here?"

"Just thought I'd warn you. Some fancy-ass guy nosing around looking for his wife. Seems to me could be trouble. Guy in a suit and tie and leather shoes in this weather asking if anyone's seen this pregnant woman. Seems his wife is hiding out on him."

"Oh, yeah?" Peter takes a big drag of the Lucky and blows the smoke off to the side.

"He's been going from house to house like one of them damn salesman types. 'Excuse me,' he says. Polite as the pope, you know the type. 'I'm looking for my wife. She's pregnant and may be in some danger.' But I could tell she must be hiding out on him. Something shifty in his eyes. Even if I knew I wouldn't be telling him nothing. Just thought I'd warn you. He might be down here and I know you don't like no one nosing around your place."

Peter thinks quickly about the woman and what to say. News will get around. Spreads like fire around here. Might as well spread the true news. *Something shifty in his eyes.* What if people find out about Elaine and think Peter has been hiding her? Folks around here hate to be fooled. Brendan would be real pissed off. He points up to the cabin. "She's in there. Seems scared. I've been just waiting for the roads to open up so I can get her to a shelter or a phone or something. She's not staying here."

"Well, I'll be fuck all," says Brendan, turning the country music down so it's barely a whisper. "Hiding from him, is she? He sure didn't look like a bum but there was something weird in his eyes. There's gotta be something wrong with anyone wears a suit and them fancy shoes to go out in this kinda shit."

"Roads open?"

"Yeah, but you gotta go slow. Well, you know how to drive around here. You been here long enough."

"Yeah, she showed up the other day. Having a hard time getting rid of her in this goddamn ice. Got the chains on ready to go."

"You'll have no trouble. Just get some momentum going before you hit the incline."

"Yeah, thanks, man. Appreciate it."

"Damn. Looks like this domestic scene might heat up. I'll see ya down at the store."

Peter slaps the side of the truck bed as Brendan turns around to head back up the driveway. The truck doesn't slide a bit. Brendan honks a couple of times and disappears up the hill and around the curve. Everyone around here knows everything about everybody. Folks leave you alone but they have to know. No one seems to care what you do as long as they know about it. So. A guy with a suit and fancy shoes. Peter guesses he'll be able to handle that but hopes he doesn't have to. He slides into the driver's seat of his old black truck with the shiny new chains attached to the rear wheels and grinds his cigarette out in the ashtray. The engine lurches as he turns the key but settles into a soft purr after a couple of seconds. He'll leave it running while he gets the woman moving in the right direction. It's been a few days since he's driven it and it could use some warming up. Besides, the windshield and all the windows are encased in an inch of clear ice which he can almost, but not, quite see through to drive. First big bump and the ice will crack like a glass shell, shatter and fall behind him in pieces. He turns on the windshield defrost and moves the temperature lever to high. By the time he comes out with her, the windows will be clear.

Big Luke

C H A P T E R   7

Peter is still sitting in his idling truck, fingers on the door handle, when he hears the other truck coming down the driveway. It drives into the yard as if there isn't melting ice covering everything and as if the roads aren't the most slippery they've ever been in the history of the state of Maine and as if the ice isn't on every TV, radio, and newspaper in the whole east coast. This could make things easier. He wishes he hadn't wasted the two hundred dollars.

The truck looks shiny. Black. Peter sees the driver's dark skin and close cropped hair through the haze of his ice-covered window. The fellow doesn't even have a beard, near's he can tell. He drives his truck right up to Peter's, stops where he can practically touch the driver's side, and rolls down his window. There he sits, suit dark against the white of the starched shirt, necktie squishing his neck. What kind of a man would wear a dark suit this early in the morning, ice storm or no?

He taps politely on Peter's car window. Taps like he's knocking on someone's door, smiling all the while, one of those salesmen smiles. If Peter didn't know who the guy was, he would yell at him to get out, leave the property, don't bother him, but he is Elaine's husband and is not selling anything. Tap. Tap. Again, on the top of the ice-encrusted

window that is no way going to open and Peter isn't sure if he can even
swing his car door without hitting the glossy black steel of the truck. He
slides over to the passenger side and tries that door. It gives with the
fifth shove sending ice plates shattering to the ground.

"Pull up over there," Peter shouts as he steps around the rear of
his rusty truck toward the husband in the dentless black one. He points
to the parking area ahead. The man's truck pulls forward into the space,
slowly and perfectly, no tires spinning, and stops just shy of the side of
the barn. This could be really easy. Just hand her over. No need to try
out the new tire chains. No need to argue with her, watch her chin
tremble, the corners of her small mouth tighten, especially no need to
watch her eyes melt like the ice, glisten with the water covering them.
But there is something wrong. Hard for Peter to put a finger on it. Just
a feeling about the guy.

"Excuse me, I am looking for my wife," the husband says as he
lowers himself cautiously from his truck to face Peter.

"Your wife," is all Peter says.

"My poor wife is confused, pregnant. I can't imagine what got into
her. I need to get her home where she belongs. Someone said she might
be down here."

The man wipes the corners of his mouth with his starched white
handkerchief which probably has his initials monogrammed into one
edge. There is nothing stuck on the corner of his mouth. No crumbs,
nothing that Peter sees.

"Your wife."

"Have you seen anyone? Or heard of anyone like that?" the husband
asks.

Just as Peter forms the words in his head, the words to tell about
Elaine, he catches sight of the man's shoes. Brendan was right. Dress-
up black shiny shoes, practically floating on the skin of water coating
the driveway ice. Black leather shoes, shiny like the black of the truck,

for Christ's sake. No scratches, either. What kind of an asshole wears dressy funeral shoes on top of ice?

"What's she look like?" Peter asks.

"Have you seen her or not?"

"Tall, short, blond, dark?"

The man pulls his handkerchief out of his pocket again and rubs at an invisible spot on his truck bed, replaces the handkerchief. His fingernails are immaculate and he turns his hand in a fist so he can check them. Peter wonders about the fist and the bruise on Elaine's cheek, wonders if there is a connection. "She's very pregnant. Fair. Very fair. Blue eyes."

"Fair? Blue eyes?" Peter thinks about how easy it is. *Sure, she's right up there in the cabin.* But he can't say the words, can't get his tongue around the *s* of *sure.* "Fair? Tall?" He wonders if the man will offer pieces of silver for her and suddenly Peter feels like Judas. Is she confused? He looks for the fist again but it is shoved into the pocket of the coat and Peter can't tell if it is hard and angry.

"You've seen her or you haven't," the man says. His hand comes out of the pocket to pull up his collar against the wind.

"Fair. Blue eyes. Can't say as I've seen anyone like that. Haven't seen many folks the past few days. Too much ice."

The man glances up to the cabin as if he doesn't believe Peter's words. "You'd tell me if you saw her, wouldn't you? She needs help. She belongs at home. We're all very worried about her."

"Got work to do. Nice meeting you, Mr . . ."

"Oliver. Here's my card. Please call if you hear or see anything." Oliver steps forward on one of his black shoes and peers through the trees toward the cabin again before he walks back to his seat in the truck. Must be a borrowed truck. He's not a truck man. "You could be in trouble if you're withholding information," he says as politely as you please but Peter feels a hard cold where the words settle into his ears.

Mr. Oliver smiles like a cartoon man just before he rolls up the window and starts the truck.

Peter waits until the truck disappears up the driveway before he looks at the business card. "Oliver Sinclair. Roofing contractor, Brewer, Maine." He can't imagine the man up on anyone's roof, especially in that blooming business suit. He sticks the card in his jacket pocket in case he needs the address or the phone number. Just in case. Peter turns off his truck and waits until he doesn't even hear the other truck's engine before he turns toward the cabin and the face in the window.

What's wrong with him? It would have been so easy. Just say, *She was lost and I let her stay here.* Easy. He pictures Elaine in the black truck, Oliver's fingers tugging at her arm. *We're very worried. You're just confused.* Is she just confused? Peter reads the card again, memorizes the phone number and puts the card back in his jacket pocket. The damn ice has affected his head, got in there and froze up some brain cells. What is the matter with him?

She wants to know everything. What did he say? Did Peter lie about her? But Peter can't answer everything now. He tells her the basics. No, he didn't give her away. He has to think about things. She touches his arm while she asks the questions about her husband. Her ivory hair catches on his jacket and he thinks he smells a trace of lily of the valley. Not strong like perfume, just the almost imperceptible fragrance you can detect in the early spring when the first blossoms open up. Her hair is damp, like she's just washed it. He's got to get out of here. Get out where it's quiet.

Peter straps on his ice-cleats and throws another log into the firebox before he lifts his twenty gauge off the gun rack attached to the far wall of the cabin. "Come on, Dog," he says. The old dog lurches forward, standing on his hind legs first and placing his front paws one at a time in front of him.

"What are you doing?"

"Going out."

"Why do you have a gun?"

He doesn't answer.

"Why do you have a gun?"

"To shoot something."

Christ's sake. Why does he have a gun? What does she think? She lives in Maine. He doesn't look at her the whole time he is gathering his things, gun, shells, gloves, a couple of crackers for his pocket. No point in looking at her. But she doesn't stop trying to touch his arm, asking imbecilic questions.

"Be back in an hour," he says to the cabin in general just before he closes the door.

He resists the urge to cover his ears with his hands partly because he has the shotgun in one hand and needs the other to balance himself on the slick surface. Even with the ice-cleats the footing is difficult. The poor old dog slides down on his ass all the way to the driveway but picks himself up when he sees they are headed for the woods. Already Peter feels better, stands up straighter, has lost that cold wad in his belly.

They walk as quietly as they can over the crusted snow. Chunks fall from the overhead trees like plaster from an old ceiling, smashing at his feet, or ahead of them, or behind the dog, giving him a short-lived speed spurt. The deer will be having a tough time of it with this ice everywhere, probably holed up somewhere till it all melts. They're no match for the coyotes and dogs until they can get better footing. Broken branches lie scattered around, some littering the path, mostly birch but some evergreen. The trees that aren't broken touch their tips to the ground like gargantuan croquet hoops. And everywhere the music of the ice. Strathspeys. Sometimes a waltz.

They stop shy of what everyone calls "the crossing." Peter kicks at a spot under an old pine tree unearthing soft needles and moss from underneath the brittle crust. "Here, old thing." He pats the spot until Dog stands in the newly made bed and turns around more times than is necessary. Peter leans his shoulder onto the side of the pine trunk that is bare, and pulls his cigarettes out of his jacket pocket. The tree has been there as long as he can remember, way back when he and his sister, Antoinette, ran through on the way to Dora and Mitchell's. It seemed even bigger then. The lighter goes out four times before it finally catches the tip of the Lucky Strike and he inhales as hard as he can holding the smoke in until he can't any more. He's got to quit. That's what Antoinette says. And Dora won't even let him in if he has them on his person. But not today. Not with this fucking mess going on.

The next drag isn't quite as good and he holds the lit end against a chunk of ice on the trunk until it sizzles, turns the ice around it into water, and extinguishes itself. He isn't quite ready to go back. What's the next step? Why the hell didn't he just tell the guy his wife was in the cabin? *She's right up there, mister*, he should have said. Oliver's her problem, not his. It's not his fault if the guy hits her. Besides, he can't protect the women and children of the world. Oliver. Maybe he's the salt of the earth. How does he know? Kind of fancy, though. Peter holds his fist up in front of him, back of his hand toward the pine tree, fingers facing him. He'll be fifty-nine in July but that isn't the only difference. His nails are ragged, cuticles torn, calluses here and there, on his palm, his thumb, streak of yellow from years of Lucky smoke trailing past. The wrinkles and creases have a permanently ingrained amalgam of grease, woodbark, harness blacking, garden soil. Nothing there that he could get off with soap and water even if he tried. He is clean. Christ, he'd washed his hands last night and took a bath in the washtub last week, before the storm. Certainly couldn't with the woman in the house. He never did take to letting his body get dirty but it is hard to keep it immaculate when you have no hot water and you work with your hands.

He leans the gun on the trunk of the pine and holds up his other hand. Things were different before the fire. He even manicured his cuticles before the highland games because he knew judges considered everything in open competition, even the condition of the fingernails bouncing up and down on the holes of the bagpipe chanter. No one had beaten him those last two years. He'd won just about everything, even Open Piper of the Day that last day in Maxville, and was ready to yield to pressure to become a judge. Three hundred dollars and a silver bowl he won at Maxville. That woman, up-and-coming grade one piper, he'd forgotten her name now, Kate or something like that, clapped loud and kissed his cheek when the winners were called. *Dinner?* he'd said to her after his name was announced as North American Professional Piping Champion, after he'd sat down with the silver bowl in his lap and the check in his sporran. *Love to*, she'd replied. Wonder what happened to her. Peter can't recall what happened after that until the call about the fire. Where had he eaten dinner? He'd eaten with Colin. He remembers telling Leslie, but he doesn't remember what they had or where they went. He stayed at the Prince Edward Hotel. He remembers that much. And he was in bed when the call came, his last minutes of sanity for a long time, just lazing around, thinking about what to have for breakfast. He didn't pick up the phone on the first ring or the second, thought it might be bagpipe business. It's the only thing he can remember of the hours before the call and it pisses him off. Forgetting those last hours of knowing he had a family.

Dog notices the movement first and raises his head, cocks one ear, emits a low growl. A rabbit blends into the bank of crusted snow just thirty feet away and doesn't seem to notice him. There are some new dark hairs mingling with the winter white. The trigger and the barrel of the twenty-gauge chill his hands as he raises it to sight. He pushes the safety off. Peter doesn't want to miss. He hates when he fires and the mere sound of the shot, instead of the pellets, ricochets against the flee-ing critter. He doesn't like to injure an animal either.

The wind dies down and there is no sound in the trees. He snugs the butt of the shotgun against his shoulder. The rabbit turns toward the gun as if giving himself up. He sights on the head, feels Dog's nose at his thigh. *Baroooom*. The sound reverberates off each frosted birch in the Crossing over and over, around the clearing. Too much noise for a

small rabbit. The rabbit drops, shudders before it stretches its front feet
out on the white mound. "Got it," Peter says.

In the old days, Dog would get there first, sniff, pick it up maybe.
But today he lags behind as Peter crunches his way to the carcass. It
looks like one pellet entered the head above the eye and a few more
along the body. A thin trickle of blood oozes from the head hole, scarlet
against the white of the fur and the ice, diffusing into pink when it finds
the water. The rest of the shot must have sprayed out onto the ice. With
his free hand, he scoops up the rabbit by the hind legs. It swings limply
against his thigh on the way home.

*You can stay one more day. You can stay two more days. He gave me
the creeps. That's why I lied. I gave you two hundred fucking dollars.*
Peter practices the responses aloud to Dog as they walk through the
woods. Once in a while, Dog stops to sniff a drop of the rabbit's blood.
*I'd like to help you but I've got a small place. I like living alone. Don't
see much of people. You really belong with your family. It's not my responsibility.* The rhythm of the ice-noise shifts from strathspey and waltz
to the cadence of his voice as he walks.

He is still trying to find the right response when he enters the clear-
ance of his driveway. When he's found it, he'll tell her. Just because he
lied to Mr. Oliver Sinclair, esquire, doesn't mean he will keep the woman
in his cabin. Only means he won't throw her out today. After dinner
he'll demand to know what's really going on. She'll have to tell him the
truth, not some Mumbo Jumbo. He didn't seem the abusive sort. Just a
little odd. Something else is going on.

"Got supper," he says after he shuts the door and kicks the frozen
pellets off his ice-cleats.

C H A P T E R   8

The right response never comes to Peter although he practices different ones in his mind over and over during the next few days. She stays and he grumbles about needing to get her to a phone or a shelter as soon as possible. He takes the truck out once to get supplies at the local store—tea, cream for coffee, flour—but leaves her in the cabin alone. The card from Mr. Oliver Sinclair lies flat behind the Luckies in his jacket pocket. He lingers at the pay phone, touches the card, greets Brendan on the way into the store.

"Hey, Pete, that guy ever get down your way? You know, the one with the shoes?" says Brendan.

"Yeah. Couple of days ago. He was a fancy one, all right."

"Ever hear what happened to the woman? Where'd you leave her off?"

"She's going soon." Peter turns to go out the door. "Hope this damn ice leaves pretty quick," he says to no one in particular.

Later on in the morning the ice has melted enough to allow the thick coverings to slip off tree branches and clatter to the ground. The birches stay bent but the evergreens gradually unfurl themselves toward the sun. Peter and Elaine and Dog make their way on the partially melted path to Dora's. There is enough bare ground now to provide safe footing except that the old dog often stops. Peter isn't sure if he is afraid of sliding or is just old and tired.

"Come on, Seamus," Elaine says, slapping at the side of her torn denim dress.

A few more days, he told her the day before. And this morning she asked to see Dora. He certainly has to find her a place to go before the baby comes. She is due in six weeks, which seems like a lot of time, but what if she's early?

"Oh, look, a rabbit," she says.

He doesn't look but keeps plodding ahead. She wouldn't even eat the rabbit he shot. Said it wasn't bled properly. Even so, she's tried. She's washed dishes, fed the stove, even made some passable rye bread, and she doesn't ask about the towel hanging over the dollhouse. There are even signs of her having leafed through the seed catalogs in the outhouse. Dog still sleeps beside her with no sign of changing his mind. Peter has stopped calling to him at night.

Suddenly he feels like a family. Peter, Elaine, and the dog, all trooping along together in the woods. It's too cute. He's had a family once and doesn't want another one. Things were fine before she arrived, so why doesn't he just call Oliver and be done with it all? He kicks at a branch in the path and it springs back at him. It doesn't take much to break it off at the ice line. He tosses it into the brush at the side of the path. From behind him he hears a low humming sound but can't place the tune. Low, like the ewes talk to their young, rumbling, resonant. He can't help placing his feet ahead of him in time to the rhythm of Elaine's humming voice.

The smoke from Dora's chimney is visible before they see the cabin. "Just up ahead," he says to Elaine.

"Wait, Peter, Seamus is lying down. Come on, boy, only a little more," she says.

Dog loves her and he obeys, even trotting the last little way. Peter wonders what Dora will think of Elaine. Dora meets them at the door, a little surprised.

"Well, who do we have here? Come in," she says. "I see the old dog is still with you."

"Dora, this is Elaine," he says.

"Gory be, but ain't you big as a house. You better come right in here so's I can get a good look at you."

"I thought you might check her out. You know. Take a look at things."

"Lordy, Mama, but you're a mess. Looks like you been sleeping in those clothes. I call all my mothers 'Mama,' don't I?" she says, looking at Peter. He doesn't remember ever hearing that but says nothing. "Shut that door. Get that old dog in here and shut that door."

"Hello, Dora," Elaine says. "Peter said you might check me and the baby. He says you deliver babies."

"Isn't that the fairest hair I ever saw. I used to have the blackest hair you ever saw before it turned color of birch bark. Soon's I give that dang dog his jerk I'll get you some tea."

Dora throws the jerky from the jar to Dog and turns away from them to make tea. She moves slower than Peter remembers. She was over sixty when he moved to the cabin for good and her hair was still mostly black then. Now there are just a few streaks of her former color left. Her thick braid hangs almost to her waist and Peter thinks it must be heavy, wonders why she doesn't cut it off. Peter loves Dora's place although he would never let his cabin get this untidy. Hunks of un- washed fleece dot the braided rug, fallen off, he supposes, when she carried armfuls of it to wash in the sink. Bits of walnut shells litter the area around the kitchen and brown liquid from the dye pot has spilled down the front of the yellow enamel woodstove. Her spinning wheel occupies the center of the room merely as a hub for baskets full of dyed and undyed fleece, skeins of spun yarn, hand cards, measuring tape, scissors, dirty teacups.

She's clean enough. Takes real good care of herself. He is sure that yellow enamel will be shining by evening and the teacups washed and set down on the table. But there will be more stuff to fill in the gaps. In the fall when she got her deer, she'd hang the jerk strips right from the kitchen ceiling where they dripped until they dried. Dog would sit under them with his tongue hanging out, trying to catch the dripping blood before it hit the floor.

"Here you go, got a little sweet flag in it, keep you from getting one of them danged spring colds."

Dora places the cups without saucers in front of them, the one with the handle broken off for herself, and sits at the end of the table. "I got a young girl from the reservation who helps me. I'm too old to be reliable any more. What if I died right there as the baby's coming? I'm well over eighty, you know. Could go any time."

"The baby is due the first of May. I don't want to have it in the hospital. There's some complications."

"Let me get my room fixed up a bit and I'll check you out," Dora says. "You stay here and drink your tea."

Dora holds her hand out to the side as she walks toward the bedroom, as if to make sure she is going the right way. Her legs wobble slightly with each step and when one of her socks falls down around her moccasin, she doesn't pull it up.

"Where you planning to have this baby? You can't have it in my cabin. Not enough room for us, let alone a baby." Peter makes himself say this to her because he needs his cabin back. He has things to do. Certain things you can't do with other people around.

"Can't we take it day by day? See how it goes? You said I could stay until tomorrow. Let's talk about it again then, okay?" she says.

There is nothing he can do now except sip the slightly bitter tea out of the cracked cup. He tries to picture Elaine underneath Mr. Fancy Pants Oliver Sinclair, her pale legs wrapped around him, and him saying,

Excuse me but shall I put it in now? He laughs out loud enough for Elaine to react.

"What's funny?" she asks.

She is beautiful, he thinks. Her eyes are the color of the Caribbean Sea, that turquoise blue that fades into aquamarine at the edge of the water. The way the two braids from her temples come together in one near the back of her head remind him of Leslie, except Leslie's hair was the color of rich garden soil and Elaine's, the color of beach sand.

"Nothing," he says, trying desperately to get the sex image out of his head, but it persists, strengthens. *May I brush that errant strand of hair off your forehead before I insert?* Peter almost hears the voice, polite, soft, damning.

"Ready?" Dora says, hands on hips. Peter notices that Dora's eyes in contrast are jet black, recessed and protected by thick brows and wrinkled skin. There is a glaze over them like that on the ice, a thin watery layer that shields old eyes from harm. "Peter, you behave yourself out here. No smoking. And leave that bread alone. Too hot to cut."

He tries not to eavesdrop but the bedroom is close and the door is thin. He remembers the questions from when Leslie was pregnant with the children. Children. That's a hard word for him to hear even in his head. He blinks his eyes hard, which usually clears the image. "When was your last period? Have you seen a doctor? How much weight have you gained?" Usual questions. He strains to hear the answers but Elaine faces away from the door and her voice is soft. "How far along was the miscarriage?" Peter moves as close as he dares to the door, feeling like a child listening at his parents' bedroom. "Things have changed over the years. I had my babies in a hospital. A white man's hospital. Lucky I got out alive. Lost two babies. Now folks are going back to the old ways, delivering at home with women who know how to birth babies."

Dog tires of his jerky and ambles toward him yawning louder than Peter thinks possible. Peter backs away from the door quietly and stands at the table, still close enough to hear. He shuffles around making some noise, pours more tea, coughs. He imagines Elaine with her dress pulled up, Dora pressing her belly, Dora's old thick fingers prying away folds to enter the vagina. He hears a low murmur now, one, then the other in response, the kind of talk women do when it's private, about private things. He remembers how erotic it was when Leslie's doctor felt for the baby, some stranger invading his space, knowing it like he knew it, and how he tried to keep the erection from being conspicuous.

He rustles through the silverware drawer looking for the bread knife. Finally he finds it in the sink, wet. He wipes it on his shirt before he starts the cut, looking at the door occasionally to make sure they are still in there. He's not going to get away with it but it's habit from childhood to keep watch when he's doing something forbidden. It is molasses bread and the steam rises instantly when the knife penetrates it. He tries hard to keep the loaf from smushing as he cuts but the bread follows the knife until it is only an inch high on the end. Dora was right. Too hot. One piece will be enough, he thinks.

Peter tears off a corner to give to Seamus. The name is kind of growing on him and he tries it out loud. "Seamus." He doesn't say it loud, just loud enough to hear it himself. Certainly a better name than Dog, but it's hard to change what you call someone. He thinks about getting a border collie pup, one he can train to help out on the island. He isn't getting younger and a dog could round up the ewes and hold them for shearing or gathering up lambs for slaughter. When he was growing up, his family had springers but Old Man Farley would never allow them on the island. Said they'd cause a terrible ruckus. Only dog he'd allow was a border collie. Irene up at the general store raised springers and he thought her bitch was getting ready to have another litter. A springer might be good for hunting bird and rabbit. Seamus wouldn't take kindly to a new pup, though, so it would have to wait.

The voices from the other room become louder; Peter brushes the crumbs off the counter to hide the evidence and stands in front of the bread.

"You spin your own wool?" he hears Elaine ask.

"I do just about everything, honey," Dora says on the way back to the kitchen. "Nothing real well, but a lot of stuff acceptable."

"Everybody healthy?" he asks.

"Right fine baby in there. Should be five or six weeks more." Elaine stands next to Dora, looking like a child although she must be thirty, and Peter notices she wears a thick gray and blue sweater that covers her belly. "Mitchell's old sweater. Remember it? He always wore it when he went out to check his traps. Been sitting on the bottom of the closet floor since he died. Might as well get some use."

"Did you spin the wool for this sweater?" Elaine asks.

"Does the bear shit in the woods? Is the pope Catholic? Only kind of wool that's any good. Just enough lanolin to keep the damp out. Keeps you warm. Looks good too. I sell tons of the stuff in the summer to the tourists."

"Could you teach me? Not today, but sometime. I'm good with my hands. I knit and crochet."

"If Peter don't mind, I'll get you set up right now. Give you a quick lesson. Won't take more than ten minutes. Then you go home and practice."

"Peter?" Elaine asks. Her eyes look directly into his and the corners of her mouth turn up like sleigh runners. The yellow mark on her face has disappeared, leaving the faint pink of her cheek.

"Why don't I cut you a piece of that bread you been staring at and you can sit and eat it while I show her."

"Go ahead. I can cut the bread. Go on. I've got a little time before chores."

C H A P T E R   9

The next day Peter leaves Elaine at Dora's and heads back home alone. Dog's days of walking through the woods any great distance are finished because the day before Peter had to carry him the last half of the way. For the first time, he growls when Peter pushes at his nose to keep him in the cabin, tries to shut the door gently against the old dog's face, because it's just too much of a walk over to Dora's. Elaine is going to help plant some seedlings in exchange for another spinning lesson and Peter has a few hours before he has to walk over and get her. She says she will walk back herself but Peter says there is still too much ice in the woods.

Actually, the ice is almost gone, leaving muddy sinkholes where frost still lingers in the ground and water can't drain through, a day for rubber boots, not ice-cleats. He is relieved to see no black truck in the driveway, or any vehicle. He expects to see a strange car or the local cop or the black truck soon because Brendan isn't going to keep it secret forever that the woman's still in the cabin, that Peter can't get rid of her.

He hears Dog scratching and howling before he even enters the clearing. The excitement he feels about having a few hours to himself accelerates as he bounds up the path toward the cabin. "I'm on my way, old thing," he calls to the dog behind the door. "Come on," he says. The inside of the door has deep gouges under the handle and chunks of wood litter the floor. "Dog. What have you been doing?" Dog slinks by on his way out and begins to pee before he gets off the stoop, whining the whole time. "Seamus," he says. The old dog looks up as if he can't believe Peter's utterance. It is a good strong name. Peter thinks he will try to use it.

The dolls have been cooped up even longer. Six days. Peter shuts the door on the world and walks with leaden feet over toward the doll-house, stopping on the way to pour himself some thick oily coffee from the morning. A few minutes ago he had been anxious to see them, move them from their frozen positions, but now he feels full of apprehension. The cabin is quiet, no one watching, no one making tea. He allows himself to stand still halfway across the room, just stand doing nothing for a moment, sipping the cold coffee.

The room seems the same as it used to be except for the extra bed on the floor and Elaine's things scattered around, but everything is different. He tries to remember sitting, reading Yeats or Roethke or Ruth Moore, the creak of the rocker and Dog's breathing the only sounds. The stove still sits in the center of the cabin. The back wall is still windowless and dark, the table still by the stove, the rocker still over the trap door.

Since Elaine's arrival, the towel has hung over the front of the white colonial dollhouse shutting his family off from his life. It's upsetting. Everything. He positions the stool in front of the blue towel.

There are two ways to approach everything. Lift the corner slowly or just pull the damn towel off. Suddenly he feels foolish and is glad no one can see him. He tugs one end and the towel gives easily, landing silently on his boot. The family still sits at the kitchen table, drinking orange juice, getting ready for school. The miniature Mr. Coffee machine is almost empty from the water he poured in it before the storm. "I'm sorry," he says to all of them. Should he put them all back to bed or just move them around in the kitchen? There is no telling how long the woman is going to stay.

Sarah's position is awkward, her leg slung over the chair like that and her arm has been holding a glass of orange juice for days. He picks her up and removes the glass from her hand. Her limbs stretch out easily before he moves the little doll through the hall, into the bedroom, onto the bed with the stuffed cats. Nathaniel still hasn't found his sneaker and is standing at the counter almost ready for school. His room is right in front and easy to access.

Leslie sits at the kitchen table, waiting for Peter to pour his coffee and she seems to know that it is too early to go to bed, still daylight outside. "Les, I didn't mean to leave you there that long," he says to the doll. Her smile is painted. Not a big smile but enough of an upturn to make her look happy. He picks her up. She is light as dust. He tries to keep the image of the live Leslie but the dead one creeps in, flesh burned black, hair gone, mouth pulled back to her ears in an open scream. The authorities told him that all three died before they burned. The burning came later after they died quietly in their sleep from the silent deadly gasses. Leslie was found far over on his side of their king-sized bed.

He tucks the Leslie doll under his shirt, settles it on his bare skin so her head lies just under his jaw, tries to press her closer, into his flesh. "Les. I'm sorry. It's been rough the past few days." The doll feels oddly cold against his chest. His hand finds her head, strokes her hair with his index finger, his rough skin catching on the brown fibers. The tangle that was his inadequate attempt to braid hair from her temples seems to have grown bigger since the last time he felt it. When all this with Elaine is finished, he has plans to spend some time fixing up the dolls. He's even thought of getting new rugs and furniture for the downstairs.

Just before Sarah was born, Leslie decided she wanted to change her look and started braiding two small cornrows, one at each temple. Sometimes she'd catch them with the rest of her hair and pull everything back away from her face. The first time she braided them, they hung loose as she sat on him naked, her belly huge, her knees bent at his chest, her face hovering over his, braids hanging down. Peter felt the baby move on his belly as if he carried the child himself. "Did you feel that," she said, smiling, waving the braids around. He raised his head to kiss her but couldn't quite reach past the belly. Her laugh went on and on until he began to move inside her slowly, rhythmically while she rocked back and forth on him, watching his face, watching as he bit his lip, groaned low when she felt him come inside her, her smile just like the doll, enough of an upturn to make her look happy. That was the day he felt Sarah was truly part of him.

"Les," he says to the doll snuggled at his neck, "the sweater. I'm going to have Dora make you a new one. A doll's sweater. She sells them to the summer people. A bright red one with bead buttons. You always looked stunning in red. Would you like that?" He knows there will be no answer but he waits an appropriate length of time before stretching out her legs and placing her on the bed, far over on his side. Dora would wonder why he wants a doll sweater but would never ask him outright. He'd just say, *I want to buy that red doll sweater, the one with the glass bead buttons.* Years ago, he placed a mandoll in the house but it made him uncomfortable, like he didn't belong there.

This time he tucks the towel in snugly on all sides, stuffs one end under a pile of books. He stands back and sees an ordinary bookshelf with the oddest looking structure covered by a fluffy blue towel. Elaine must think him totally mad but she hasn't asked about it. Certainly she's taken a peek. If this goes on much longer he'll rethink the whole doll-house thing, perhaps put it in a less conspicuous place.

After he lets Seamus back in and stuffs another log into the stove, he hauls the old rocking chair over to the kitchen table and plunks himself in it. A cigarette. He pats his pocket. There they are just in front of Mr. Sinclair's card. He pries off his boots and slides his stockinged feet onto the edge of the table. The first drag of the Lucky catches in his throat and he coughs a bit, tries it again. This time it goes down smooth, warms his chest. A cognac might taste pretty good, he thinks, but he never drinks before dinner. The silence unnerves him. No one rattling dishes, pouring tea, humming so low you can barely hear. He hates to break the mood but leans forward and flicks the radio on. Mozart. His head nods in rhythm up and down with the tempo of the piece. Drilling. Staccato. His neck hurts and he rubs the back of it. Not in the mood for Mozart. Country. Talk. Advertising. Dylan. Bach. He leaves it on the Bach station until the movement is finished but he's not in the mood for Bach either. He needs some Mendelssohn or Stravinsky or even Frank Sinatra. God. He hates Frank Sinatra. He turns the radio off, drags his feet off the table, stubs out his cigarette in this morning's coffee cup, and gets up.

It's been a long time since he's played his chanter. There is a small crack in the mouthpiece which he covers with a piece of black tape pulled off one of the holes. African blackwood. The first chanter he ever had. Must be over fifty years old, a gift from his father. He's had many plastic ones over the years but this one was always the best. The wood feels warm and smooth under his fingers and the ivory of the sole feels cold like alabaster, like satin, like ice. Hard to buy real ivory now.

He runs off a scale. The reed still sounds in tune except for the high G because he pulled the tape off it to fix the mouthpiece. He sits on the red highback chair, places the sole of the chanter on the table and the mouthpiece between his teeth. He covers the holes, raising one finger, lowering another, playing tunes only in his head, tunes he remembers from years ago. He doesn't blow into it so the chanter makes no noise. Every once in a while over the years he has picked it up and played a short reel or a jig once and then put the chanter back on the shelf. Twice he's replaced the reed.

Some of the grace notes he's forgotten, but the tunes are always there except for the piobaireachd. When he was competing, he knew most of the piobaireachds by heart, and the rest were at least familiar. Regular folks didn't know about them because they were never played in parades but Peter loved all the ancient tunes, loved the structure, the haunting movements, even the name, impossible to spell. *Pee-brock. Give it a guttural ending,* he'd say to students, but it took years for the youngsters to learn to say anything in Gaelic. *Pee-brock.*

He's never played any of them since the fire, never could manage to think of them, couldn't even play an air or a slow march, let alone a piobaireachd. The first part of "Speed the Plough" is easy but he forgets the second part in the middle, goes back, begins again, and this time he plays it all the way through. Then he tries the jig, "Paddy's Leather Breeches," out loud but it reminds him of Mozart and he stops. His fingers are thick and slow. His right little finger is crooked and a bit swollen, which makes his low G sound fuzzy. It's hard to listen to bad piping, even on a practice chanter, so he makes himself play movements over and over until he feels his finger loosen up as if he'd sprayed WD-40 on the joints.

It's been years since he played a strathspey and he chooses "The Devil in the Kitchen" because he loves the title. The beats, strong, weak, medium, weak, not straight like the reels and jigs but hold and shorten, a lilt, a dance piece. Damn. Too round. He begins again. *Hold those dotted notes,* he hears in his head, he hears the judges when he was fifteen and sixteen and eighteen, before he became an open piper, before he became one of the best in the country. This time it sings. His foot sways in a dance and he holds the dotted notes until there's barely enough time left for the cut ones and it sounds good. Not good like he used to sound. But good for someone who's hardly played in twenty years.

After the woman leaves, he thinks, he'll try a slow air, just to see how it goes, see if he can do it, see if he can give it the passion that a slow air demands. And the piobaireachd? Not ready for that yet. Maybe never again. Playing a piobaireachd requires too much emotion.

The sound of a vehicle outside stops him and he is embarrassed to be caught playing his chanter, although he has plenty of time to put it away before anyone can see it. He hears the banging on the door before he even gets over to the shelf. Christ, the guy must have run up the path. He steps into his boots but doesn't bother to lace them. He wanted to meet them outside before they had a chance to knock. It must be the husband because Brendan would have honked or just opened the door and hollered. No one knocks around these parts. More pounding, this time louder and longer.

"I know someone is in there. Please open the door." He's right. It is Mr. Sinclair. Seamus whines on the other side of the door in unison with the husband as Peter stands, door latch in his hand, trying to think of what he will say.

"Hold on," he says through the door.

More knocking, not as frantic this time, but insistent, low down as if a child were out selling Girl Scout cookies or collecting for a charity, knock, knock, perpetual, like a clock, four-four time, a march. Suddenly he is terrified of what is on the other side of the door. He hears shuffling and low voices in rhythm with the knocking before he raises the latch. The noise ceases. Seamus is the first to push through the opening door, leaving three men standing on the landing. Actually two stand on the steps because there isn't enough room. Mr. Oliver Sinclair himself is at the front. They are all wearing suits. Peter hasn't seen three men together in suits since the funeral. All dark suits. And black shoes.

He glances down at his clothes. Boots scuffed and reeking from horse shit, pants with a red patch on one knee, jacket frayed at the bottom and the edges of the sleeves. He impulsively runs his hand through the front of his hair as if that would make it neater, tugs the end of his beard to pull the straggling beard hairs together.

"What can I do for you?" he manages. He knows damn well what they want. Three of them. Odds are a little unbalanced.

Oliver steps into the cabin and the others crowd behind him. "Folks in the store said they thought Elaine might be here."

Peter sweeps his arm toward the back of the cabin and back to the men. "Only person here is me, far as I can see."

"Then you won't mind if we come in and look around. We're very concerned."

The men are all in the cabin now and the last one, a very round man with a too-small suit, pulls the door shut behind him. The dog slinks over to the bed and jumps into it. Seamus has never seen that many people in his cabin before. Peter backs up so there is room for all of them and so he doesn't have to breathe their breath.

"Suit yourself," he says backing up all the way to the kitchen sink. "Cup of coffee?"

"No, thank you." A wizened man with thick horn-rimmed glasses speaks for the group.

Peter has a momentary flash that he has gone to heaven and these are the keepers of the gate. Or perhaps it is hell. Or at least undertakers.

"We don't want to accuse you of anything but someone in town did say she was here," says the round man. "We just want to talk to her."

"Why is there a bed and a sleeping bag on the floor? Does someone else live here?" says Oliver, moving toward the bed. "She must realize what this means, to go off like this, everyone worried." Oliver fixes his stare at the two cups on the table, one with old coffee, one with old tea. "She's been here. I know it."

"Oliver," says the man with the big glasses, "let me talk to this gentleman. My name is Christopher. I am an elder. I'm one of Jehovah's Witnesses. We mean no harm."

Peter takes the fleshy hand in his. "Peter," Christopher says. "You must realize we are worried."

"Look. She is trying to sort things out," Peter says. "She doesn't want to go home right now."

"We believe that wives should be obedient to a loving husband," the man says. " 'Let wives be in subjection to their husbands as to the

Lord, because a husband is head of his wife as the Christ also is head of the congregation.' Ephesians 5:22."

Just like that, he says the Bible mandates that Elaine go home. Just like that. Memorized. As if he says it every day. The four men stand still, eyes all averted to table, woodstove, dirty dishes, pile of logs on the floor. Peter and Christopher stand very close to each other. Peter needs to speak. Needs to say something for Elaine. What kind of shit is that, saying that women have to obey. "I never read anything like that in my Bible," he says.

"Where is she?" Oliver says.

"Out. And that's where you better go. She doesn't want you to know where she is."

"She is carrying my child and I will know where she is. Now. Right now," Oliver says, calm as could be, his voice low and even, "now, right now," as if he were saying, "cream and sugar" when asked what he wants in his coffee. He sits down in the rocking chair without asking first.

"Loving husband," Peter says, looking at Christopher. "Does that sound like a loving husband? This is my house and I'm telling you to get out," Peter hears himself say. "Get out." The thought of Elaine's bruise causes Peter to look at Oliver's hands. They are gripped on the arms of Peter's red rocking chair.

It takes a minute or two but Oliver rises from the chair. Peter is afraid Oliver will take a swing at him but doesn't back up. "Please give her this," he says, placing a small black Bible on Peter's table.

Peter doesn't answer.

"I'm sorry," Oliver says. "She isn't strong. We need to talk. Just talk." He offers his hand but Peter can't take it, can't bear to touch it.

"I'll tell her you were here," Peter says, still staring at the empty hand in front of him.

Oliver's hand drops to his side.

"Please tell her we love her," says Christopher.

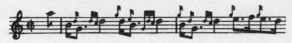

East Wood Cottage

CHAPTER 10

*P*eter waits until he no longer hears the car's engine before he turns away and heads for the woods. It is easy walking, at least compared to what it's been lately. The patches of ice are ringed with bare ground where he gets a firm footing for his cleated boots. He misses the dog and once he lowers his hand searching for a furry head. Then he stops because he thinks he hears the dog whining at his cabin door to join him. The old thing can't keep up anymore but Peter hates to leave him cooped up, thinking that no one wants him.

Peter hears her struggling before he sees her on the ground. He hears thrashing of tree limbs and thinks it's a deer or moose until the words come. "Damn," he hears. "What a dumbo." Then more thrashing. He jogs ahead, watching for ice patches until he glimpses Mitchell's old blue sweater through a crisscross of birches.

"Elaine?"

"Over here," she says. "My foot's caught."

He senses the fear in her voice, not from her words, but from an innate feeling, like he sensed an underlying current of warning in Oliver's polite retorts. When she looks up at him, he sees the fear, in her eyes, her flushed cheeks, her chin. He kneels beside her and touches her leg, detects the shivering underneath her thin denim dress.

"Under that root. I slipped on that patch of ice and my foot slid right under that root. I can't get up. My foot won't come out."

"Hey," he says back to her. "You're aren't going to get unstuck yanking on it like that." He is afraid to touch her leg again, even to calm her, so he crawls to her foot. He'll have to stand her up first. "Swing your arm around my neck." No other way to do it. "Just take your time. I've got you." He holds her just under the ribs and feels her hand at the back of his neck. "Come on," he says while he pulls her up with him. She feels like a rag doll stuffed with lead, far heavier than he thought possible.

"Ow, ow, ow," she says in rapid succession.

"Hold on."

When she is standing upright, the heaviness of her body against his disappears and the shivering begins in her belly. He feels it against his hand and doesn't know what to say. Her right foot is jammed under the stump of a large uprooted pine. "Put your hands on the stump while I steady you." She obeys him without question, does exactly as he says.

"I fell hard," she says. "I don't feel the baby kicking."

Peter's hands are around her foot, pulling. The root gives just enough for him to jerk the boot free. He knows her arms are going to go around him when he stands up. Her crying is quiet and desperate, the kind that causes women to need comforting. What will he do if she needs him too much?

When he can't stay on the ground any longer without explanation, he steadies himself on the stump and gets to his feet. She doesn't throw her arms around him. Her arms are around her belly.

"We'll go to see Dora. She'll listen for the baby," he says.

Elaine doesn't reply. The sobs abate slowly. He touches the sleeve of her sweater. "The baby. It kicked," she says, still looking down. "It kicked," this time directly to Peter.

"Come on, then, let's get you home. Can you walk on that ankle?"He hopes she can.

"It'll be fine. Just a bruise." Just a bruise. Just a bruise.

Peter allows her to go first. The way back is slow and she limps. Once she turns back to tell him that the baby moved again. "Good," he says.

"Peter."

"Yes."

"I want to show you my spinning. When we get back."

By the time they reach the cabin, Elaine is out of breath, bulky as she is and favoring her right leg. She stands at the edge of the cabin clearing, leans on the corner of the barn and pulls off her cap allowing her hair to tumble down like oats from the winnower. "Your husband came back," he says when he is next to her.

"What? Oliver?" She steps back, glances around the yard, up to the cabin.

"He's gone. Came with two other men. They know you're here."

"What did he say?"

"He wants you home. He says they're all worried."

"He'll be back."

"I told him you didn't want to go home, wherever that is. Hell, I don't even know where you live."

She moves close to him. Their sweaters touch. Her hair ripples around her face. "Thank you, Peter," she says.

"He left you something."

"Oliver? A small black book?" she asks.

"Yes, a black book. A Bible."

"Are you sure? A Bible?"

"Small. Black. 'Holy Scriptures' printed in gold across the front."

"Holy Scriptures. Yes. That's a Bible."

A wisp of hair covers her eyes for a moment and he pulls it back from her face with his little finger. "There," he says before he heads toward the cabin.

At the door, the old dog pees again before he gets all the way outside and Peter has to wipe up the urine with a rag. Won't be long.

"Look," she says. "Watch me spin."

She is like a child with a new toy as she twirls the drop spindle, drawing out the fluffy white wool in the air above it.

"See? It's almost smooth."

"Dora makes some money doing that. Well, on the wheel, of course, not the drop spindle. Looks pretty smooth to me."

"I love this. It feels soft on my fingers when I draw it out. Look. Dora said I had the knack."

"Got to get some stuff in town," he says to her while he shoves a chunk of maple into the stove. "Just a few things. Milk, coffee, salt, sugar."

"Oh, please, may I come?"

"Won't be long. I'll fill the woodbox for you before I go."

"No. You can't leave me here alone. What if he comes back?" She stands beside the door, her heavy sweater still pulled over her denim dress, her hat back on her head.

Peter's not going to be able to smoke if she comes with him and he hasn't had a cigarette since early morning. Maybe she'll call someone from the store. "Have you got a friend you can call?" he says.

"I don't know," she says.

"Come on, then."

They help the old dog into the back of the truck and Peter slams the gate. Maneuvering up the driveway is easy except for a couple of icy patches which he avoids. No need for the chains today but he has thrown them in back just in case. There is hardly a spot of ice or snow on the roads but the bushes and trees off to the side are still covered in the shaded areas and the deep pockets into the woods still sparkle when the sun fills them. Peter flicks on the radio at the top of the hill. Handel's

Water Music. He turns the dial. Country. *"Why'd you leave me, baby, I'm crying all the time."* He swings the truck out onto the wet macadam and changes the station again. *"They paved Paradise and put up a parking lot,"* blares out of the speaker. He turns it down. She turns it up.

"Don't it always seem to go, that you don't know what you've got till it's gone, They paved Paradise and put up a parking lot." Elaine sings in counterpoint to Joni, her voice high and sweet, like a wood thrush. She knows all the words, even to the verses. Peter remembers singing that song on a trip, the children joining in the chorus form the back seat, always in a raucous tone, but Elaine's is solemn and doesn't quite go with the song, as if someone really is going to pave Paradise.

Peter shifts down before a patch of icy road, jerking the truck, stopping the song, and he regrets interrupting. "Sorry," he says.

Elaine turns away from him toward her window.

"We're almost there."

There is no response from Elaine and Peter turns the radio off. He hasn't seen her like this before, pensive, quiet, withdrawn.

"Just up ahead," he says.

"I'd like to go to a secondhand store," she says, after an uncomfortable period of silence. "I need some clothes. I have the two hundred dollars you gave me. We'll need to get a baby car seat. It's possible we might have to get the baby to the hospital after delivery and we need to have a car seat."

Christ, that could be more than a month from now. She can't stay with him all that time. He starts to tell her that, starts to form the words in his head. *No way. You've got to go home. One more day, but that's it. I need my cabin back. You took my two hundred dollars, so go.* But the words don't come out of his mouth. "Oh," is all that he hears himself say. He swallows and tries again. "A car seat. Well." He touches his jacket pocket. Luckies, and in behind the package, the business card of Mr. Oliver Sinclair. If he says any of the things in his head out loud, she will cry. He knows that. For the first time she seems weak.

"Here we are. I won't be long. Then we'll go to the Goodwill store. It's just down the road." He swings himself out of the driver's seat and hops to the ground. She doesn't even turn. Good. The thought of introducing her or explaining her is very unpleasant. *Peter. The hermit. The guy who lives in the woods alone and hates people. Now he's got a woman.*

The store is crowded with folks released from the ice by the thaw. They line up at the register with basics: milk, bread, beer, videos, candles and batteries, just in case. Peter roams up and down the aisles picking up sardines, pepper, milk, batteries.

"Hey, Pete. How'd you make out with that pregnant girl?" It's Mason, Brendan's stern man. Christ, it's all over town.

Peter turns. Mason can hardly wait to hear. It's written all over his face. Pete, the guy who lived in the woods for twenty years without a woman. Now he's got a pregnant one. That's big news in these parts. "It's just temporary. She's going home soon as I can reach her family. Couldn't throw her out in the ice." He feels he has said too much. That he doesn't need to say anything. Mason nods, smiles, doesn't believe him at all. Probably thinks it's his kid in her belly.

"Where's she from?"

"Bangor way."

"You got her in the truck?"

Peter turns away without responding and heads for the checkout, piles his groceries on the counter, throws a couple of peppermint patties on top. "Pack of Luckies, nonfilter," he says to the kid behind the counter. They keep the cigarettes on the wall where customers can't get at them. "Better give me two."

"Make out okay in this freaking ice?" the kid asks. "Four days and no juice. Wasn't too bad except for the TV. Missed everything. Just came back on this morning. Guess you don't care about that, do ya?" Peter doesn't reply. He never replies but the kid always asks, makes small talk about weather. As soon as the bag is packed with groceries, Peter grabs it and heads for the door.

"I'll drop you off at the Goodwill. Got a couple of errands to run," he says as he climbs into the truck. She turns and smiles and he sees that she is feeling stronger than she was.

"Thank you," she says.

The music store is only a block away from the Goodwill, a few minutes' walk, just enough time for a smoke. He pulls the pack from its spot in front of the business card and taps out a Lucky. He finishes the cigarette in front of the store. Guitars and mandolins crowd the display window and in the corner are several violins. He wonders if Elaine plays an instrument. Her voice is probably instrument enough. He catches a drip from the side of the building with the lit end of the Lucky and drops the butt into his pocket.

Next to the music store is a place called Pleasant Dreams. Godawful name for a store, but in the window are some inexpensive mattresses with bright covers. He thinks of the hardness of his cabin floor while he opens the door, causing a loud buzzer to go off. The girl behind the counter is watching a television talk show and barely looks up.

"How much for one of those mattresses?" he asks.

"You mean the futon? They're ninety-nine fifty plus tax." She still doesn't look up at him, but swipes the edge of her fingernail against an emery board and blows at it. She turns the television down with the remote thing and continues to file her nails.

"I'll take it," he says.

After he loads the futon into the bed of the truck he enters the music store. The store is hot, stifling, bad for the instruments; probably turn the heat way down at night and on Sunday. Bagpipes would crack under these conditions. Guitars and fiddles probably do too. He wouldn't buy an instrument in this store.

"What've you got for bagpipe chanter reeds?" he asks the old guy who's dusting the drums.

The man wobbles over to the counter and pulls out a small box, placing it on the glass between them. "That's all we got," he says.

Peter lifts the tissue paper, exposing the cane reeds nestled at the bottom. "Mind if I try them?"

"Be my guest."

Peter picks them up one by one and blows into the end of each one, listening for sound, a crow, anything to tell him about the reed. He separates three out of the bunch and tries each of them again. One has a nice crow but may be too easy, soft, mushy. The other two are a bit on the hard side but are clear and strong. He holds up the one with the crow. "I'll take this. How much?"

"Seven dollars," the man says. Peter struggles to hide his shock, like a man just out of prison. When he was competing, a top notch reed went for about three bucks. "Seven bucks plus tax," the man says.

Peter slips the padded reed between the business card and the Luckies and pays the man. Might not even play the damn thing. Could be a big waste of money.

C H A P T E R 1 1

*P*eter's hands move quickly over the straw, raking it with his fingers, exposing the tender garlic shoots. "They're planted four across. Just pull the straw off into the paths," he says to Elaine, who is on the next row. She is cumbersome and slow as she inches her way down the rows of garlic, pulling the straw toward her bulky body. The sun warms them and they have both removed their hats and gloves. Her hair glows when she turns her head, the little waves created by the braids mirroring the sunshine. It sways as she leans to scoop the straw and for a moment he can't tell the difference between the straw and her hair. He thinks of the young maiden spinning and spinning the straw throughout the night, trying to turn it into hanks of gold thread to please Rumpelstiltskin.

It's hard to believe that just three weeks ago everything was covered with ice. Folks around said it was the only spring ice storm this late in the season they could remember in the history of the whole state of Maine. He nips the tip of one of the garlic shoots and pops it into his mouth. The first thing from the garden is always the best. "Try one," he calls over to her. "Just pinch it off near the top."

She sits, legs spread out in front of her, chewing the tiny shoot as if she had never tasted garlic before in her life. Strands of straw decorate Mitchell's old blue sweater. "Do you use the shoots in cooking?"

"In the spring sometimes. Mostly I wait until August, till the tops begin to die down, and pull the bulbs. They last through the winter. Gone now, though, ate most all of them before the ice storm. I think you used the last one in the potatoes."

His hand slides over a frozen spot on the ground, pushing the straw off as best he can. Bunches stick to the frozen ground. *It will take a week or so to thaw out,* he thinks. Past the chunk of ice, he feels an emptiness under the mound of straw, pushes his hand further into the space until his fingers touch something warm, moving. "Elaine, shhh, come here. Slowly."

She hefts her body off the path, moving like a waltzing whale over to him. He gently pushes the straw aside enough for her to see the babies. They look like one being, huddled in a hairless blind heap. Six or seven squirm together while one shivers off to the side, alone. Peter scoops it up along with some straw so his scent won't transfer to the infant and places it on top of the mound. It is smaller than the end of his thumb.

"Oh, Peter. Look." Elaine lowers herself onto a mound of straw next to the babies. "They're naked. Wouldn't you think they'd freeze to death? I guess the mom keeps them warm." Her arms circle her round belly as she speaks.

"This seems kind of early for mice to be having their young. If we cover them up, the mother will probably come back and feed them. Let's check next week."

"But what if the mother is dead or is afraid to return?"

"There's nothing we can do. No mouse milk in my cupboard." His laugh surprises him.

"Mouse milk. What a weird concept. Mouse milk. But, of course, mice need milk too." Her pale hand rises to her sweater, pauses over her breast. She looks up at Peter, unaware that her fear projects in her

eyes like a movie on a screen. "I will have milk soon," she says. A dread
of something horrendous, not the pain of childbirth. Something primordial, something terribly primordial, eats at her. He can see it. It has
something to do with the baby, the husband, the miscarriage she spoke
about behind the closed door of Dora's bedroom. Something to do with
the religion. He knows she wants to tell him but won't until he asks.
He's not sure he's ready to do that. Asking about personal things means
commitment.

"They'll be fine. I've done this before, exposed baby animals. If you
don't get your smell all over them, the mom will be back." He pats her
shoulder lightly and hopes her horrible fear won't materialize into tears.
"Come on. Flowers are next."

The flower bed at the side of the barn is all perennials begun by his
parents years ago when it was just a summer property. Doesn't take a
lot of work except this time of year and in the fall when he weeds and
mulches everything. The vegetable garden always looks better than the
flowers. His sister brings him a shrub every year and plants it for him.
"You've got to keep replacing the dead plants," she said during the last
visit. "This garden gets smaller and smaller every year." The peonies
grew better here than at the house in Connecticut, something about the
sun and heat from the barn. They were the only plants that didn't get
scorched because they were over by the garage rather than against the
house. This year he planned to divide them but he's said that every year
for the past fifteen. He'll be glad to get into the vegetable garden where
the plants have a purpose, a reason to grow.

Elaine lumbers along carrying a bucket for winter flotsam and jet-
sam. The feeling of dread flickers when he looks back. Flickers and
disappears. "Tell me what the plants are. I've done some gardening. Not
much, but I know daisies and lilies of the valley when I see them."

Peter is surprised that Elaine is still able to get down on the ground
and then get up again. She lowers herself onto a heap of straw with a
grunt.

"The peonies line up along the back of the barn. White and rose. Just pull the straw to the side and break the old sticks off into the bucket. You'll see deep pink shoots growing in the woody center. They're brittle."

Elaine has been with him just over a month. Dora said yesterday that the baby could come any time but most likely it would be a couple of weeks. Peter wonders why the husband hasn't been back. Letters arrive in the mailbox every other day from him to Elaine but she never tells him anything about them. "Another letter from Oliver?" she says as if they hadn't been arriving regularly. Her letters to him are not quite as frequent. Three times Oliver has driven down the driveway allowing them enough time to hide in the barn. He called out, honked his horn, and left.

They talk about the dog, Seamus, about Dora, about the sheep out on the island, about her religion. She's a Jehovah's Witness and talks about paradise on earth being much like the cabin and the gardens and barn and the walk through the woods to Dora's. He always thought the Witnesses were holy rollers, talking about hellfire and brimstone and purgatory and heaven but Elaine doesn't talk like that. The pain in her eyes fades when she speaks about Jehovah and the life on earth after Armageddon. Peter watches her on her knees, heavy with her child, brushing back her oat-colored hair and wonders how she can believe that, how she can pray and give thanks to a God that doesn't even exist. He knows. He tried it, after the fire.

Elaine works quickly and meticulously through the peony bed, pulling away the straw, snapping the old dead stems, exposing the fragile new shoots. She mounds the straw around the plants to keep weeds from growing and to retain moisture. He works on the lily of the valley bed because it's more difficult, requires experience, but his fingers are older and stiff and thick and it is hard to remove the straw from between the small circles of plants.

She hears the car first and looks up from the straw. It's not the black truck this time but it certainly is Oliver Sinclair driving. She sits back on her heels, brushes her hair from her eyes and stays where she is, no attempt to hide but no attempt to greet. Peter considers fleeing, but just briefly. They've avoided Oliver so far by hiding in the goat stall. It's too late for that. There's going to be trouble. He can feel it.

A woman is the first out of the car. Peter scrambles in the straw like a child, tries to gain his footing in the slippery ground. He feels he has lost the first round. He brushes the bits of debris from his clothes, pulls his hat over his head, positions himself in front of Elaine. The woman lilts as she walks. She is dark as maple heartwood and her lime-green dress swings around her with each step. Peter thinks she must be connected to a sky hook that allows her to barely touch the sodden ground with her feet. In the background, the figures of two men alight from the sedan, shadowy, vague, but he's sure the one in the suit is Oliver. The woman is almost to the flower garden before Peter sees the age on her face, her neck, her hands. Wrinkles in the smooth brown skin seem out of place.

She stops abruptly an arm's length from Peter with a plea in her eyes, a plea for permission to approach Elaine. Peter nods to her but holds his arm as a barrier to the men who have barely moved from their little car. When he turns his back to them to help Elaine up from the heap of straw and broken twigs, he worries that they won't heed his warning, but Elaine needs to be standing. The woman waits at his side while Elaine struggles to rise, holding on to Peter's hand with an anxious grip.

"Elaine," the woman says, opening her arms. Peter is in the middle, two women on one side, two men slowly approaching on the other. He moves a few steps over to position himself directly in the center. "Elaine," she says again.

Elaine glances at Peter before she advances toward the open arms, her hair loose down her back. The brown hands stroke the length of the flaxen hair while Peter watches Elaine's arms encircle the woman at her waist. Who the hell is she?

"I love you," he hears, but isn't sure who says it.

"I love you," again, in Elaine's voice this time.

The woman talk hovers between them, unintelligible to outside ears until the embrace is over, until they separate, clasp each other's hands, Elaine's white against the dark.

"What is it? Why are you staying here? Can we talk about it?" The woman's speech is like her walk, light, lilting, Jamaica, or perhaps Trinidad.

"After the baby. I can't talk now, Mama. As soon as the baby comes, we'll talk." Elaine's voice is too loud for conversation but doesn't sound angry. Noise to hide the fear, he thinks.

"We all love you. Oliver is beside himself. He doesn't understand why you won't come home." The dark woman certainly isn't Elaine's mother. Must be Oliver's. Peter hears the men approaching and barricades them with his arm again. "Wait, Oliver, Bruce—just wait a minute," the woman says.

"I want to know when she's coming home," says Oliver.

"I think he's been patient enough," says Bruce. He is ruddy. Looks like he drinks. His skin is like Elaine's pale, except for his red face. They step forward again, almost touching Peter's arm.

"Elaine says she will talk after the baby comes," says the woman.

"She's a whore, that's what she is. Living with this old guy. What does she think? She can just do what she wants?" Bruce is angry and Peter wishes the trap door to the root cellar was out here under him.

"Dad," Oliver says. "Don't call her names. She is not a whore."

"I call a *spade* a *spade*." Peter feels Bruce's spittle sprayed onto his cheek, some close to his mouth. To wipe it off would be to give in, he thinks. Peter sets his jaw forward and allows the spit to dry on his face.

"You don't know what you're talking about," Peter says. "You don't know anything about our relationship." A feeble attempt to fix everything.

The woman wraps her lime-green arms around Elaine again, shields her from the anger of the men.

Mr. Oliver Sinclair, esquire, steps forward in his suit, as if he is going to give a sermon. "Elaine, the elders agree. We will have no recourse other than to have you disfellowshipped if you don't return home and repent." Peter wonders why the polite gentle voice of Oliver stings worse than the angry, spit-ridden profanity of Bruce. "You know what that means. You don't want that to happen, do you?"

Peter is afraid to look up, afraid that he will punch the polite mouth just to stop the words from flowing out.

"No," she says without moving from the shelter of the arms.

"Just take her. You have a right. Take her if you want her. A goddamn fornicator. Look at her," Bruce says.

Peter moves to the left just enough to catch the spray, just enough to keep it from touching Elaine.

"Elaine," Oliver says, as if he is speaking to a frightened child. "Go to the car. Right now. Remember the lesson of Jezebel. Remember the teaching of our Jehovah. Obey your husband." He stands with his hands clasped in front of his crotch, thumbs flicking each other, playing out their own little dance or their own little battle.

"Just take her, son."

"Stop it," the woman says. "Just stop it. Elaine needs some time by herself. Give her some time."

Peter wonders how the glorious woman in the lime-green dress with her arms around Elaine could possibly be married to spitting Bruce and have mothered someone like Oliver.

"Now," Oliver says. "It isn't too late. Please, Elaine." He reaches toward her belly, his fingers touch the outside of her dress. Elaine doesn't move.

"We will talk after the baby is born. I'm fine here. As soon as the baby comes, I will come to you and the elders. We'll talk then. Not now. Not here."

Oliver steps forward. Peter feels a rumble deep down in his intestines.

"Get to the car. If you don't obey me, Jehovah will never forgive you. We need to talk about the blood."

Elaine moves away from the woman, pushing her gently, until she stands alone, arms around her beloved belly. "The journal. I want my journal. It's mine," she says. "It's private."

"Private? Not anymore," Oliver says. "Get in the car." His arm sweeps toward the sedan.

"You will have to carry me." She glances at Peter, who isn't sure he can handle things. "You will have to carry me and I'm heavy."

"I'll take the child. It won't be too heavy," Sinclair says, his voice less polite and more like his father's than before. "Because of your sin, Elaine. Because of your sin."

"You'll take no one from this place," Peter says. "No, you won't take anyone. Get your fucking ass off my property. No one threatens me or anyone who lives here." he is surprised neither of the men tries to hit him. "I mean it. Get out of here."

Oliver takes a half-step toward him but stops. Peter senses that Oliver is too close and has to force himself to hold his ground. They glare, like children in a schoolyard, glare without blinking, without flinching, until Peter leans forward just an inch.

"This isn't finished," Oliver says, turning away from them toward the car.

The father, Bruce, follows. "Come on, Virginia," he says.

The woman, Mama, kisses Elaine's pinked face, smoothes her hair away from her brow. "You know my phone number. Please call when the baby comes," she says before she follows the men to the car. "I know you will follow your heart."

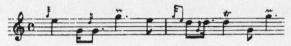

CHAPTER 12

*E*laine stands at the stove sniffing and stirring potato soup. It's the first time he has seen her wear the purple dress from Goodwill and he guesses that she's grown out of the denim. Her basket of yarn on the floor has filled almost to the top.

"Better start knitting some of that or we'll have to get a bigger house," he says.

"Is that all? No package?" She's looking at the mail in his hand.

"That's all," he says. He drops a letter for Elaine on the kitchen table, and heads back out the door to feed Alice and Ruby. He thinks she expects Oliver to send the journal, the black book that looks like a Bible. His rubber boots slide in the mud at the bottom of the lane but he steadies himself on the corner of the barn.

The goat, Ruby, stands like a toy balloon, her belly looking oddly lopsided. She refuses her grain. Alice is quiet. She snorts wet breath onto Peter's neck, swishes his rear end with her tail. He slaps her shoulder. "Garden, tomorrow. You ready for that?" Her front hoof stomps for grain. She doesn't require much because she's got some pony in her but he does have to buy a lot of hay to get her through the winter. He takes a big load in August which usually lasts until pasture time. "Here you go, you hussy," he says, throwing her a couple of leaves of the older hay. She's been out in the corral all day so there is no manure to scrape up. It's been weeks since she's had a harness on her. Before the ice storm. She'll probably fuss about the bit in her mouth and kick at the traces but she loves garden work once she gets going. They've already planted some radishes and lettuce in a small garden off to the side but tomorrow they'll get the big garden ready for spring planting.

The chickens are out of water. Peter's been meaning to get a new waterer since the old one has a slow leak and the water often doesn't last through the day. He writes "chicken waterer" on the clipboard hanging by the barn door, just under "goat feed."

Things are going fine, even with Elaine. They seem to allow each other their private time in the cabin and he's gotten used to her presence. He pours her tea, adds the honey, passes the cup without her asking. Sometimes their hands touch and the place where they touch feels warm on his fingers. He does chores, cuts bent birches, she visits Dora, works on the flower beds, plants herbs. Nights are the hardest although the futon isn't uncomfortable. The old dog still sleeps by the old bed and sometimes he hears Elaine cry in the night. Nothing that would wake you up if you were sleeping but soft, almost inaudible sobs under the blanket. It makes him uneasy, afraid to make noise adjusting his position or coughing for fear she will know he is awake and has heard her pain.

He plans to ask her why she has run away. Maybe tonight at supper. He wants to know more than, *I need time away from everything*, or that she is *trying to sort things out*. What things? She owes him that. But something inside him is afraid to ask.

He hears the crying from the landing before he opens the door. She is kneeling at the rocking chair, sobbing into the pillow. He hates crying. He will have to pat her back, tell her it's all right. His rubber boots are filthy and fall to the floor, splashing muck and manure around. She doesn't look up but the noise of her wailing softens. He offers his hand to her. Perhaps she has fallen. Or something in the letter. He gently tugs under her arms to get her up and she doesn't help him. He can't get her up without a struggle unless she helps. Seamus whines at her side, breaking into a howl when she continues her soft sobbing. Peter stops, stands beside her in his socks, hands folded in front of him. He feels like tapping his foot or finding another activity, maybe pour some wine or go out and have a smoke, but he places his rough hand on the back of her head and pats it. What else can he do?

His hand feels sweaty where it touches her head but he leaves it there. She begins to speak into the pillow of the rocking chair and he has to lean forward to hear.

"What is it?" he asks.

"I was only sixteen. It was a boy from school, a Witness, too. We went to a crowded movie and got lost from the rest of the group. He had a flask of something, brandy, I think. We didn't drink much but the night was warm and the ground was dry and we were in love."

Peter wonders what to say. His arm aches and her hair feels damp under his hand.

"Cameron, his name was. He said things to me. Sweet, tender things. Words no one had said to me before. We did it in the bushes at the park. It hurt and I thought I'd never do it again but he loved me, told me I was his *star in the heavens,* and we thought we'd get married after graduation."

The cabin is still except for her low voice telling private things and Peter is glad he can't see her face. He moves away from her and pulls up his red high-backed chair. The grating noise on the floor causes her to shiver and he isn't sure if she will continue. He pulls the shawl from the back of his chair and places it over her back as if it is the cold that causes the shivering. "There," is all he says.

"His family moved away that July. We had talked about visits and letters and the senior prom and the wedding but only one letter came from him. I wrote and wrote and then stopped sending them. I knew I was pregnant but couldn't tell him in a letter. I couldn't tell anyone, even myself. Only my journal. Just a small entry. *I think I'm P.* That's all."

Elaine slumps closer to the floor but keeps her face buried in the pillow. Her sobs have calmed to slight sniffs between sentences.

"My mother was very strict and religious. She hadn't used the riding crop on me for over a year but I knew this would bring it back. I knew she would whip me until my skin opened up. I knew the elders would shame me in front of everyone. I prayed to Jehovah to take the child, prayed quietly under my blankets so she wouldn't hear, prayed for hours at a time. In our religion, to disobey Jehovah's laws is a very bad thing. It was wrong. I went to meetings, went to school, wore a girdle to hide the fetus inside me."

"You don't—"

"Stop. Please. Let me continue." She turns to him, her face blotched under light wisps of hair stuck to her cheeks.

"Okay," he says, slipping down off the chair onto the floor himself. He leans on the edge of the red chair, stretching his legs out in front of him. Seamus plunks himself down between them.

"I was desperate. One night during my prayers, Jehovah answered. The elders would help me. If I was penitent they would not disfellowship me. I made an appointment with the elders for the next day." Elaine's sobbing ceases but an occasional tear runs down her cheek following the shallow furrow by her nose, drying on her chin.

"The cramps started that evening. I told mother I was sick and went to my room. The cramps got worse and blood appeared on my underpants. I thought I would just get my period and it would be over, that Jehovah had answered my prayers and there really was no fetus, no pregnancy, that it was all going to go away."

Peter shifts himself on the floor and wishes he had the guts to light a cigarette. He's not going to say anything until she is finished but he isn't sure how long he can stay in this position. His hips ache.

"The cramps became excruciating and I knew that I was wrong.

That it was not going to go away. It was night and my parents were in bed. I dragged my bureau across the front of the door so no one could get in and prepared the room. There were some old clothes in the closet that I piled up by the bed. I dumped my old stuffed animals out of a large plastic bag. I stuck a wide piece of duct tape over my mouth so I wouldn't yell out and the labor progressed. My water broke and I mopped it up with the old clothes. The pains went on and on and I thought I would die, that they would find me half naked, bleeding. I pictured in my mind my mother and father and all the elders knocking the door down, pushing the bureau out of the way, and there I'd be, dead, bloody, a baby half out of me. At least I'd be dead and would never get a whipping with the riding crop. I threw the key to my journal out the window, hoped they'd just toss out the journal if they couldn't open it. Throw it out unread, unopened. I didn't have the heart to destroy it."

Peter struggles to look at her while she speaks. He is embarrassed and wants to look away but she continues, seems to need to tell the story, and he is polite.

"Between contractions, I mopped and tidied so when they came in, it wouldn't look so bad. I covered myself with a blanket, stayed on the floor so the blood and fluid wouldn't stain the bed. I prayed for forgiveness, in my head, yearned to speak aloud, to yell with the pain, to open my mouth. Then I thought that the baby might live. It would be very small. Only four and a half months along. What would I do with a tiny baby?"

"Didn't you have any—"

"Don't interrupt me. This is hard enough. If I stop, I might not be able to continue. It's something I need to do."

"I'm sorry. Go ahead."

"Then I felt the head and pushed as hard as I could, grunted against the tape, pulled the blanket aside to see. She was about the size of a small puppy, a head smaller than a tennis ball. Her skin was translucent with rivers of blue veins just under the surface. Her chest heaved up and down as if to gasp for air but no air went in or out. One hand, like a dolly's hand, stretched out to me and I took it. It was tiny and white, with bones like toothpicks. Her eyes never opened and after a minute, her chest stopped moving. I held her close to me while she continued to move, to be warm and soft. The cord held us together and I felt it as it slowly collapsed, ceased carrying blood between us. Gradually all movement stilled until she became lifeless. The placenta came out quick. A couple of pushes and the baby was separate from my body, no longer part of me. I sang to her. 'Rock-a-Bye Baby,' I think, the only lullaby I knew, held her and sang until the body was cold as a fish. She was perfect. Tiny. So tiny that she was difficult to hold. Slippery. And so cold. I wrapped her in my old sweater. I remember, it was deep pink with spring flowers embroidered around the neck. I tucked her together with the placenta into the arm of the sweater and wrapped the rest around her. I remember thinking that the placenta was my sin, part of my body that would be gone forever because I was disobedient."

Elaine stops for a minute and Peter wants to make tea but he is afraid to say it. She slowly pulls herself up from the floor and Peter does the same, thinking that it is finished. That the story is over. And he wonders what it has to do with why she is here. She sits in the rocking chair, covers her legs with the shawl and waits for him to sit. It feels good to get off the floor. Her rocking is the only noise in the cabin now except for their breathing. No sobs. No talk. Elaine wipes her face, inhales sharply.

"I'm not finished," she says. "Can you listen to the rest?"

"Yes," he says, resting his head in the crook of the red chair.

"I cleaned up all the mess from the floor and shoved all the dirty clothes into the plastic bag. It took a long time because I had to keep resting. I hid the bag at the back of my closet to save for trash day. It was the end of September and still warm out. The sun wasn't up but the clock said four so I didn't have a lot of time left. The bureau was too heavy to move. I leaned into the side until my strength was gone. Mother would be up at six and would know everything. I removed each of the drawers one by one to lighten the load and was able to move it back. I wanted to use one of the drawers to bury the baby in."

Peter opens his mouth once to ask her to stop. He doesn't want to hear all the detail. But he says nothing.

"I took a small shovel and a flashlight from the garden shed and went to the park, to the spot where we made love the first time. My legs were shaky and I remember shivering although the air was warm. I dug up a bed of petunias from the edge of one of the gardens and shoveled out a hole as deep as I had the strength to. The soil was light, fluffy, easy to dig and I laid the baby in the hole. It took a long time to cover the pink sweater with the garden soil. I replaced the flowers and walked home. I had to sit on a bench, and later, lean on a telephone pole because I felt faint. My mother was awake by the time I got back. I told her I couldn't sleep and went to the park. She believed me. I had never lied to her before."

"I'm going to make us some tea," Peter says. He pumps the water into the kettle, glad for the diversion. He has difficulty holding the kettle straight under the spout and his legs ache. The image of Elaine cradling the dead baby fills his head and even the pumping of the water isn't enough to shake it. While the kettle heats on the stove, he places some camomile tea in the teapot and readies the two mugs on the counter. He stands by the stove waiting for the water to heat, hears her rocking behind him, steady, slow, quiet, on the small rug. When he turns with the steaming kettle, the soft light reaches the back of her hair, that certain slant of light that says *winter's over,* different from the crisp late winter afternoon's glare. A muted suggestion of warmth. He senses a calmness about them that wasn't there before, senses that perhaps he will tell her about his family. The tea smells sweet as he pours the water into the teapot.

"I kept a small bit of cloth from the pink sweater, a piece with our blood on it. All I have left of her. It's taped in the journal."

There is more to this story. Why is she telling him all this? Seems too personal to tell just anyone. He pictures her going from her parents' home to Oliver Sinclair's home and he understands a little bit why she won't go back. Elaine tells him they've been married over seven years. Too long to stay with someone like that. Peter wonders why they'd gotten married in the first place.

"Almost ready," he says. The tea is light yellow and clear. He pours each of them a full cup and offers her the lamb mug, a small gesture, perhaps some comfort. She rocks even as she takes her tea. She holds the mug in both hands as if her hands were a cradle. *Rock-a-bye baby,* he thinks. *And down will come baby, cradle and all.*

"*Bheir me o, horo van-oh,*" she sings, *Bheir me o, horo van-ee, Bheir me o, o hooro ho, sad am I without thee. When I'm lonely, dear white heart. Black the night or wild the sea.* She sings without embarrassment, looking fully at Peter, voice strong and confident. Not loud but clear and unwavering like a thrush. "If I had known that song when it happened, I would have sung it instead of the other," she says, her eyes open full and dry. He's never known anyone who sings totally without embarrassment.

"Have your tea," he says. They sit together in the cabin like lovers, sip their tea, pat the old dog. No need for talk. They need the respite. "Is there more?" he says finally.

"My blood. I'm Rh negative. When we married, I asked Oliver to have his blood tested. He is positive. I don't know what the first baby was. If she was Rh positive, my blood might kill this baby. I'm running out of time."

"What?"

"Oliver knows about the other pregnancy, about Cameron, that I disobeyed Jehovah's law. Not the details. Not that I buried her in the garden. But I told him about the miscarriage the day that I left."

"What happened? The bruise?" Peter asks.

She doesn't answer, just touches the spot below her right eye, high on the cheekbone, with her fingertips.

"Elaine? Did he hit you?"

She doesn't answer.

"Elaine?"

"I had to tell him because of the blood. He's the father. He has a right."

"Did he hit you?"

"My sin. My sin. It's my fault. He didn't mean to hurt me. He writes almost every day. *I'm sorry. I'm sorry,* he says, over and over."

"A man has no right to hit a woman."

"If this baby dies, it's my fault. Because of the blood."

The silence becomes thick. He waits for her to continue, afraid to intrude, to probe.

"He called me *whore.* He said my sin would kill his child. I fell and he left me there, on the floor. I lay for an hour, my face stuck on the cold linoleum, counting the squares, afraid to get up, wondering what to do. I watched the hands of the clock move, listened to the tap drip into the kitchen sink, until I knew I had to tell someone. The elder. I had to tell the elder and he would know what to do."

"Christ, Elaine."

"He forgives me for that. Even for the lies. But not for my diso-bedience. When I reached the elder, he said a man can take only so much disobedience. He said my sin was great."

"Great?"

"I hung up and left. Just left. Then I found you. But it is my sin. Not theirs. My fault. Not theirs. The elder was right. My sin is great and hard to forgive. My fault. I came here because I thought, like Jesus in the wilderness, that something would come to me if I was away from people who knew me and prayed hard enough. I thought the answer would come. And now they're disfellowshipping me for living with you and refusing to come home." Her eyes shift to the opened letter crumpled on the floor by the rocking chair. "They say I disobeyed my husband and am living in sin."

The rocking slows and she sips the steaming tea. Peter feels her urge to cry but she is cried out, dry, finished with that, and he is glad. "But you're not living in sin."

"I lied to him about seeing a doctor. He didn't know about the miscarriage then. I think he thought he was my first lover. I was afraid to go because the tests might show the antibodies in my blood and he would know about Cameron and the baby. Each month, I left the house dressed for the doctor's and went to the country. Just pulled the car to the side of the road and sat for an hour and then went home. I lied every time. Told him the doctor was pleased with everything. He wanted to go with me but I said, 'wait until next month.' Now he probably knows that I never even had a doctor."

Peter remembers Oliver sitting in the rocking chair, not even asking, and wonders if he has a riding crop in his closet, thinks that maybe he spits needlewords into her face like his father, imagines that he strikes her with the crop. He's too polite to use his hands, too polite.

"Peter, are you all right?"

"Yes," he says.

"I lied to Dora. Said that I'd have the doctor's records sent to her. But there are no records. No test results."

"Maybe the baby is negative. Maybe everything is fine."

"I'm afraid to know. I can't have the baby transfused. We can't accept blood, for our children either. I thought I would find the answer here but I don't know what it is. I feel safe in the cabin but the baby is coming soon and I don't know what to do. I can't go back to him until I know."

"Do you love him?"

"I don't know."

The beam of twilight from the front window moves until it falls between them, bathes their hands and he feels the warmth of it. He tries to reposition himself so it will illuminate her hair again, but . . . gone.

"I was married once."

"Dora told me."

"I loved her."

"Yes. I know. Dora said she was beautiful."

Peter has never spoken of Leslie to another except Dora. Never spoken of their love or his sin to anyone. He's said enough. Enough.

"Well, what about Oliver?"

"He loves me. He's gentle. He thinks I'm beautiful."

Peter follows the light from their hands up to her face. *Beautiful*, he thinks. Yes. Very beautiful. The most exquisite face he has ever seen. Like soft porcelain. But beyond her eyes he sees the pain and he doesn't understand about the blood. "There must be something else they can do besides a transfusion," he says.

"I've looked into it. If I have antibodies and the baby is Rh positive, it will require a total blood transfusion and we can't do that. It would be against the will of Jehovah. 'Any soul who eats any blood, that soul must be cut off from his people.' Leviticus 7:27."

"The Bible is just a metaphor. Only a story. Not a law."

"Yes, it is a law. For me it is a law. I believe it. 'Keep abstaining from things sacrificed to idols and from blood. If you carefully keep yourselves from these things you will prosper.' It's very clear. Acts 15: 29. The baby will die and it will be my fault. Because of my disobedience, my lies."

"But you disobeyed before, with Cameron."

"To disobey again doesn't make things better. God knows about blood. There is a reason for the law. I would do anything to help this baby live. Anything."

"Blood?"

"Not blood."

Peter waits for more. An explanation. Something to make him understand. She sits silent, her mouth drawn tight.

"Why not have Dora test your blood? Then you'll know. Maybe there's nothing to worry about."

Elaine's head drops to the side. Her hair is loose, shiny like the hair of an ermine, fine like chick down. Her tea is almost finished and he pours her another half-cup.

"I'm so tired," she says and closes her eyes. "Too tired to think."

C H A P T E R   1 3

*I*t is another week before Peter sees the signs of impending birth below Ruby's tail. He's been watching carefully for a couple of weeks, feeling her bag, checking to see if she is eating her feed, listening for mother sounds, watching for pawed spots in her stall. Since the Sinclairs left, since the night Elaine told him her story, he and Elaine have talked some, mostly about her love and respect for the mother, Virginia, but little about her fear of Oliver. They have both been jittery. Ruby is overdue to kid. They worry about Oliver coming back. Each time Peter hears an unfamiliar noise he rivets his glance to the driveway, expecting the black truck or the little blue sedan to come inching down into the yard. They haven't talked about personal things but occasionally their hands touch in passing and they do not pull away.

When Elaine checked on Ruby the previous night just before bed, she said the goat was restless, pacing back and forth, licking her hand more than usual. Peter got up at midnight, then again at two thirty, and now, at five.

"Ruby, you going to have those babies?"

Ruby plods to the corner of her stall, lowers her head as if to speak to the hay, and paws until she has exposed the floorboards. Peter flicks on the flashlight and shines it on her tail. Finally. A string of clear mucus drips down, catching on her rear leg. She lies on the bare floor and rises almost immediately, paws the same spot, talks to the bare floor with guttural chatter.

"Hold on, girl, I'm going to call Elaine."

Ruby barely looks up from her pawing. Peter calls into the dim early morning until Elaine answers with a sleepy, "On my way."

He enters the stall, not bothering to latch the door. Ruby doesn't mind his presence but he chooses a place on the hay at the opposite corner and lowers himself onto the hay covered with marble-sized pellets of goat shit. It'll be a little while yet, he supposes, and he might as well be comfortable. He stretches his feet out in front of him, crossing the rubber boots at the ankle. He pats his shirt pocket, checking to see if his cigarettes are there. Of course, he would never smoke in the barn, but after it's over, a Lucky might be good. One package has lasted him all week and there are still two left. They don't seem to taste as good lately. He finds himself taking a couple of drags and putting them out before they're even half smoked.

"Grab a couple of leaves of that hay on the way in, will you," he says to Elaine, "and you probably ought to latch the door behind you."

Elaine moves like Ruby does, deliberately, ponderously, with a little sway. He tucks one of the leaves of hay behind his head for a pillow and gestures for Elaine to sit.

"She's getting ready. See that string of mucus? That's the first sign."

"She's got the corner all pawed. I thought it would be just a little pawing but she's got the whole corner dug up. Why do they do that?"

"Holdover from the wild. It doesn't really work in a stall. Just exposes the winter's shit. Hear that? She's talking to her babies. Hear that? Real low and throaty. That's the only time they make that noise. Kind of like when you sing to your baby, I guess."

Ruby lowers herself onto the bare spot, curls her lip up, shoves her rear leg into the manure-laden hay, and begins to push. Peter points the flashlight on her belly and the ripples on her abdomen catch the glare thrown by the beam. Waves take over her body and her black hair shimmers like phosphorescence in the night ocean.

"Look," he says. "See the bubble coming out? That's the water bag. Each time she contracts, it will get a bit bigger until it bursts like a balloon."

Ruby moans with the contraction, pushing her head forward on the dirty hay unearthed from the floor of the stall.

"Shall I put some clean hay under her head?"

"She's going to move in a minute. I'll spread some around."

The standing time is less with each interlude but he has time to spread clean hay over the wet manurey mess before she lies down again, this time pushing the water bag out to the size of a baseball.

"Come on over closer, she doesn't seem to mind," he says.

Elaine scooches across the packed hay and Peter tries not to laugh out loud at her awkwardness.

"Don't laugh at me," she says. But her mouth is turned up and even in the near dark, her eyes sparkle.

The laughter bursts from his mouth before he can stop it. "What a sight," he says.

Ruby is on her feet again, circling around and around the bare spot. She paws away some of the clean hay Peter has laid for her, exposing the hard-packed excrement of winter. "Come on, Ruby, that's enough of that." He throws some clean hay on the dark areas. "Here, shine the light," he says, handing Elaine the flashlight.

This time the bag fills as if someone inside were blowing it up, grows to the size of a cantaloupe and bursts into the clean bedding. The smell of birth surrounds them, permeates the air. Ruby looks surprised although she has had many babies and broken many water bags. She turns her head to the wetness and licks, talking all the while, the slurping sounds almost deafening in the early morning stillness before the wind rises, before Alice belts the boards out of her stall. There's no more sound of ice tinkling or branches breaking, it's too early in the season for many bird songs, and the frogs don't start for another month. Ruby stops her guttural noise and there is nothing. No sound at all except for the breathing of the three and Ruby's intermittent lapping. Ruby licks and talks to the steaming liquid by Peter's foot and Elaine inches closer until she touches the goat on the head by her ear, strokes down the side of her neck to her shoulder.

"Should be able to see some hooves on the next push," he says as Ruby lies down for another contraction.

"There's a foot. Just one, though. Is that a problem?"

"Not necessarily. Usually they can push them out with one leg back. Sometimes I'll help them, just pull the other leg forward, or give the whole thing a tug."

The contractions continue but only one foot is visible. "I'm going in," he says when the other foot doesn't come. He's left soap out by the barn pump just in case and the water is cold on his hands. He scrubs his right hand shoving the soap into his fingernails, lathering almost up to his elbow. On the way back to the stall, he picks up the Vaseline and lambsaver.

"What's that?" she says. "Looks like a torture device."

"Lambsaver. You hook this plastic noose over the lamb's head and pull hard as you can with this handle." Peter shoves his fist into the noose and tugs at the other end to show her how it works. "Sometimes the head's just too slippery to grab with your bare hands. This thing's saved a lot of lambs and goats. Might not have to use it. Just want to see what's coming out and what isn't."

"Is everything all right? Something's wrong, isn't it?"

"Maybe. Maybe not," he says, crouching near his goat. "Hold this, will you?" He hands Elaine the white plastic loop before he smears the Vaseline around the goat's external area and firmly inserts his hand into her vagina. Ruby pushes against it and makes little grunts. He feels one foot. Just one foot. No second foot. No head. His hand pushes in further until it reaches the cervix and still no head.

"I'm going to have to push it back in and see if I can locate the head. Be ready to pass me the lambsaver." Elaine moves in close, gripping the lambsaver, her bulky body swaying on all fours on the edge of the pawed-up area. "It's okay, girl," he whispers to Ruby. She strains against his hand and moans, the sound cutting into the stillness with a jolt. His fingers pry forward into the uterus, push back the kid's leg. He stops, holding the leg from coming back out until the contraction is finished, then pushes hard against her again. His hand gropes, searches for the other front hoof and nose. The baby's tongue is unmistakable against his fingers.

"Give me the thing," he says.

He eases the noose through the vagina, up into the uterus. He's done this before. Once. Slipping the noose over the head is easy once he finds it again and he tugs it taut behind the ears and positions the nose at the cervix.

"I'm going to grab the front foot and I want you to pull the handle when I say."

"I'm ready." Elaine grasps the white plastic handle attached to the noose and settles against him.

"She's going to holler."

"I'm ready."

"Pull," he says, holding back on the feet until he feels the head slip forward into the birth canal. "Keep pulling as she contracts."

Ruby screams long and hard. Gone is the sweet low guttural mama talk, the gentle licking, but Peter feels the baby slipping down the vagina. It stops suddenly as if caught on something.

"Pull, dammit—pull."

Peter hears a deep growl behind him that is not the goat, feels Elaine's foot push against his thigh, and the head slides a few more inches.

"Almost there."

The kid plops out onto the hay, shaking its head, sending mucus flying in all directions. Steam rises from the spot and Peter turns Ruby's head toward her rear. "Look, Ruby."

"Oh, my. Oh. Look at that baby," Elaine says, still holding the lambsaver attached to the head of a black kid with a small white spot on its shoulder. "It's alive. It's moving. Alive."

"It's a boy," he says as he lifts the tiny black leg. Ruby becomes interested and staggers to her feet. She licks the face, pulls off large sheets of mucus, and Peter's knees are soaked through with the stuff of birth.

"Everything looks fine."

"Looks fine to me, too, but she's probably got another one in there. Have you ever seen anything born before?" The question is out before he remembers. Too late to take it back. "I'm sorry," he says. "I forgot."

"I've seen puppies, too," she says.

The next contraction brings two front hooves and a white nose with the pink tongue already protruding. Three more pushes and a white kid with a brown saddle slithers onto the newly strewn hay, tearing the cord on the way. Ruby leaves the black kid and moves to clean off translucent membranes from the muzzle and eyes of the new one. The boy staggers and falls behind her, nudges at her back legs. Both kids make noise and Ruby responds, deep from her bowels, and continues to lick the new baby.

"Think it's a girl," he says. Ruby licks the ears, down the neck, shoulders, all the while talking to the black one at her rear. When she gets to the chest, she stops, cocks her head, kicks at the small white thing nestled in the hay, paws like she did at the bedding, and turns to the other.

"There's something wrong," he says.

"No. Please. Nothing wrong," Elaine pleads.

Ruby kicks with her rear foot at the white baby when it thrusts its head against her hocks, struggling to stand. Peter scoops it away from the hooves and begins to rub it down with scattered hay. The blood and mucus come rolling off until he comes to the chest. Hanging from the center of the breastbone is a plumsized brown blob, jerking back and forth. "My God, it's a heart."

"What?" Elaine says, scooting over to Peter's side. "What?"

The baby raises its head with a "maaaa," until Peter shoves a finger into its mouth. The kid grabs hold and sucks. "If this was a human baby in the hospital, it would be easy. They'd just open the chest and shove the heart back in."

"What will happen?"

"It will die soon. A few minutes maybe."

"May I hold it?"

Peter cradles the kid, balancing the still pulsing heart on the edge of his hand. "Here," he says. "Mind the heart. It's still beating."

He has never seen anything like this before. There've been petrified fetuses, newly dead ones, some that died the first day of some inability to suck or born in the cold night and chilled. But never a kid with its heart on the outside of its body. Never. Ruby continues to lick and mumble to the healthy baby who is now on all fours, struggling to locate the milk source.

Elaine begins to sing, just a humming at first, then with unintelligible words, he thinks it might be Gaelic, a tune as haunting as any piobaireachd. Then in English, *"Thou'rt the music of my heart, Harp of joy,"* she sings, soft and low. The baby lays its head on the old blue sweater of Mitchell's, right at the elbow, and Peter sees the heart still beating, nestled in the palm of Elaine's hand. *"In the morning, when I go, To the white and shining sea, In the calling of the seal, Thy soft calling to me."* She begins again with the Gaelic and he tries to learn the words but the voice is too low and the language too guttural. The small heart slows as her voice slows, as if it is being led by the cadence of the song. The ears are the last to move. They flick almost imperceptibly just before the last pulse of the heart, until the organ lies still, purple against the white of Elaine's palm.

The humming continues, all notion of a tune gone. Just a low hum, like a drone. Then the image of the baby goat with its heart hanging from a string changes to a fetus with a head the size of a tennis ball and he feels like he might sigh out loud with the pain of it. Her tears flow like water from a pitcher, run down her face unaccompanied by motion or sound and he leaves her with the dead kid while he attends to the live one.

"I'm going to lift this baby just for a second," he says to Ruby. The bottle of iodine is left from last year and as he opens the top he makes a mental note to buy more for next year. He guides the umbilical cord attached to the baby into the mouth of the iodine bottle, holds the bottle close to the belly, tips the baby upside down allowing the liquid to cover the area around the navel. It's a simple way to keep out infections and he's always careful to do it soon after birth but never before the mother claims the baby, loves it. The sheep on the island don't need it because they deliver out in the open, not in a manure-packed stall.

Ruby sniffs the iodined baby, decides that it is acceptable, and resumes with her licking and talking. She has paid no attention to the dead one. Peter always leaves the dead young with the mother until the mother turns away but in this case, Ruby turned away before the baby died. He's never seen that before, either. She must have known something was wrong.

Elaine's humming is barely audible now but Peter is hesitant to interrupt her grief and he doesn't know what to do with tears. As soon as he hears sucking sounds and sees the black tail wagging at Ruby's side, he struggles to his feet. His hips and ankles ache until he is all the way out of the barn. His clothes are covered with iodine and bits of bedding stuck on with baby goat mucus. The old dog joins him for the walk up the lane to the cabin. He pauses just inside the door to peer into the round mirror his sister gave him because she thought no house was complete without a mirror. His fingers slide through his disheveled bangs, pushing the hair back from his face. Time for a haircut, he guesses. Dora trimmed it about this time last year. He's forgotten what he looks like without a beard but he won't find out soon. Don't want to have to shave every day. He might ask Dora to trim it just a bit when she cuts his hair.

There is no sign of Elaine when he looks out the front window. Peter pulls off his rubber boots, lowers his filthy jeans to his ankles and sinks into his futon. Figures he can use it as a chair after she leaves. Almost as comfortable as his bed and it was a bargain at the new furniture shop. He has given up trying to entice Seamus to leave his old bed.

He has long ago abandoned the idea of getting Elaine out of the cabin before the baby comes but other complications take the place of that. Complications he isn't clear about. Elaine doesn't speak to him anymore about the blood and he doesn't really understand. Her Bible stays on the kitchen table next to his book of poetry. He knows she is afraid of something. He knows that her husband is an asshole. He also knows that the mother-in-law loves her and would do anything for her. So what is the problem? Something to do with this religion and Armageddon and paradise on earth and Jehovah and blood. They haven't talked much about the future. Peter isn't one for talking, but she's promised to leave as soon as she and the baby are able. Leave for where? She hasn't said. Just that she'd like to stay in the area. She loves the ocean and the mountains together, the idea that you can grow food for yourself, that deer and moose live behind trees that you see from the window.

Elaine is probably still sitting with the dead kid. He pictures her hands laced with blue lines holding the limp body, the small heart in her pale palm, the low dirge emanating from her thin lips, her hair, white as the baby goat's. His hands rest on his bare thighs, either side of his pubic hair. His right hand moves to cover his penis, not small like a fieldmouse but struggling against the flat of his palm. His fingers curl around it and he looks away toward the ceiling, closes his eyes, begins to circle it with his index finger. His hand slides down the taut skin which feels kind of foreign to him now. He feels movement on his fingers until he hears Seamus scramble to his feet and the shuffle of feet on the landing, the latch rising. He pulls the quilt over himself.

"Please, I'm changing. Please go back out for a minute."

She stands in the crack of the door, holds the doe kid at her breast, its heart bobbing from a cord of bloody tissue. "I want to bury it. Where is a good place?"

"The shovel is leaning by the barn. Put it just outside Alice's north wall. It'll be easy digging."

"Do you have an old towel or something I can wrap it in?"

"Use the old red shirt hanging up in the barn. It's got holes in it anyway." He remembers the pink sweater with the flowers on it and believes she has buried too many babies.

She eases herself out of the cabin backward and he hears her heavy footsteps plodding down the landing toward the path. His clean jeans are cold on his slightly damp skin and it's difficult getting them zipped up. He changes his shirt and throws the dirty laundry into his laundry bag at the bottom of the futon. Before the chores he takes care of his family. He stands Leslie at the counter and sits the children in the chair. He places Leslie's coffee cup in her hand, gives the children orange juice glasses. Nathaniel's sneaker is still missing and Peter can barely stand it. "I'm sorry," is all he can say today. "I'm sorry for everything." But the dolls look happy, have small smiles on their faces, and he hates to cover the house with the old blue towel. It has to end. This fucking charade has got to end. But he is too weak to stop it. He can't imagine how to stop.

C H A P T E R 1 4

The night of the white kid's death is hard for both of them. Peter watches Ruby with her baby until he is sure Elaine is asleep in the cabin. The black kid stands at her side, bumping at the udder, while Ruby chews her cud. The milk isn't much good for people to use for a couple of days until the thick yellow colostrum turns to foamy white milk. Once he made a colostrum pudding from a recipe he found in one of those homesteading books and thought he'd gag before he had a chance to throw the stuff to the chickens. He feeds Ruby half her usual grain that night because he doesn't want her milk to come in too fast and stuffs two leaves of green hay into the rack. "Sorry about the other one," he says, but Ruby is concerned only with the one living, the one sucking her thick teat, not the one wrapped in the red shirt under the garden soil.

Life between Peter and Elaine changes over the next few days, since the death of the goat and since Elaine told him about the miscarriage and the problems it is causing with the new baby. The subject of her relationship with Oliver no longer hovers between them like thick haze. He asks her questions like *Why did you wait so long to have children?* and she answers, *Because I was afraid.* She doesn't ask and he doesn't volunteer anything more than telling her that he had a wife and that he loved her. That is enough for now. They don't speak of the dollhouse.

Elaine walks like a duck. Dora says it will be any time and he knows that Elaine is scared to have the baby come out because that is when she has to decide. The blood test, which Elaine finally allows Dora to take, shows antibodies from the miscarriage built up in her blood. Antibodies that will kill this child if it is Rh positive like its father.

Dora explains it to him over lukewarm coffee the day he goes over alone to bail his rowboat after a spring rain.

"Here's a Rh negative mom," she says, positioning a heavy glass salt shaker between them. "Here is the Rh positive dad." She plops the pepper shaker next to the salt. "The baby could be positive or negative. If it's negative, everything's fine. If it's positive, everything's fine the first time. But during pregnancy and delivery, the blood of the mother and baby can mix. The mother's blood, the negative blood, creates antibodies against her baby's invading positive but not soon enough to affect the first baby."

"So, what's the problem?" Peter asks. "This is her first baby."

"The miscarriage. During and after the miscarriage, Elaine created antibodies against positive blood, should it happen again. The blood thinks it's protecting Elaine from something foreign."

"This baby could be damaged, right?"

"Those antibodies are just sittin' there waitin' for some positive blood to attack. During delivery and sometimes before, the blood crosses and, *wham.*"

"Wham what?" he asks.

Dora fiddles with the shakers for a minute as if taking up time, allowing her old mind a few extra minutes of thinking time.

"It's a disease. They're born with it. Erythroblastosis Fetalis, it's called. Kills them in a few weeks without a transfusion."

Peter's never spoken with Dora about anything like this. Technical medical things. Only wool and weather and surviving Maine winters.

"So the baby really could die," he says, as if the thought had never occurred to him.

"If it's Rh positive, it will die without a transfusion," she says, knocking over the salt shaker with a thud. She pushes them both over to the end of the table and brushes the spilled salt onto the floor.

"She thinks it's her sin, the antibodies."

"In a way, she's right," Dora says.

Peter and Elaine go about their days as if each day is the same as the one before and the belly would stay the same size forever but the old haze of her past is replaced with the haze of decision, or indecision. He knows she thinks about it all the time and hears her at night, whispering under the blankets—praying, probably. Sometimes he catches a word or two. *Jehovah. Please. I beg you. Sorry.* It won't be much longer and he wishes he could help.

Tonight they are having a big dinner. A spring celebration of sorts. The thaw. Their first meal from the garden. They discuss it at breakfast over their tea and coffee. It's to be only food made today or killed today or picked today from the garden and surrounding woods. Those are the rules and they agree.

The layer hens aren't even a year old yet. Peter brought them home from the feed store last May and they have been laying eggs since January. Elaine comes with him but hangs back as they walk toward the chicken house. The white fluffy chicken, Snowball, hasn't started to lay yet and is small but plump. Peter scoops her up by the feet, carries her upside down to the block over by the woodpile. Peter loves chicken feet. Not eating them, but the way they are, different from the rest of the chicken, scaly, yellowed, distinct toenails. The chicken's feet turn into tight yellow fists and then relax. Seamus yips a couple of times but doesn't get up. He used to try to bite the heads off before Peter even got them to the block but now he is content to watch from the cabin landing.

Peter holds the hen over the block, neck stretched out politely, while he grips the hatchet until it is comfortable in his other hand. "They don't have a chance to worry," he says to Elaine, who is standing a few feet behind him. The hen looks around, surveys the woodpile, the newly cultivated garden. *Whack*. Peter flips the head off the block with the edge of the hatchet and holds the hen by the feet. The wings flap frantically while the blood spurts onto his boots. "The heart pumps for a few seconds after the head is gone. It isn't feeling anything." He guesses he believes that but thinks about people who have been beheaded and whether their eyes can see the inside weave of the basket covers used to catch the heads. The hen's head lies at the base of the pine stump, mouth opening and closing slowly, eyes getting a last look at the heap of maple logs.

He feels awkward holding the flapping bird, his back to Elaine, waiting for the headless hen to relax. It seems to take longer than usual but there is nothing to do but wait.

"Guess there's no blood left in that chicken," she says.

The bird jerks as he plunges it into the pot of hot water. The fire has gone out but the water is just the right temperature. He moves the bird around, counts to fifteen, watches as the water turns pink. At fifteen, he pulls the bird out and tries plucking. The long white wing feathers pull out easily.

"Here, try to pluck," he says, slapping the bird down on the back of the wagon. She steps forward, close to the wagon, peers down to watch. His hand rakes the back of the bird and the feathers roll off the bird but stick to his fingers. "Easy, try it."

Her hand reaches forward, fingers extended, and plucks a few of the soggy white breast feathers out. "Yes. It's easy."

He finishes the rest, tossing the feathers randomly out onto the ground. The neck area is his least favorite plucking place and when he is alone, he leaves it, cuts that part off in the house, but she is watching and he plucks each small feather from the wound until the bird is totally naked. He slits the skin at the neck down to the base and cuts the neck

off at the chest. The next slit is aft of the rib cage and around the anus,
following his finger down to the chest bone. He doesn't want to slip and
cut into the anus while Elaine is watching. The intestine pulls easily and
the gizzard follows. He reaches into the cavity and digs out the lungs,
heart, liver, scrapes until the hole is empty of loose organs. He places
the organs except for the lungs into the bowl and tugs back and forth
on the trachea. The left hand wins and the trachea slides out in one
piece. The crop is a little more difficult but comes out without breaking.

"Come here. I want to show you the gizzard." He dips the organ
into the bucket of water to clean the blood from it. The knife blade slits
the muscle clean to the center, exposing a core of gravel. "Look," he
says as he pushes the small stones out with the tip of his index finger.
"Stones. They grind the food. Hens have no teeth. Ever hear anyone
say, 'scarcer than hen's teeth'?"

"Yes," she says.

"That's because they don't have teeth. The chickens swallow the
little stones and the food goes into the gizzard and get rolled around
with the stones. As good as teeth," he says.

"My dad used to cook me the gizzard. I never knew what it was. I
don't think he did either."

Peter scoops all the stones out onto the ground and swishes the
open gizzard around in the water again. "Here, look," he says, sticking
his knife into the edge. "You peel the inner skin. Just like a banana but
it's on the inside, not the outside. Once you get it started, it comes off
in one big hunk." His fingers grab the corner that his knife exposed and
pull the skin away from the inside of the gizzard all in one piece, tossing
it on top of the lungs and placing the gizzard with the heart and liver.
"As soon as I cut this bile off the liver and the feet off the body, it's
done." He throws the feet toward the woods, doesn't want them around
the woodpile, and rinses the whole chicken in the bucket of cold water.
"See? Just like a store chicken. All we need is the plastic bag and label."

Elaine laughs. Can't help herself, Peter figures. He piles the saved organs into the body cavity for the journey back to the cabin. "Be right back to help you," he says.

By the time he returns to the garden, she has covered the bottom of the basket with bits of sorrel and lettuce leaves, small and fragile, the lettuce gleaned from under plastic. "Here's another basket for the radishes and asparagus. That way we won't even have to wash the greens."

At first glance he only sees three or four asparagus spears shooting up in the row but he gets right down beside the first, aims the knife below the soil surface to get the largest spear he can, and notices the rest. Every foot there's a spear, some just nubbins showing. He leaves the very small ones but soon has a good handful littering the bottom of his basket.

"I've found a few radishes. Not very big but very red." She plops them into his basket on top of the asparagus. She stands by the row, arms circling her belly, and he can't imagine how she gets around. Wherever she walks, her arms hold the weight of the unborn baby, keep it high up, away from her pelvis. As if to keep it from being born.

They gather some dandelion greens and onion shoots left from the previous year. He watches as she pinches off a few garlic tips, her thin white hand stretching out from the too-large body, the other hand still holding her belly. The thought occurs to him that she might not allow herself to give birth to the baby, that it would just grow and grow until her skin was stretched as far as it could go and she would explode.

After a quick lunch of leftover soup, Peter leaves Elaine in the cabin to stuff the chicken and hang the cheese and keep the woodstove going, although the air outside is warm. In the summer he does most of his cooking outside but the air is just cool enough to make a fire comforting. The heat in the woodstove oven is a little uneven but she knows about that and can turn the chicken halfway through the cooking.

Alice has been inside all morning and is just beginning to kick as he enters her stall. "Don't you dare, you old gluepot," he says to her. "Going to finish the garden today." She seems to understand and quiets down. Peter slides the bit between her teeth and buckles the throat latch. Her collar is just a hair tight. Seems she's gained a bit of weight over the winter. Her harness needs cleaning but it is still black and shiny. He hefts it onto her back and straightens all the traces and straps, secures the hames to the collar, buckles the belly band, flips the crupper around the base of her tail. She loves garden work. Sometimes she balks at hauling logs, especially if the ground is icy, but garden work, he thinks she'd even go out there herself and get everything ready just fine if he'd trust her. The plowing is all done and most of the harrowing. He wants to go over everything once more before the major planting begins and before they get any more rain.

Her shod hooves plod through the barn to the spring-tooth harrow parked by the garden. "Whoa, girl," he says. "Back. Back." Peter tugs on the whipple tree attached to Alice's traces. "Come on, you bag of bones, half a step back'll do it." Alice sways backward just enough for him to hook up the harrow and they are off down the side of the garden, Peter walking just to the side, the harrow digging into the soil, exposing rocks, smoothing out the ridges made by the plow. They go back and forth over the surface until Alice is out of breath. "Whoa." While she rests, Peter stoops to pick up witchgrass unearthed by the tines of the harrow and throws it toward the edge of the woods. By the end of the week, all the root crops and possibly the broccoli will be in the ground.

Except for checking on the sheep and a small carpentry job for Brendan, he has the next two weeks free for the garden and Elaine. He hasn't thought much beyond mid-May. Kind of scared of thinking that far into the future. Funny how that goddamn witchgrass keeps growing year after year and you think you got it all pulled and the next spring it's back worse than ever. All you see are little green tips, like blades of grass here and there and then you start pulling and you can hardly stop.

Roots going everywhere. The pile builds up at the edge of the asparagus bed. He'll take the stuff into the woods later. See how it likes hard-packed forest dirt and shade.

When the garden is finished it looks square and dark. Perfect. No witchgrass visible on the surface of the soil, just black loam covered with the pattern of the spring-tooth tines.

"Good girl." He slaps Alice's rump, gives her tail a little jerk. "Gee, a little," he says. She turns toward the barn, a bit reluctantly, although she is tired. The hair on her neck by the collar is covered with white foamy sweat. Froth seeps out of the corners of her mouth. Back in the barn, his face brushes her moist shoulder while he hefts the harness off her back. It's the smell of her that makes him keep a horse. The smell of her and the sound of her hooves on the wooden floor. Otherwise, he'd get a tractor.

Ruby gobbles her grain with the little fellow sucking at her udder. Too bad about the other one. Christ. He's never seen anything like that in his whole life.

By the time he's finished with everything it is close to five o'clock. Just enough time for a bath before dinner. He draws water from the barn pump into a black enamel pot of water and places it on the propane cooker. While it heats, he pumps more water into the round galvanized tub by the side of the barn. First outdoor bath of the season. When he adds the hot water from the black pot, the bath is tepid, perfect to scrub off the horse and garden grime. His skin looks white from a winter's covering except for his hands. He scrubs his beard and hair, slides down into the tub to rinse. Tomorrow he'll show Elaine how the outdoor tub works. He uses his sweatshirt to dry himself off before he puts the dirty work clothes back on. If he were alone, he'd just go and get clean clothes but he doesn't want her to see him naked.

Smoke trails off from the top of the chimney. That's a good sign. Seamus doesn't get up to greet him, just raises his head and emits a grumble, low and barely audible. She's found a cloth for the table. An old milkbottle sits in the center of the table brimming with dandelions and mayflowers. He hasn't seen a set table in years, or at least, a table with a cloth and real napkins and flowers with silverware placed where it's supposed to go. Her flaxen hair is piled in braids onto the top of her head, an apricot blossom stuck in the side by her temple.

The chicken steams on a platter on the side of the woodstove and beside it a pie with a crisscross crust. "It's rhubarb. I picked it. It's a small pie because there wasn't much rhubarb," she says.

The urge to hold her, breathe in the scent of her apricot blossom, overwhelms him almost to the point of doing it. She is his mother, his wife, his sister, his daughter. What if he loses her? What if she leaves him, goes back to Oliver? What if they leave the country? She leans forward, touching a lit match to the charred wick of a white candle. He tries to remember if it's his birthday. No. Not until July. Anyway, he doesn't think Witnesses celebrate birthdays.

"Here, wine. And cheese on the table from Ruby. I mixed it with the garlic tops. Try some on the bread." Her hand reaches out to him holding a wineglass full of last summer's rhubarb wine. The cheese is soft, creamy, garlicky, and he spreads it on two more slices of French bread.

"You've been busy," he says.

"Everything is fresh. Except for the bread and the pie crust. I used the old lard and flour. I was going to just make stewed rhubarb but thought you'd like the pie better so I broke the rules." Her smile is serene, tranquil. Not happy exactly, but not as troubled as she has been.

Everything tastes like itself. The asparagus is barely steamed, crisp and tasting of the rich earth. The chicken is stuffed with parsley and onion tops mixed with a little of the French bread. Chunks of diced gizzard, liver, and heart pour out with the brown gravy from the pitcher. She's found old wooden bowls for the small salad of fresh greens and radishes that she serves after the chicken. With pie, she pours him a demitasse cup half filled with brandy. The pie oozes juice and is tart. His mouth puckers and the inside of his lips swell just a bit when he has a second slice. He thinks about a man faced with a death sentence. *What do you want for your last meal? Fresh killed chicken stuffed with herbs, asparagus lightly steamed, tangy rhubarb that makes you swear under your breath.*

She doesn't let him help with the cleaning up. "A present, for your kindness," she tells him. He says he's never tasted as good a meal, and all from the garden. He sips his brandy. She might like the chanter, he thinks, a little after-dinner music. He rests the ivory sole against the bleached linen tablecloth and plays "The Clucking Hen," but doesn't tell her the name of it, then "The Skye Boat Song," a slow march, plays it just a bit up-tempo the first time. She wipes her hands on the dishtowel that is thrown over her shoulder.

"I know that song," she says.

Speed bonnie boat like a bird on the wing,
Onward, the sailors cry
Carry the lad that's born to be king
Over the sea to Skye.

Her voice follows his chanter notes, and she knows all the verses. He goes into another repeat and her voice breaks into a high harmony.

Loud the waves howl, loud the waves roar
Thunder claps rend the air
Baffled our foes, stand on the shore
Follow they will not dare.

Tho the waves leap, soft shall ye sleep
Oceans a royal bed . . .

Then he sees the corner of the towel. Folded up under itself. He sees Leslie holding her coffee. He never would have left it that way. His fingers suspend themselves over the holes as the blowpipe slips from his mouth. She sings a few more bars alone before she realizes he is no longer playing.

Rock'd in the deep, Flora will keep
Watch by your—

"What have you done to the dollhouse?" His voice scares him but he asks again. "What have you done?"

C H A P T E R   1 5

*T*he towel, Elaine."

"What?"

"The towel. Did you move the fucking towel?"

"Peter, please."

"Just answer. Yes or no. Did you touch the fucking towel? Answer."
Peter feels his own saliva spatter on his hand when he says *fuck*. Elaine's
eyes squeeze shut when he says it. He wants to say it over and over and
over. He wants to feel that he can't stop saying it. "What were you doing
there? I hope you got your fucking jollies." He turns away from her,
puts himself between her and the family, wishes she would just get out.
Leave. He never wanted her here in the first place. He stands, his fists
clenched in front of his waist waiting for her to respond. He doesn't
think he wants to know if she lifted the towel. If she has seen his family,
he doesn't think he can bear it.

He's crazy. A crazy man who plays with dolls. She knows about him
now, that he moves little dolls around and feeds them coffee and orange
juice. His family. His dolls.

"Peter, please," she says from behind him.

He feels her hand on his shoulder and shrugs it off. It is cold. Like

ice. The family is where he left them, having breakfast. With the corner
flipped up like that, she can see them all. Leslie holds her coffee, Sarah
and Nathaniel sit in chairs. Nathaniel's sneaker is missing.

The silence in the cabin is chilling, as if everything alive is frozen in
place. The statues game. He remembers little Brett Sutherland, sixth
grade, yelling out, *statues*, and the whole gang freezing in place. Not a
word. Not a movement. This silence is like that. The old dog's head is
halfway under the bed and the tip of his tail flicks, the only motion in
the whole cabin. Her hand is back on his shoulder.

"I'm sorry for invading your privacy."

Her voice is quiet and steady and he wishes he'd ignored the whole
thing, just pulled the corner down when she wasn't watching. "I'm going
to bed," he says. "Be careful of the shotgun if you have to use it tomorrow. Remember, hold it firm against your shoulder like I showed
you. I'm going out on the island first thing in the morning. Three shots
will get me. Dora will hear them and let me know." He can't bear to
look at her.

For the first time, Elaine is the last to bed. She pushes Seamus out
the door to pee and brings him in again, covers the leftover pie and
roasted chicken, blows out the kerosene lamps. Peter's jeans are still on
and he loosens the waistband and pulls them down over his hips, slips
his hand between his legs. His hands are cold and clammy as he pushes
the jeans down past his knees and ankles. His feet push them off the
futon onto the floor before he brings his hands back to his genitals, still
frigid. He listens to her night noises for a long time before he falls asleep.

The pale mauve of the rising sun fills the picture window just after
five and Peter reaches for the jeans, slides them on the floor along the
side of the futon. If he can get out to the island early enough, he won't
have to talk to her. She will be sleeping. Seamus doesn't even raise his
head when Peter lets himself out of the cabin with his cup of yesterday's
greasy coffee.

He stubs his boot on a chunk of granite in the path and the coffee sloshes over onto his arm. "Shit," he says aloud, shaking his arm. "Where the hell did that rock come from?" The rest of the way, he watches the ground, holds his coffee away from his body until the cup is empty. He places it on a stump to pick up on the way back.

Dora is out in the garden when he arrives. "What? No old dog?"

"Nope. I think those days are gone," he says.

Dora wears a pair of Mitchell's old overalls, several sizes too big, over her flowered housedress, sticks out her boot-clad feet in front of her. "Trying to get these cabbage plants in the ground. Getting too big for the windowsill. Should be all right s'long as we don't get another ice storm," she says. "What you doing? Going out on the island?"

"Need to check on the lambs, dock their tails. Castrate, too. You seen anything?"

"Even with the binoculars it's hard to see the little ones. Mothers been feeding in the meadow, though."

"I'll stop for coffee on the way back. If you hear three shots, stick that flag in the ground, will you? She's getting close. I'll keep watch."

On the way to the skiff, he grabs the bag of tools from Dora's shed and checks to see that everything is there. No elastics. He rummages through the chest of supplies until he finds the small plastic bag full of doughnut-shaped green elastic bands. Must be a couple hundred of them left. He squirts a spray of WD-40 onto the hinge of the elastrator and squeezes the handles a couple of times to work the oil into the joint. *That's it*, he guesses, and heads toward the haul-off line.

The boat hauls easy. No seaweed on the line this time. He's got a couple of hours before the tide goes out enough to make getting back difficult. *Stroke, stroke, stroke.* The skiff glides across the still water, hesitating for just a moment when he pushes the oarblades back into position. *Stroke, stroke.* The black and white eiders float close to each other, forming a raft twice the size of his cabin. They move as one silently away from the boat as he approaches, just drift off to the side. When he is almost to the shore, he turns to look. One sheep stands on the shore. He thinks it's the ram.

The last stroke takes the skiff up onto the pebble beach and Peter jumps out with the anchor and tool bag. The ram runs off at a trot down the beach and Peter follows, leaving the anchor hooked on a piece of granite. That's where they'll be. In the meadow to leeward. A couple of years ago, he built a chute which leads into a low-sided holding pen. Because of the lay of the land, he is able to get them all in there himself. Unless he puts the top rail on, the ewes are usually able to jump out, leaving the lambs inside.

The ram heads up toward the meadow with Peter behind him. He almost steps on the black lamb before he sees it. The ram had trampled right over it. He bends down to examine it and sees that it is newly dead, a day, maybe two. His thumb pulls back one of the eyelids. Empty socket. Goddamn black-backs. Every year he loses at least one lamb to the rotten gulls. He picks up the lamb by the tail and tosses it into the bushes at the side of the path. No point in letting the sheep keep walking on it. He looks around him to make sure there isn't another before he climbs the rocky hillock into the meadow.

The meadowgrass is greening up and the ewes are mowing it faster than it can grow, leaving little but a few clumps of wildflowers. The grass will catch up in a week or two. He tries to count but they move. He counts again. Twenty-seven. Should be twenty-nine including the ram. He tries to count again, this time grouping them according to color. The whites first, then the blacks. Twenty-nine this time. He won't even attempt to count the lambs until he gets them into the pen. They begin to move when they become aware of his presence, float like eiders, one mass of black and white, and Peter advances methodically behind them. Slow. Close to the ground. "Git," he says. "Move on in there." They veer suddenly just before the chute and Peter sprints to the right, shakes the tools at them. The ram goes into the chute first and the rest follow.

Peter nudges a couple of errant lambs toward their mothers and shuts the gate of the chute behind him. The passage is narrow. Just wide enough for two sheep to jam themselves through together. When they are all in the pen, he locks the gate to the chute.

The ram is gone, leaping over the fence as if it were a line drawn on a tennis court. Most of the rest follow, leaping and scattering, blatting at their lambs to follow. The noise of confusion always excites Peter. The lambs all scream at once, trying to find their mothers. "Just hold on there," he says to them. "Got a few things to do first."

He hangs a clipboard on one of the cedar posts, its pencil dangling from a string. "Who's first?" From what he sees, half the lambs are black and half white. He's got some buyers for a bunch of black ewe lambs out of that romney ram. Handspinners. He'll get a hundred dollars each for them in the fall. He scoops up the closest lamb. Solid white. Female. He dips the end of the elastrator into the jar of iodine before he squeezes the handles, opening the prongs. The dime-sized elastic band stretches to the size of a fifty-cent piece before he pulls the white woolly tail through. When he relaxes the handles near the base of the tail, the lamb wiggles almost enough to escape. "Oh, no, you don't," he says as he peels off the elastic from the prongs and settles it around the tail. In a month, all the tails will be gone, dropped off. He likes this method better than just cutting off the tails. Bloodless. And the pain goes away in seconds.

Sometimes he finds the tails stuck behind a rock or at the edge of the tide line. He leaves them a couple of inches of stump to keep the black flies off their private parts. If you dock them too close they prolapse, anyway. Fancy show people. That's what they do. Dock them right close to their asshole so they have no protection. After he throws the lamb over the fence to her mother, he jots down on the clipboard pad, *White ewe.*

The next is a male. Black. Peter doesn't dock the males because they will all be slaughtered in the fall and the presence of a tail makes it easy to select the males. Besides, the lambs aren't eating that new meadow grass and aren't likely to get loose stools like the ewes. He's seen ewes die in the spring from getting their tails stuck to their bodies so their shit can't get out. He doesn't like to have ewes with tails but sometimes he misses one, or the elastic breaks. There are two tailed ewes in his flock and he keeps a close watch on them this time of year.

"Sorry to have to do this, fella. I know. It's no fun." Peter dips the elastrator into the iodine and spreads the elastic wide. He holds the lamb belly-down and feels the scrotum. Testicles already. His thumb and fore-finger secure the marble-sized balls down into the scrotum while he sets the elastic at the base. The lamb cries in surprise when Peter releases the elastic around his sack and pulls off the elastrator. When he tosses the lamb to its mother, it falls to the side, staring toward its injured organ. Its hind hooves kick at the air a couple of times before it rights itself and heads off down the meadow. "Sorry about that. Don't want you breeding your mothers too early." Strange about animals. They don't care who they're screwing. Mothers, sisters. Anything in heat will do. *Black ram,* he writes on the pad.

The notes build up on the clipboard. One large white lamb escapes over the fence. He watches it fly by close enough to see there is nothing hanging between her hind legs. He looks at the list. More ewes than rams. He lets her go. She'll be part of the meat group. There are plenty of ewes for replacements and to fill the orders for the handspinners.

After he finishes the last lamb, he checks for the flag. Nothing. Just Dora's house and Dora still sitting in the garden. At least, there's a lump the color of Mitchell's overalls in the middle of the tilled-up rectangle. He counts forty-nine lambs in all. Mostly ewes. Mostly black. Mostly twins. That's good. And they all feel like they're getting plenty of milk. One of the tailed ewes is stuck but he is able to pull the tail free and trim the wool around her rear end.

The image of Elaine slams at him on the way back to the boat. He hasn't thought about her the whole time he was working with the sheep but now she is there, looming with the apricot blossom in her hair, singing "The Skye Boat Song." He pictures her lifting the corner of the blue towel, chuckling to herself. *How cute.* Her voice says the words. He hears them in his head. *How cute. How cute. Peter has dollies.* Does she think he just plays with dolls? That he is a closet toddler? Like men who wear women's underwear in private? Shit. He was almost ready to talk to her about Leslie and the children and she has ruined it all. She just couldn't wait for him to tell her. Probably thought it was her right to know because she told him about the miscarriage and the blood thing. He shakes the tool bag at the ram who has been following him down from the meadow. "Get the fuck out of here," he says. "Go on. Git."

The skiff is up on dry land and he has to push it over the pebbles into the water. The water smooth as glass is gone and in its place, small chops breaking on themselves. *Stroke, stroke.* The oarblades intermittently strike the tops of the waves on their way back to the water, making the boat hike to the left or the right.

Stroke, stroke, stroke. He hears the coxswain in his head and he follows. The eiders are gone but gulls circle over Dora's house. The radio didn't say anything about bad weather yesterday but it sure is gearing up to gale. The chops become higher and he pulls his orange watchcap out of the tool bag. A glance back to the house shows him that Dora has gone in but there is no flag stuck in the ground. He wishes he had brought his mittens or at least his gloves; the Christly Maine cold pierces right through the skin of his fingers. A wave breaks over the bow and soaks the back of his neck. *Stroke. Stroke. Stroke.* He begins to say it aloud. "Stroke. Stroke. Stroke." He rows hard on the right to straighten the boat. Fucking spring gale. "Dora's got the coffee on. Dora's got the coffee on." He says it slow and loud, dips the oars in on *Dora* and *coffee,* and the boat makes progress. A black raincloud gathers over by Indian Point and he rows so hard he thinks he might bust a blade.

The haul-off line is just ahead and he reaches for it with the oar.

Got it. He follows it to the ring, ties the painter onto it, and jumps off onto slippery rockweed with the tool bag. The tide is going out and he only has to haul it about ten feet to the mooring.

Dora's been watching because she is pouring the coffee into two mugs when he gets into the kitchen. Half a rhubarb pie balances on the corner of the woodstove, two forks leaning on the lip of the plate. "Quite a gale out there, yes sir," she says. "Find yourself some lambs?"

"Some nice ones. Got everyone docked and castrated. Gulls only got one that I could see."

"How's my clip look? Wool good and long?"

"Real good. Clean, too."

"That Elaine. She's going to be a right good little spinner, she is."

He doesn't want to talk about Elaine so he sips his coffee. Dora pushes the pie plate to the center of the table and stabs a piece of the pie. "Go ahead. Have some. First rhubarb of the season."

"Don't think I'll have any. Had a big breakfast."

"Well, that's a first. Peter don't want no pie. You sick?"

"Nope. Just don't feel like pie."

"Made some anadama bread yesterday. It's over on the counter. Have some of that and I'll eat the pie."

"Thanks," he says as he goes toward the bread.

"You know, this past winter was kind of hard. The ice storm and everything. Fell on my butt a couple of times out in the yard. I'm not sure's I want to spend another winter alone down here. Got a phone and all but I don't feel comfortable driving in the ice. Always said I'd never leave the house Mitchell and I built, but . . . It would only be for a couple of months. January and February, maybe. Mitchell's sister Thelma said I could go over to the reservation and stay with her. Hate to do it, but it's something I've been thinking about."

Dora's giving up? Not Dora. She's strong. Old, but a body like an ox. When he sits down he notices her hand shaking just a bit as she brings her forkful of rhubarb pie to her mouth. "What are you talking about, Dora? You're an institution. How'm I going to keep my sheep if I have no one to make me coffee when I get out of the boat?"

"I know it. I always said I'd never leave. But last winter I got scared. I thought, What if I fall and break my hip and lie here all day on the ice. By the end of a couple of days I'd be froze solid. I don't mind dying but I don't want to be no popsicle. Takes too long to do that."

"Yeah, you sure are right about that. Takes a long time."

"That bulging mama getting ready to drop?"

"They say it's not a bad way to go."

"What?"

"Freezing to death. Not that you'd want to, but . . ."

"But what about Elaine? She getting ready?"

"Pretty close," he says. *Pretty close to what? Pretty close to having her baby die? Pretty close to going crazy?*

"Some bitch of a problem with that blood thing. She won't let us schedule an amnio to check out this baby. But those antibodies. Just waiting. They're killers, they are. She been talking about the blood transfusion? She even thinking about it?"

"Don't think so. Says Jehovah will never forgive her. She's going through a terrible time. I hear her praying at night, quiet, under the covers."

"Poor thing. She's got demons fighting inside her. There's a bunch of Jehovah's Witnesses around here. I told Elaine that. I'm sure they got elders here too. The other day when she was here, she tried to call Joanie Willis to find out. She goes to that meeting hall up in Steuben. Thought she would know who the elders are. But no one answered. I thought I might call for her, you not having a phone and all, just see what I can find out. But we don't have a lot of time. She's right ready to have that baby."

How could he have yelled at her last night? Elaine who is already full of her own demons doesn't need his too. "Yes. She's getting close. Has she told you what her plans are after the baby comes?"

"Not really. Just that she doesn't think she'll go back to that Mr. Sinclair right off anyway. I think she'd like to stay around here."

"Wait a minute. . . ."

"I don't mean at your cabin. Just in these parts."

"Maybe she ought to move in with you, Dora. She could take care of you."

"I surely don't need no taking care of. Just that the ice . . . Well, the winter was hard. But don't have room here for a woman with a baby."

"She's going to have it in the cabin. She's determined to do that. Afraid that husband will get ahold of it, make the decision for her, I guess, or maybe afraid the authorities will force a transfusion on the baby."

"What a mess. Well, will you look at that. I've eaten almost the whole pie myself." She puts her fork down into the near empty pie plate and sips her coffee.

"Dora. If I can do anything for you, just holler." She pours him another half-cup of coffee, no tremble to her hands now.

"Oh, don't you worry 'bout me. I'm old, about washed up. But you. You got a few years left."

"You know, Sarah would be Elaine's age if—"

"Christy's sakes, you're robbing the cradle." Dora laughs. Peter loves it when she laughs. "The young 'uns keep us old fogies youthful, follow your heart. Don't you think I know how you feel about that woman?"

Peter feels the flush begin at the base of his neck. No. He's too old. *I grow old, I grow old. I shall wear the bottoms of my trousers rolled.* "I think she loves him," he says. "Oliver. She has a beautiful voice. She sings."

"I know," Dora says.

"Did you know I play the bagpipes?" He is surprised that he asks her.

"Everyone knows that. I used to hear you practice in the summer when you were a kid. Over by the rabbit crossing. There's talk in town about how good you was. A professional, won lots of money. And that you stopped playing after your family died. I got a picture of you in my scrapbook winning that prize just before the fire. It was in the paper."

"I've been playing a bit on the practice chanter. Just getting ready. You never forget. Of course, I'm stiff and some of the tunes I forget halfway through. I bought a reed for the pipes a couple of weeks back. Haven't tried it yet."

"Everybody needs some kind of music. You asked me once if I sing. Mitchell used to call me his wind-up canary. Said I never stopped making some kind of noise."

"I've been thinking about checking out the pipes. They've been at the bottom of that trunk for years. Something been keeping me from playing them," he says. "Can I get another piece of that bread?"

"Sure you don't want the rest of the pie?"

She smiles at him as he picks up the other fork. If Dora leaves, he won't have a friend except for the old dog and that terrifies him. "Rhubarb's my favorite," he says.

C H A P T E R   1 6

When Peter arrives back at the cabin, Elaine is feeding the baby goat, which she has named Dizzy. For some reason he hasn't asked why. They separate the goats during the day so they can milk Ruby in the evening for themselves. Ruby licks the baby through the slats between their stalls and on nice days she goes outside to graze on alders and wild raspberries. Dizzy is content to lie in the hay and romp by himself in his stall. At night Dizzy sucks at her with loud slurping noises, back and forth from one teat to the other.

"Do you think he needs more?" Elaine asks, holding an empty beer bottle, acting as if no one had yelled at her, no one had said the *f* word at her, no one had left her alone for the whole day, so close to term like that. "He still seems hungry."

"Don't want him to scour. They get loose stools from too much milk. He's growing like a weed. Keep an eye on his ass end and if he gets the runs, just give him water. Happens fast sometimes. Ruby's got enough milk for ten kids."

"Could you put him back?"

"Sure," he says, lifting the kicking Dizzy into his stall.

"How was the island?"

"Great. Lots of good lambs. Going to have a beautiful clip of wool this year. Gale came up on the way back. I'm surprised it isn't more windy here."

"Peter, I'm sorry about the dolls," she says. "I wanted to know about you, who you are, what you were hiding. I'm sorry if I hurt you."

Peter wishes he could be as direct as Elaine, tell her that he's sorry she miscarried, that she has a mean husband. He wishes he could tell her about Leslie and Sarah and Nathaniel and why he has dolls in a dollhouse hidden by a towel. And why he was upset that she looked.

"Sometime I'll tell you about it," he says.

"Thank you." She stands up quick, her hand on the small of her back, her face drawn and serious.

"What? What is it?"

"Nothing, probably."

"Elaine."

"Yes."

"I'm sorry too. I'd like to help you through this."

"Thank you."

Her eyes water but the water doesn't hide the fear of the blood from him. He sees it clear and strong, the fear that her body will kill her baby. But it's not her sin. It's a medical condition. Not guilt, but misguided blood cells. "Wait here," he says. "Won't take a minute."

The Bible is there on the table beside his Langston Hughes. A Bible is a Bible. Has to be pretty much the same as the one he knew. He remembers from childhood, the Psalm about forgiveness. He thumbs the Psalms, thinks it's the twenty-fifth or sixth. Psalm twenty-five. He closes the black Bible over his thumb and runs out to her.

"Look, here. Read," he says. "No. I'll read. 'For your name's sake, O Jehovah, you must even forgive my error, for it is considerable.' And here: 'See my affliction and my trouble and pardon all my sins,' and then," he says, pointing hard on the page, holding the book close to her eyes, "here, 'May I not be ashamed, for I have taken refuge in you.' You see? it's not your fault. God forgives you."

Her tears gather and fall softly. "Thank you," she says as she takes the Bible from him and slips it into her dress pocket.

They walk together out of the barn. He watches as she shuffles to the outhouse, as if she doesn't want to open her legs even to walk. It's going to be today, he thinks. "Come here, old dog," he calls to Seamus. He doesn't look up. Peter walks over to him and scratches behind his ears and Seamus lifts his head, whines, drops it again.

"Peter," she says as she shuts the outhouse door behind her. "It's starting. There's blood. Just a little. But enough to know." Her arms which have been encircling her belly for so long hang limply at her sides. "I need to be alone for a while. No reason to go for Dora yet." Her arms wrap around her belly, her hands clasped tight underneath, holding the baby inside. Her face is white as wool and he remembers the day she stood out in the ice storm. He thought she might be a ghost or an ice-mirage leaning on the birch tree staring up at his cabin. Her hair hangs loose down her back, catches the light from the noon sun as she walks like a bound Chinese woman, taking half-steps up the path to the front door of the cabin.

What is he supposed to do now? If he works with the chain saw, he won't be able to hear if she calls out. He can't just stand staring at the cabin, waiting to be useful. The sacks of potatoes he bought at the feed store seem heavier than they should be as he drags them out of the barn to the old picnic table. Thinks he'll try some fingerlings this year. He dumps the twenty-pound bag of Austrian Crescent potatoes onto the surface of the table and unsnaps his knife sheath. His hand pushes most of the potatoes to the far side of the table and brings a few to the area right in front of him. The first few only have one or two eyes in each so he tosses them whole into the empty bag. The next he cuts in half, some in thirds, making sure each has at least one good eye.

The cutting is quick once he gets going and soon he is dumping the Irish Cobbler bag. These are covered with eyes but he makes sure each one has plenty of potato attached to it. His knife is sharp and slices through the potatoes as if they were butter. Most potatoes he cuts into four or five pieces. The work is mesmerizing and his mind wanders away from potatoes and blood and ice and his cabin to the last highland games, just before the fire. That last day he was happy.

He tries to remember how it was that afternoon, listening as his name was called over the loud speaker after the piobaireachd competition. *And the winner of the open piobaireachd, Peter MacQueen.* And the young grade one piper, Kate something or other, kissed him on the cheek. After he sat back down with the silver bowl in his lap, she'd asked him to have dinner. She was lovely. He thought she'd placed third in grade one piobaireachd. Red hair, short and fluffy, skin covered with freckles and straight quick fingers. *Congratulations, Peter,* she'd said. *I knew you would win.* Peter had become somewhat nonchalant about winning but it was always nice to bring home a check, sort of proved that it was all worthwhile taking time away from the family to go to the games. Sometimes Leslie and the children came with him, especially to the ones closer to home.

That Kate woman sent him a sympathy card. He remembers because it seemed to be a little strange. Kind of personal. Something she said. . . .

The knife shears off a tiny chunk of the end of his finger. "Shit," he says under his breath. He sucks it, tastes the salty blood. "Damn." The blood drips to his knuckle and he shoves his finger back into his mouth and sucks again. He sits with his finger in his mouth, looking up at the cabin. It's been about a half an hour and he's heard nothing. He needs a Band-aid to stop the bleeding and doesn't want to bother Elaine, but what if she's having the baby all by herself? It's his house, for Christ's sake. He keeps his finger in his mouth on the way up the path. At the landing he sees her through the window. She has pulled the mattress from her bed onto the floor and is spreading it with the pads she bought in town when she sees him.

"Come in," she says, gesturing to him.

He wipes his boots on the landing and takes them off just inside the front door before he reaches for a Band-aid on the windowsill. The odor in the cabin is unmistakable. Not strong, not so just anyone else would notice. The same odor that Ruby's stall had when she kidded. The odor of birth, the inside of the uterus, the inside of a woman.

"Don't you think I should get Dora?"

"Yes," she says quietly. "I'm scared."

He decides to drive. Dora can follow him if she wants her car.

A half hour later when he pulls back into the yard with Dora, all seems the way he left it. Dora has called the young Passamaquoddy girl who helps her with births and she is on her way to the cabin. She also called one of the elders to say that Elaine was having difficulty and might need contact with someone. She says he seemed very kind and concerned. He said he'd be glad to talk if Elaine requests him but doesn't feel comfortable coming uninvited.

Dora's bag is much like his own sheep tool bag with some additions, plus she insists on bringing a three-legged thing she calls a birthing stool. When he tells her that Elaine has the bed ready, Dora says that all women need choices. Peter rushes to open Dora's door and help her down from the truck. She holds onto his arm with one hand and steadies herself on the doorhandle with the other.

"Don't fret so. I can do this," she says.

"Just don't want you to fall and sue me," he says.

"Can you get my bag? Just leave the stool in the truck until we see what she wants."

Peter feels for his Luckies in his chest pocket but decides against having a smoke. Too much trouble. Too much complaining. He guides Dora as she walks up the path, just keeps his hand behind her in case she stumbles. "Haven't been here in a while. Just like the old dog, too old to walk all that way in the woods. Seems cheating to drive over," she says.

Elaine greets them at the door, as if it is her house and they are visitors. "Come in," she says. She has changed into the knee-length red dress she bought at the Goodwill store in town. He hasn't seen her in it before. Actually, he hasn't seen her legs before, not much of them, anyway. The long wool socks that Dora gave her collapse around her ankles and her legs are bare from the socks up to the hemline of the dress. The skin on her legs is so white that it looks like it has been painted, like the ice-encrusted birch trunks, and he wonders if they are cold.

"Please sit down." Elaine offers them a chair. Her chin quivers and Peter knows she is distressed. "You sit here, Dora," she says, offering Dora the rocking chair.

Elaine sits on the straight-back. "I'm due for another contraction but I want to make sure you understand me. I am not going to allow the baby to be transfused. I've discussed this with both of you and I've prayed for hours. This is the way it will be. It's in Jehovah's hands now."

"Do you know what this means?" Dora asks, no longer gruff and sarcastic.

"Yes. I know the baby might die. I will love it more than life itself whether it is positive or negative. If the baby is negative, we have all been blessed. If it is positive, I will hold it and nurse it and sing songs. And if Jehovah chooses to take it, so be it." Elaine's voice is passionate, strong, clear, although he has never seen such tears on anyone. The streams flow down her face, roll into the corners of her mouth, drip onto the new red dress, and her jaw shivers as if she is cold. The urge to warm her with his body becomes almost overwhelming and he fights to stay in his chair. Dora is the one who moves toward her, fleshy arms enfolding her. She does what Peter is not able to do.

"We respect your decision, Elaine, although we may not agree with it. We'll help you through this."

"There's someone here," Peter says, getting up to look out the window. "Must be that girl, Susanne. She has a medical bag like yours," he says.

"Here comes another contraction."

"Tell me how it feels," Dora says. "And don't forget to breathe. Just remember Ruby. Humans forgot along the way. Forgot all the instinctual things like breathing."

Peter opens the door for Susanne. She is dark, like Dora, but young. Not even twenty-five. "Hello," she says as Peter steps aside.

Dora begins to give quiet orders. Peter has never seen her so serious and efficient. "Get this mattress elevated. Piece of plywood on a couple of boxes. Peter, start boiling water. Susanne, make sure there's towels available."

Peter fills the kettle with water from the pump and places it on the woodstove which is barely warm. He stuffs a couple of birch logs in the firebox and tilts the cover. He knows damn well that boiling water is just to get the men out of the way.

"Susanne, can you help me?" he says. They lift Elaine's mattress with the plastic sheet and disposable pads onto the mattress of his new futon. "How's this?"

"Perfect," Dora says.

"Sorry about the bed, Dora. I didn't think you would be able to see anything if I left the mattress against the wall," Elaine says.

"It's fine. I'm just too old to bend down that far. It's fine now."

"Here's another," Elaine says, under her breath. "Oh, please, God, let me keep this baby," she says. Her arms tighten around her belly and she stands straight, legs tight together. " 'Show me favor, O God, according to your loving kindness. And cleanse me even from my sin.' "

"Move around if you feel like it," Dora says.

A noise comes from Elaine, thin Elaine, a noise that sounds like it comes from deep in a mine, a kind of rumble. "Please don't come out," she says to her belly. "Please. I love you, little one."

Peter hears the splash before he notices the water soaking the new red dress, cascading down onto her socks. She moves her feet apart and stares down past her belly. The odor wafts through the cabin, the smell of goat stalls and island sheep shelters. The smell from Leslie when she had the children. You never forget what some things smell like. Baking bread, your mother's perfume, a woman's womb.

Susanne kneels before Elaine with a white towel and soaks up the water while Dora guides Elaine away from the puddle. "I want to sit down," Elaine says. Dora leads her to the kitchen chair, the wooden one with no upholstery and holds her arm while she sits. "I love you, my baby." She murmurs to her belly as if no one else were in the room. Things like "Please slow down, no need to rush, Sssshhh." Peter tries not to listen, tries not to hear.

" 'May you purify me from sin with hyssop, that I may be clean; May you wash me, that I may become whiter even than snow,' " she says.

It's another psalm, Peter thinks.

"I'm scared," she says again, her face showing everything.

Peter grabs the scissors from the hook by the door on the way out. There used to be a patch by the barn. Purple flowers in the summer. Sometimes he puts it on fish. Hyssop. He finds it behind the pineapple mint, tiny green leaves on a woody stalk, and clips off seven branches. Seven for luck. Dora will know what to do with them.

She nods when he passes the stems to her. "Hyssop," he says. "For the water."

"Yes," she says, taking them. "This is going to be a while. Do you have something you want to do?" Dora asks.

"Are you trying to get rid of me?" He doesn't mean to be funny, it just slips out before he can think of a serious answer.

"Yes. I have to examine her. See how far along she is. Now get." Dora looks younger all of a sudden. Her sunken eyes have more sparkle, her tremor barely noticeable.

"I'm going outside for a bit," he says to Elaine. "I'll be back in to check." She sits in front of him still wearing the wet red dress, her socks still dripping onto the wood floor. "Dora'll get you cleaned up." His hand goes to her face, just touches her cheek with one finger. "Do you want me to call Oliver?"

"No. Not until it's over," she says. "Not until we know."

Peter lifts his chanter off the shelf and tucks it under his arm. On the way out the door he hears her. "Why did I do this? Please, baby, stay safe inside. Dora, please don't let the baby come out."

And then Dora's soft replies, "The baby is coming, Elaine. It's coming and Susanne and I are here to help you. I'm going to wash you with the hyssop." Then soft female voices murmur back and forth as he shuts the door behind him.

Peter sits at the picnic table. Remnants of potato eyes and flesh and skin stick to the wood even after he brushes his hand over them. He rests the sole of the blackwood chanter on the first board and blows into the mouthpiece. He plays a scale and adjusts the tape on high G hole to flatten the note. It sounds better. His fingers feel a bit more agile today as he begins a slow march, "The Cradle Song," easy, melodic, appropriate. He repeats the tune before he pulls the mouthpiece out. Something a bit faster, he thinks. The strathspey he plays is familiar enough for him to play all the way through before he registers the name of it. "The Devil in the Kitchen." The devil in the fucking kitchen. What was he thinking of, playing that tune?

"Shit," he says aloud and brings the chanter down hard on the surface of the picnic table. "Dammit, Jehovah. You better do something here. Do something. Are you fucking listening to me?" He hopes the women are too busy to hear the rawness of his voice. He might as well try. How can it hurt? Maybe it doesn't work every time. But this time it has to.

He places the blowpipe into his mouth again. It's time, he thinks. "The Old Woman's Lullaby." He begins the ground of piobaireachd, the first movement, slowly, tentatively. The first time he's played any piobaireachd since the fire. The As. The Cs. Back up to high A. The movements are not as precise as he'd like but the eloquence of the notes saturates the space around him, the speech of angels, *please God, listen to this, listen to this*. The drips coursing down his face fall onto the surface of the picnic table like rain, seep into the wood and disappear along the grain. When he hits the high A in the fourth measure he feels his heart break inside him and waits for the blood to pour out of his eyes, his nose, out of the holes in the chanter. He finishes the entire ground before he ceases blowing and places the chanter in the space between two boards of the table surface.

"Please, God. Was it good? Was it enough?" he says.

The Transfusion

C H A P T E R 1 7

*P*eter stays away until the sky begins to darken. He nods to Susanne when she fetches the birthing stool from the back of the truck. She nods back but doesn't give him any news. The animal chores take up some time and he plants most of the potatoes, but he isn't sure that he does everything properly. He is afraid of himself, of what he has done wrong, and tears repeatedly well up in his eyes. He'll have one cigarette before he goes in. The tapping sound of the package against his finger calms him but when he lights the tip, the smoke he sucks into his mouth tastes like bile. For the first time in years, he wants to vomit, to throw up everything foul that sits at the bottom of his stomach and begin again with fresh water. He grinds the burning end of the cigarette into the end of the picnic table until there is nothing left of the butt except a bit of paper between his fingers.

The kerosene lights flicker in the window and flashlight beams make faint patterns around the room. Although it is not yet dark, Peter stumbles on an exposed root in the path, catching himself on the railing of the steps. He wonders if he should knock. Knock at his own door. He doesn't. "Hello," he calls when the door is open a crack. They are singing. All of them.

"Old MacDonald had a farm, eeiieeiioo, and on that farm he had a pig, eeiieeiioo, with an oink, oink, here and a—"

"Here comes another one."

"Do you feel like pushing?"

"Yes, pushing."

"Hello," he says again and opens it enough to enter. He thinks they've lost their minds. The sound of a growl fills the cabin. He knows it is Elaine but it sounds like an animal, low and strong and menacing. Elaine squats on a three-legged stool that doesn't look strong enough to hold her as Dora hovers over her. Susanne stands at the kitchen table arranging instruments on a towel. No one looks at him. The growl waxes and wanes until the room is silent.

"Please, sing," Elaine says.

"I'm running out of songs," Dora says. "How's this one?"

The fox went out on a chilly night
Prayed for the moon to give her light
For she'd many a mile to go that night
Before she reached the town-o, town-o . . .

Susanne wipes Elaine's forehead with a damp cloth while Dora sings loud and off-key.

She ran till she came to a great big pen
Where the ducks and geese were kept within
Sayin' "A couple of you—"

"Sing a lullaby," Elaine says, interrupting Dora's song.

"A lullaby. Lordy. A lullaby. Always thought that was a lullaby. Guess I'll have to repeat myself."

Sleep my child and peace attend thee
All through the night

Guardian angels God will send thee
All through the night

Dora's voice mellows with the song and it almost sounds pretty.

Soft the drowsy hours are creeping

Elaine's clear high voice joins the old gravely one and Peter can't help but look at her. She is naked, except for a silver chain holding a small key between her breasts, her body shiny with sweat, white, white, white. Her head leans back on Susanne's body, her hair the color of oats now sodden, hangs in strings down her bare shoulders.

Hill and dale in slumber sleeping
I my longing vigil keeping,
All through the night.

Susanne squeezes out the cloth and places it on Elaine's forehead.
"Remember, no blood," says Elaine. "Peter." She notices him standing just inside the door and makes no effort to cover herself. "Peter. No blood."
"Yes," he says. "I know."
Susanne crouches down with a small blue bottle, tips it over her fingers, places her fingers where the baby will come out. "We'll keep doing this until the baby crowns," she says, moving her hand in circles. Peter has barely heard her speak and is surprised at her confident voice.
"Another one," Elaine says.
Susanne keeps her hand down there as the contraction begins. Elaine's voice begins high and frightened.
"Low," Dora says like an angry parent. "Low. Elaine, low."

Elaine's voice immediately lowers a couple of octaves and her face contorts. Dora has taken Susanne's place behind Elaine and places the cloth on her brow, covering her eyes. " 'Deliver me from blood guiltiness, O God, the God of my salvation," she says, low and strident.

"I feel the head," Susanne says.

"Peter, can you come and take my place," Dora says. It is not a question. It is a command not to be disobeyed. The soles of Peter's boots feel like magnets on an iron floor. "Come on," Dora says. "Now."

The growling surges as Peter feels his feet lift one after the other over to the birthing stool, over to Elaine, angelic Elaine, glistening white like alabaster.

"Put your hands on her, right here," Dora says.

Peter obeys her, places his coarse hands over the neck chain, over the bones of her shoulders just as the sound ceases. The flesh softens under his fingers as she leans her head against his groin.

"A couple more," Susanne says to everyone.

Peter hears Elaine's prayers almost before they begin. "Jesus, please give me the strength to give birth and the strength to do what I have to do. I can do this with your help. Please, God, make me strong enough to be obedient to your words." The words are spoken toward the ceiling as if God were sitting on the roof, listening. He is afraid his fingers feel cold on her skin and he wills his blood to go there, to the tips of his fingers, the pads of his hand, where they touch her. She reaches up and touches his hand. "Thank you, Jehovah, for sending me Dora and Susanne and especially Peter. Thank you for giving me this time." Peter moves his hand onto hers. "Here it comes," she says.

This time, Elaine sits up straight, pushes her legs toward the back of the stool, grunts hard. When Peter moves his hands from her shoulders and squeezes out the cloth for her forehead, he smells the hyssop, dank and rich. "Never mind that now," Dora says. "Hold her."

Peter circles her head, wraps his arms around her neck, his hands close to her breasts, brings his body to meet hers. "Lean on me," he says, close to her ear. "Lean on me." She pushes against him until he feels like he will burst.

"The head's almost out," Susanne says, as the contraction subsides. "One more will do it."

"Come on, God, do something here. We need you." Peter hears his own voice, shouting toward the ceiling where God sits waiting to hear it. "Jesus Christ, save this baby, dammit, come down here and save this baby."

Elaine slumps back on him, her face serene, tears flowing freely from the corners of her eyes. His jeans feel wet from the sweat, the tears, the water dripped from the browcloth.

"I'm sorry," he says to her. "I don't really know how to pray."

"Sounds like good praying to me," Dora says. "Come on now, Mama. One last good push and this baby's going to be breathing."

"No blood," Elaine says again.

"No blood," says Dora. "If that's what you want, no blood."

"No blood," says Peter.

Dora stands by with scissors and string and a blanket while Susanne lies on the floor in front of the stool. "This will be a long one. Just keep going," Susanne says.

The contraction begins without Elaine's introduction, just grows and swells until her muscles tense against him. He encircles her head again and presses against her. "You can do this, Elaine. I'm helping you," he says above the grunting.

"Here it comes," says Susanne from the floor. "Keep pushing. Push." The last command is one which no one would ignore and Elaine pushes and pushes and pushes, straining against Peter, against the stool, against herself. "Okay. Stop. Stop pushing." Elaine pants like a dog, her body still tense but the noise gone, the straining finished. "Yes. Here it is." Dora passes Susanne a towel. Susanne cradles her arms under the stool as Elaine leans forward. "It's a girl, Elaine. You've birthed a baby girl." Elaine collapses back onto Peter. Susanne places the moist infant on Elaine's bare chest and Dora covers her with a baby blanket. Peter knows the cord is being cut but he can't see it. Dora pulls a quilt off the bed and places it over Elaine's shivering body. Elaine nudges the infant toward her full breast, steers the nipple toward the open mouth. The cry is like a kitten cry and the baby's mouth sucks at Elaine's skin around the nipple until it is successful.

"Look at that, will you," Dora says. But the baby begins to cry again and Elaine looks at Dora. "This nursing thing is harder than it looks. It's going to take some patience. Do you want me to test her now?"

"No. Not yet," Elaine says. "I'd like to have an hour with her first."

"The blood may be coagulated by then and we'll have to take a few drops from the baby." Dora milks the cord that is still attached to Elaine into a test tube. It fills quickly with red blood. "Baby's blood," she says as she corks the tube. "Usually I test it right away but should be all right to wait."

The next hour is filled with housekeeping chores and medical procedures. Seamus walks around a few times, sniffing at the floor. Dora trims the cord and sets aside the afterbirth in a plastic bag for burying later. They fill out a paper, birth certificate, he thinks. They help Elaine into the freshly made bed after they dismantle the bed in the middle of the room that Elaine never even used. They bathe her skin and help her into a clean shirt. Susanne cleans up the bloodstained pads and washes the floor. Elaine holds the baby close to her until they hear sucking noises. Elaine says it is painful, something she hadn't expected, but smiles and says it feels good. No one speaks of the blood that even now might be attacking the baby. They have given her an hour. She sings songs, lullabies mostly, songs that Peter remembers from his own children, songs like "Itsy Bitsy Spider" and "I'm a Little Teapot." Dora and Susanne join in on "Summertime," their voices disparate, Elaine's soaring over the rest. They laugh at the end. There is no crying for the whole hour. No tears. No sadness. Only music and laughter and mamatalking.

The tube of blood rests against the inner rim of a water glass in the center of the table.

At eleven twenty-six, Elaine points to the clock. "The hour is finished," she says. Dora rummages in her bag for something, pulls out a small packet. "Eldon card," she says when she notices Peter staring at her. "To test the blood."

The air is tense, figures moving about as if in a trance. Elaine holds the infant close to her, eyes closed. She begins to hum a pretty tune Peter has not heard. The words come but the song is to her baby and Peter strains to hear.

Like a ship in the harbor
Like a mother and child
Like a light in the darkness
I'll hold you awhile

We'll rock on the water

Dora holds the tube over the Eldon card, allowing a few drops of blood to fall.

I'll cradle you deep
And hold you while angels
Sing you to sleep

Peter looks toward the ceiling. *God, you better do this right,* he thinks. Elaine begins the song again and Peter isn't sure he can listen to the last verse without breaking down.

"Elaine. It's negative," Dora says. "The baby will be fine."

"Negative," Elaine says. Her laughter comes from deep inside her and she allows the tears to flow. "Thank you, God." She looks at them one by one, her face pink and joyous. "Jehovah answers all prayers. I'm so happy he decided to answer mine this way." Dora throws her head back and laughs, hands on her ample hips. Susanne rushes to Elaine and bends to kiss her.

"Well, holy shit, a baby." Peter needs to get outside quick but first he goes to Elaine, strokes her forehead, touches his finger to the crown of infant hair at her breast. "A baby girl. Imagine. All that praying must have patched through," he says to her. Dora opens the windows, flicks on the radio. Late night jazz, Monk, he thinks. They begin to pack their bags, instruments, papers, a bag of dirty towels.

Elaine holds her up, naked. "Look. Her toes. Do you see? The second is shorter than the others. Azelin. Her name is Azelin," Elaine says. "It means *spared by Jehovah*."

"Azelin. That's pretty," he says before he races out the door into the starless night. He fumbles for his Luckies and his lighter. The cigarette smoke goes deep into his lungs and he holds it there until he coughs.

CHAPTER 18

The days following Azelin's birth are quiet except for her intermittent wailing. She sleeps at night between some nursing spells. She is a good baby. Her skin is dark, like her father's; her features are lovely, like her mother's. Her fingers stretch out long and her mouth sucks and kisses the air until Elaine gives her the breast. She smells like Elaine, especially when Peter holds her so Elaine can have her supper. The nurse practitioner comes from the clinic to test the baby for things Peter doesn't understand. Metabolic disturbances and reflexes. She is perfect, except for the short second toes but the nurse says that might never cause a problem. For a few days, he empties Elaine's waste bucket but now she walks easily around the cabin and outdoors to the garden and to the outhouse. Seamus follows some of the time but two trips in a morning prove to be too much for his old limbs.

Dora gives her a month's worth of diaper service. The truck has come twice, picking up the sack of dirty diapers and leaving clean white folded diapers in exchange. Elaine rinses out little undershirts and socks and blankets in the sink and hangs them out on the line to dry. She butterfly-kisses Azelin's stubby toes, one then the other. The warm air and soft rains encourage the garden, especially the weeds, to grow. Peter plants the rest of the potatoes, beets, more lettuce, cabbages, onions. They eat radishes and lettuce out of the garden. Asparagus soup appears every noon and no one complains. Peter has made two rhubarb pies and Elaine says she will make the next one.

Her breasts are sore and sometimes she cries out when Azelin begins to nurse but Dora says that is normal for a first baby. At the end of the first week, Dora plans to come to check them and stays for supper. The seriousness of the midwife is gone and her old strident self is back. Peter is glad. He knows she has to be organized and professional when she delivers babies but is relieved to see her old self. *Nasty old thing,* he thinks. He loves Dora. Can't imagine life without her. She is his only friend. He has a few acquaintances but no one except for Elaine and Dora that he talks to about anything other than ice and rain and whether he's got radishes yet.

Elaine works all that day in between nursings. She carries Azelin tight to her chest in a baby carrier. Peter helps pick the asparagus and gathers wild greens from the nearby field. Some meadow mushrooms sprout up after the spring rain and he pulls up the largest. Brendan comes down earlier in the day with half a dozen lobsters. Heard the woman was still here and had her baby. "Sort of a baby present," he says. Peter tells him that Elaine is staying a few more days and will be off on her own. "Sure," Brendan said, "and the pope goes to temple on Sundays. One of them lobsters is notched. Don't tell no one. The fucking feds don't know nothing about fishing anyway. One goddamn female with eggs ain't going to make a difference."

Probably not, thinks Peter. He's certainly going to cook them. Two for each. That's the only way to eat lobster. Make sure you have plenty. If he buys only one, he always wishes he had more. That's no way to eat it.

Peter drives to the general store for butter for the bread and ice cream to go on the rhubarb crisp. He buys some crackers and cheese to have before supper with the blueberry wine. It's Dora's favorite and he has three gallons left from last summer. He figures he and Dora will put away a bunch. He doesn't drink much unless they get together to celebrate something like a good clip or the first frost or the end of slaughter day.

Peter sets up the propane cooker just below the landing and secures the black enamel canning pot with two inches of water on the rack. Too hot for the kitchen stove. The spring has been warm. Buds swelling on the maples, flowers on the fruit trees earlier than usual. He's opened all the windows to allow the spring smell inside.

Elaine has set the table with a cloth and napkins. A glass pitcher full of mixed white blossoms, mostly apricot, he thinks, mixed with some popple, takes up the far end of the table and the scent of them is intoxicating. She sets little cups at each place.

"What's that for?" he asks.

"Butter. For the lobsters." Peter usually just plunks the butter pot down in the center of the table for himself but the cups make sense. "How do we crack the lobster shells? Do you have those lobster crackers?"

Peter grabs a hammer out of the junk drawer and sets it on the table. "That ought to do the trick."

"Dora should be here. It's after six," she says.

"She'll be here. She's always late," he says. "Elaine?"

"What?" she says, turning toward him.

"It's worked out okay, hasn't it?"

"Yes."

Dora arrives with her baby tool bag in one hand and a plastic bag from the grocery in the other. "Got something for the baby," she says.

"Oh, Dora. It's beautiful." Elaine accepts the sweater knit in the colors of Joseph's coat as if it were an offering, a sacrifice. Reds, oranges, purples, colors he can't name, bits of fluff, Angora maybe, checkerboard around the bottom of natural grays, browns, and whites. Elaine holds it up to Azelin. "It will be perfect by next winter," she says. "Thank you."

"It's all made from the island fleece. Some even from old Zelda. And there is bunny fur from my old rabbit Mitchell bought me for my birthday years ago. Been storing it just for something like this."

"Look, Azelin," Elaine says. "The most glorious sweater in the universe."

"Well, you can thank Peter's sheep and the black walnuts and goldenrod and even some foil packages of color. I hate those wimpy little pink and blue and yellow sweater things they put babies in. Babies need color just like big people."

"How about some blueberry wine?" Peter says.

"You get out. Go play with them lobsters while I check out this mama and babe. Go on with you." Peter, like a naughty child, obeys her immediately, grabbing the bucket of lobsters on the way out the door. "I'll call you. Won't be ten minutes."

He pulls off his long-sleeve flannel shirt and tosses it onto the landing. He pats the pocket of his T-shirt before he realizes his lighter is still in the flannel shirt pocket. "Shit," he says under his breath. "I'm rowing with one oar these days," he says to Seamus who lies under the shirt. "Fetch. Get the shirt," he says to the old dog. Seamus hasn't fetched the stick of wood for the past two weeks. The last time Peter gave the command, Seamus looked at him as if he'd lost his mind and closed his eyes, continuing to sleep. Today he has no interest in fetching someone's old flannel shirt. He doesn't even cock his head or raise an ear. Peter ambles over and pulls his Luckies and the lighter out of the pocket, gives Seamus a pat on the head. "No more fetching for you, old thing. It's all right. No need to." Seamus growls quietly as Peter lights the propane stove. Peter's never heard him growl for no reason.

He'll just have one. He's going to quit the goddamn things. Taste like shit lately. But he pulls the smoke into his lungs and it feels just fine. Good old Luckies. He smokes it down to a nubbin and tosses it into the fire. The water is boiling. He drops the lobsters in tail first and shuts the pot lid tight. Twenty minutes. He glances at his watch. Just enough time to check the animals. Alice is calm for a change, munching on a leaf of the previous summer's hay. "Going to start hauling your manure tomorrow, girl. You ready for that?"

Dizzy is blatting and Peter realizes he has forgotten to put him back with Ruby for the night. "Here you go," he says. Dizzy kicks at him, chews his hair, bites the lobe of his ear. "You little shit," Peter says. "Here. Go to Mama," he says, putting him down on the run. He drains her in seconds, both teats. He's glad Dizzy won't be as cute come slaughter time. No way he could kill that little thing.

There're five minutes left by the time he gets back to the propane stove. Steam puffs out the side of the black canning pot.

"Where's that infernal blueberry stuff?" Dora says from the doorway.

"Coming right up," he says.

Elaine sits at the table, Azelin close to her chest, sleeping. "We're both fine," she says.

"Would you like a little blueberry wine? I made it."

"Just a tiny bit," she says. "Azelin might not like it." Peter covers the bottom of her glass and stops when she holds up her hand. "Plenty," she says. "Just a taste."

"Well, you can fill mine up," Dora says.

"To Azelin," he says, holding up his glass.

They drain their glasses before he goes to get the lobsters. When he tips the pot, the boiling water flows out onto the ground, seeping in when it hits the grassy area. The lobsters have turned red but one has lost a claw. "Where the hell did that go?" he asks the lobsters. No sign of it. He plops the lobsters back into the pot and heads to the cabin. Elaine has found a chipped platter to put them on and he piles them up. Six lobsters. One with one claw. He'll have that one. One female with eggs. He'll have that one too. He pours Dora and himself another glass of wine and sits in his red highback chair. Peter is happy. He doesn't remember being happy in a long time, since the fire, maybe. He loves living in the woods and working with the sheep. He loves old Alice and Ruby and Dora. And tonight he's happy.

They smash the red shells with the hammer, open the claws dripping with seawater, pull out the sweet meat, suck on the ends of the legs, push out the firm tail meat with their thumbs. Dora doesn't dip hers in the melted butter. "Too damn fat already," she says. The asparagus is perfect, crisp, tender. That goes into the butter too. They don't talk until Elaine serves the rhubarb crisp, until she tops each with a spoonful of vanilla ice cream.

"I've been going round and round with what to do," Elaine says. "This has been kind of like Jesus's forty days in the wilderness. But I still don't know. I wrote to Oliver today to tell him about Azelin. He'll be down. I'm sure of it. I said he could see her."

"Well, I've never met the fellow, but from what you said, he isn't none too loving," says Dora.

"It's his baby. He deserves to see her. But I was thinking. I love it here. Living in town just isn't for me. I've always felt there was something missing and I think it was soil and plants and animals. You need someone to move in with you. We could do that, Azelin and I."

"Oh, I don't know. I've never lived with anyone but Mitchell except for my folks. I'm awful set in my ways."

"I haven't made up my mind yet. I need to talk to the elders. Think about everything. I just thought it would be an idea."

"Things sure changing around here. Dog's getting so old he can barely get up, Peter playing his music again. You having that baby. Wanting to live around here. God, I can hardly keep up," says Dora.

Peter wants to say, *You can live here, you can live here with me,* but he doesn't.

"I'd like to be able to stay here a few more weeks, if that's all right," she says.

If that's all right. He can't imagine waking up without her in the other bed. He can't imagine sleeping through the night without stirring because of mewing and sucking sounds. "Yes, of course," he says. "But that husband of yours isn't going to stand for much more."

"I've told him he can come and see Azelin but that I need three weeks. At the end of that time, I will have an answer. I hope he respects that."

A few weeks. Three weeks. It's always two more days or three more weeks. The words from his memory gather in his mouth until he can't hold them back any more.

> *Do I dare*
> *Disturb the universe?*
> *In a minute there is time*
> *For decisions and revisions which a minute will reverse.*
> *For I have known them all already, known them all—*

Peter hears his own voice and isn't sure where it's coming from. He thinks from years ago. College. Dr. Emerson's class. Listening to a tape of T. S. Eliot reading his own poem.

> *Have known the evenings, mornings, afternoons,*
> *I have measured out my life with coffee spoons;*
> *I know the voices dying with a dying fall*
> *Beneath the music from a farther room.*
> *So how should I presume?*

The words spill out onto the table as the women stare, gape-mouthed, and Peter continues, unsure of what the next words will be but knowing they will come out.

> *And I have known the eyes already, known them all—*
> *The eyes that fix you in a formulated phrase,*
> *And when I am formulated, sprawling on a pin,*

When I am pinned and wriggling on the wall,
Then how should I begin
To spit out all the butt-ends of my days and ways?
And how should I presume?

"Christ almighty," says Dora. "Where did all that come from? 'Pinned and wriggling on a wall'? 'Measured out my life with coffee spoons'? What the hell does that mean?"

"I know that I've been talking in time limits. An hour for this, three weeks for that. I'm sorry. I owe you more than that," Elaine says.

The words of the poem scare Peter. He remembers memorizing it. The whole thing. Pages of it. But he hasn't thought of it for years and years. And now it pours out and she knows how he feels. "I am afraid to disturb the universe," he says.

"I know, Peter," Elaine says, "but it's too late."

"Please. Stay as long as you need to."

C H A P T E R   1 9

The next morning, the sun streams into the cabin through the front window. After breakfast of stewed rhubarb and oatmeal, Elaine rocks gently in the chair, sipping her tea and nursing Azelin. She kisses Azelin's odd toes shorter than the others. Peter washes dishes at the sink until there are no more. From the sink he is able to watch her back, her hair in wisps turning light from the window into tiny crystals. When she rocks, he sees the black of Azelin's hair against her white breast and hears the quiet sucking. After he finishes washing the last mug, he wipes the area around the sink until it is immaculate. Usually he leaves the dishes to air dry but today he pulls a dishtowel from the nail by the dish cupboard and dries the plates, the glasses, the cups, puts them away on the shelf, watching. His breathing seems loud and he struggles to soften it so that she won't notice and she continues to rock. The dishes are dry, put away. Peter swings the dishtowel over his shoulder and stands behind the rocking chair.

Her shoulders are covered by a deep blue T-shirt, one of his old ones with a picture of a beet and the words *Common Ground Country Fair* silkscreened on the bottom, the thin silver chain dipping into the hollow by her collarbone. He places his hands there, like when she was in labor. The rocking stops. Her shoulders feel delicate against his palms, just a thin layer of flesh covering the bones. Statues. Freeze. Brett Sutherland hollers *freeze* and they stop all movement. Like statues. Except for Azelin who bobs her head with each suck. Peter's heart thumps against his chest wall loud enough for her to hear. He feels Elaine's pulse through the skin below her left shoulder, fast but faint. Fluttering, like a hummingbird heart.

Her hair catches on his shirt, soft as goose down, and he lowers his face toward her. He closes his eyes as the fragrance of baby milk rises from her and he sees Sarah, her dark hair like Azelin's, sticky on her face from dripped milk. He rests his hand on Azelin's head as she nurses and Elaine allows it. They stand still as statues except for the slight movement of the tiny head and his own rough hand. The chair pushes into him as her head rests back. The blue vein at the base of Elaine's neck pulses and he runs his finger along the length of it up to her chin where it lingers until Azelin pulls away from the nipple.

He brings his other hand away from the baby's head, suddenly embarrassed he is so close to Elaine's naked breast. The chair begins its rocking, patting against Peter's waist each time. She begins a song. He tries to place it, to remember the words, but it is unfamiliar.

"I've got to order some seeds and pay a few bills," he says. "Do you need me for anything?"

"No," she says. "Go ahead. I thought I'd put a couple of those tomato plants in the ground, just in case we don't get another frost. They'll have a jump on the others. Can you spare them? They might freeze. Then they'd be wasted."

"Sure. I got lots. Put in half a dozen."

He helps her buckle on her baby sling. "I'll take the old dog with me," she says. "Come on, Seamus." She waits patiently while the dog hauls himself up and staggers toward the door. Her hand stays at his neck as they wend their way toward the garden. Peter watches them from the window.

The old trunk by the back wall is covered with a square of mirrored material his mother brought back from the Orient. It is heavy and as he lifts it off, dust fills the air around him, the air he is breathing. The lid creaks until it leans back against the wall. Leslie's jacket lies on top. He lowers his face into it but it smells like cedar. Underneath is an assortment of clothes and toys he hasn't seen for a long time. Nathaniel's sneaker he found in the garage, Sarah's stuffed raccoon she had left at her friend's house, Leslie's melted Mr. Coffee machine. Peter piles them on the floor beside the trunk. Leslie's silver flute lies under the heap, its original shine now tarnished black. It takes him a long time to finally expose the bagpipes, lying at the bottom of the trunk underneath his MacQueen tartan kilt. Some moths have eaten parts of the red stripe in spite of the cedar lining.

Peter shines the flashlight into the trunk because it is dark at the back of the cabin and the trunk is deep. The pipes look fine. No obvious cracks. The moths have invaded the bag cover and left holes around the chanter and the tenor stock fringes. He cradles them carefully in his arm over to the kitchen table, which he moves to get out of the sun. Henderson pipes. 1922. Engraved silver and ivory mounts. When folks heard he quit playing, his mother said three or four pipers called about buying his pipes, but he'd never sell them. He strokes the length of the bass drone stock feeling for cracks, runs his fingers over every piece examining the blackwood for imperfections. Smooth. No cracks he can detect.

At the bottom of the trunk, he fishes around for the bag of tools and extracts a can of almond oil and a cotton brush from the bag. He removes and separates all five pieces and rubs the oil into the outside and inside of the three blackwood drones, blowpipe, and chanter. The old cane reeds will have to be replaced. The bass reed snaps with hardly any pressure and he tosses them all into the firebox. The bag covered with the black silk velvet looks like some dead animal sprawled on the table. He pulls off the black cover exposing a crinkled stiffened lambskin. He tries to smooth it out, examine it to see if it can be brought back. The bag at the blowpipe end crumples in his hands, changing to disassociated bits of stiff leather spewed out over the surface of the table.

"Shit," he says aloud. "What a fucking mess." He'll have to get a new bag and new drone reeds. The music store in town might have to order those things. He can buy the almond oil at the health food store. The pipes will need oiling for a while to prevent cracking. He'll hold off playing them to give the oil a chance to permeate the wood. But he wants to try the new chanter reed, the one behind Mr. Oliver Sinclair's card in the pocket of the red plaid jacket that he hasn't worn for weeks. Where the hell is it? He rummages through the shirts on the pegs by his bed. Nothing. The barn. He left it out there. He remembers seeing it on a hook by Ruby's stall.

Elaine squats by the area Alice prepared for the tomatoes and peppers, digging with a trowel. "I've got four in," she says when she sees him running down the path. "Two more to go."

"Great," he says. "You might want to spread a bit of that fertilizer mix over the surface. This part of the garden had corn last year. Probably drained. It's in the bucket by the back door of the barn. Lime, phosphate, a little blood meal. Just something to give them a bit of a boost. Don't want to add much to tomatoes or you'll get all leaves and no fruit."

"No. I can't use blood meal. I got a bucket of compost from the pile out back. No blood, remember?" Her smile is wide and infectious. He smiles back. "How's your work going?"

"Fine. Need to get something in the barn but I'm almost through."

He pats the pocket of the jacket hanging on the nail. The tissue package is still there behind the business card. The reed looks intact when he pulls the tissue back. He blows into it, he hears a rough crow sound. Good. He blows again. Crow again. He's surprised that the dinky music store carries such a good reed.

When he gets back to the cabin, he oils the wood pieces again, slathers the rest of the oil from the can all over them, then wipes them down with a clean cloth. He picks up the chanter with its ivory sole. A couple of the holes are still taped from the last time he played that day at Maxville. He'd been having trouble with the high G and his D was a tad sharp so he remembered taping them just before he competed. He tries to seat the reed into the small hole at the end of the pipe chanter but it's loose and needs hemp. The roll of hemp is still in the bag at the bottom of the trunk. He fishes it out and wraps a piece around the base of the double reed and tries it again. He pushes it in until it seats itself snugly.

Elaine is still in the garden, too far away to hear from inside the cabin. He moistens the reed with his lips, just a little, holds his fingers on the holes. It feels a bit awkward. He places the entire reed in his mouth and wraps his lips around the base. His first breath sounds the low A. Loud. It's louder than he remembers. He blows as hard as he can and goes up the scale. B, C, D, E, F, G, high A. The high A is still a bit sharp so he moves the tape. Again. This time he starts with the low G, which sounds a little off, but the scale is better. The whole thing is a bit flat, he thinks, but after he adjusts the reed, he isn't sure.

"The Brown Haired Maiden" sounds pretty good. It's an easy tune, slow, simple fingering. He hates to play the pipe chanter by itself out of the pipes but he knows the drones might crack if he plays them too soon and, anyway, he has no bag. He probably should stop. He's tried it and it feels good. No point in chancing a crack in the chanter.

Before he piles the family things back into the trunk he notices the old *Scots Guards* book in the corner. He flips through it and brings it to the table. He knows them all. Well, almost all. At least the tune if not all the grace notes and embellishments. He plays "Hot Punch" and "Kilworth Hills" and "The Green Hills of Tyrol." His lips are tense and sore. Spit drips onto the table from the sole of the chanter. He is holding the chanter when he hears the noise, feels the vibration in his hands. It hits him like a shot, although the sound is barely detectable. He knows what it is, feels the crack with his thumb, follows it down the length of the chanter to the sole and back up to the reed.

"Dammit. Dammit."

He bangs the chanter on the edge of the table, sending the reed to the floor. Why did he play so soon? Ruined an excellent old chanter. The crack extends all the way along the back of the chanter.

"What is it? What's wrong?" Elaine asks, opening the door.

Peter throws the chanter against the wall. "Not a goddamn thing," he says. The dried bag lands against the counter by the sink. "Not one goddamn thing." His hands pick up the drones and the blowpipe.

"No," she says. "No. Do not do that."

He stops, his package in midair.

"No. Don't throw them. Give them to me."

She holds out her arms like an angel, holds them until he places the pieces of his bagpipes onto the crooks of her elbows, against the sleeping Azelin.

CHAPTER 20

*T*wice a day, Peter oils the pieces of his bagpipes. The day after his chanter splits, he goes into town to buy some more oil, a plastic chanter to use until he finds a blackwood one to match the rest of the pieces, and to order a new bag. "Sheepskin or Gore-Tex?" the pimply kid behind the counter asks him. Gore-Tex? Isn't that some kind of plastic stuff they use for outdoor clothing?

"No," he tells the kid. "Give me the sheepskin." The store doesn't even carry real cane drone reeds. Haven't had them in a couple of years, the kid says. The kid lines up the packages of reeds, all more than fifty dollars, on top of the glass case. Most are black plastic with clear plastic tongues. *Crap,* he thinks, until he reads the blurbs on the backs of the packages. Colin Robertson. My God. Couldn't be the same Colin Robertson. He'd have to be about Peter's age. Peter hasn't thought about him in years but they had been pretty good friends. Had to be okay if Colin was using them. He reads down the list. Pipers who'd been around for years were switching to the new drone reeds. He thinks he'll try them. He has to buy a new chanter reed, too, because the other one splintered into tiny chips when he banged the chanter on the table.

Everything comes to almost three hundred dollars and that doesn't even include the new bag.

Peter writes out the check, leaving very little in the checking account. He stops to call the trucker on the way home to remind him to pick up the pulp wood in his wood yard. Peter doesn't want to dip into that insurance money from the fire. He's never done that since he lived in the cabin. Elaine has been costing something. More food. Clothes for the baby. Susanne's pay. Dora wouldn't take anything for the birthing. Elaine didn't have health insurance but it probably wouldn't pay for a midwife anyway. She said that Oliver Sinclair let it lapse just before she got pregnant and now they wouldn't cover the baby's birth or anything for another year.

Peter spreads a sheet of clear plastic over the table when he oils the pieces. He's been doing this for a week, twice a day, carefully spreading oil over the outside and inside of the tenor drones, the bass drone, the blowpipe, and he notices the difference. The dull dead pieces, although beautiful to look at, felt inanimate, but after the oil, they seem lighter, full of energy. When he finishes wiping the excess oil from the pieces, he rubs a small amount of polish onto the silver until the discoloration is gone and the silver shines.

While he is at it, he might as well polish Leslie's flute. The area around the pads is difficult to get at but the rest shines up quickly. The rag is soon black from the tarnish. He wraps the flute in a soft piece of sheeting and places it back at the bottom of the trunk. Lucky it was at the repair shop when the fire broke out. The old guy sent it back to him in the mail. No charge.

On the way to town he stops at the bank to deposit the check from the paper company for the pulp wood. Almost a thousand dollars. He tries to remember if the music store had any bag covers but it doesn't matter if they don't. It's just for looks and he can order one. The important thing is the bag itself.

The old guy is back and the kid is gone today. Peter can't decide which is worse. The man is dusting the drums again and Peter figures that's the thing he does to look busy. Dust drums. "Did my bagpipe bag come in?" Peter asks.

"Let me look," the man says, rummaging through a pile of boxes on the shelf behind the counter. He pulls one out with a note on it. "Tell Mr. MacQueen that the wrong bag came in. We can send it back and reorder or he can have this one for the price of the other." The old man reads it very slowly as if he were just learning to read and Peter waits until he looks up.

"Let me see that," Peter says, aware that he is somewhat rude.

Canmore is written on the thin green plastic bag. Gore-Tex, Peter thinks. Fucking Gore-Tex. But he doesn't want to wait another week. Everything is ready at home. Elaine plans to be back from Dora's right after lunch for the concert. "All right, I'll try it," he says, sorry that he jerked the package away from the old man who coughs hard while he writes out the sales slip. He forgets the sales tax and has to redo everything.

"Oh," Peter says. "Have you got any bag covers?"

They have one left. Black like the one in the trunk full of moth holes—well, not quite the same, but black velvet with black fringe. He buys the cover and a new set of silk drone cords to match. The old man begins the third sales slip and this one takes him a long time. Peter stuffs the cover and cords into the box on top of the Gore-Tex bag and writes a check. Over two hundred dollars this time. He's glad he got the check for the wood.

"You in that band that plays parades?" the old man asks.

"Nope," Peter says.

"They ain't bad. Come from Ellsworth. Heard they won some trophy up to New Brunswick last year."

"Thanks," Peter says, pulling the sales slip from the old man's hand and heading out the door.

Next to the music store is a store that says PETER PAN SHOP, with

CHILDREN'S CLOTHING underneath. Peter stands at the window of stuffed bears, rattles, kid's bathing suits. There's no one in there except for a woman about his age sitting on a stool behind the counter.

"Can I help you?" she asks.

"Do you have a baby dress? For a girl? She's not quite a month old. Tiny little thing."

"Sure," she says. "Are you the grandpa?"

"Yes," Peter says. "Azelin, her name is."

He chooses a dark green dress with violet trim, remembering Dora's comment about babies needing bright colors. It's the only one that isn't light pink or light blue or light yellow.

"You sure this is the one you want? Color's kind of strong for a newborn."

"That's the one." It's almost fifty dollars. Just for a little baby dress. But Peter writes out another check and passes it to the shopkeeper. "Thank you," he says on the way out.

The drive back to the cabin is difficult. Images of Leslie and the children won't leave him alone. For years after the fire their faces would loom up at him while he was driving down the road and he would have to pull over to the side until they left, but they haven't bothered him for a long time. These are different. Alive. Not blackened and distorted. Leslie smiles at him and the children banter with each other, old memories of good times. Then another image. A woman. Kate. That woman, Kate, from the highland games, the day he won the open competition at Maxville, the day of the fire. She smiles like Leslie and the two faces come together and blend into one frightful composite.

He veers over to the side of the road without signaling and the car behind him beeps going by. "Christ," he says aloud. "What the fuck was that?" No one answers. The visions vanish. In their place are shadbushes coming into bloom, a dead pine, an old ice-fishing shack on the back of a trailer. No family faces. No face of a woman he hardly knows.

The rest of the way home, he drives like a ninety-year-old, slow, cautious, distracted, until he arrives in his dooryard. He feels better. Elaine walks toward him with Azelin in the baby sling. She isn't afraid of being left at the cabin because she says Oliver will respect her request of a few weeks to sort out her life. She says that he understands and will honor her wishes but Peter isn't so sure. He waves the packages at her. Her grin widens into a broad smile and her pace quickens.

"Hey, be careful coming down that path," he says. He steps up his stride to meet her. "I've got something for you," he says to the sleeping baby.

"For Azelin? What? Let me see."

Elaine has asparagus sandwiches and coffee on the table for lunch. While they eat, he pulls out the green dress and holds it up. "Green. Dark green. Dora said babies need color," he says.

"Oh, Peter," she says. She throws her head back and rocks in the chair. "It's wonderful." She extracts Azelin from the sling and holds her up. "Try it."

"It's a bit big now." The hem goes past her toes. "But it suits her, don't you think?" The baby kicks at the green hem and begins her squalling. "I'm not sure she likes it." They both laugh, like old times, like a family, like his family, and Peter relaxes, pushes aside his thoughts about the images, pats Elaine's hand. "I'm going to tie in the bag today. They sent one of those infernal plastic ones by mistake. It'll take me a couple of hours to get everything ready. Then we'll have a concert," he says.

The whole process takes more than two hours. First he tries the new reed in the plastic chanter. Not as much crow as the one he broke but clear and full. He hovers over the spot that he has marked for the chanter, afraid to cut in the wrong place, but he finally makes the slit. The other four are precut rubber-ringed holes that seem too small for the drones and blowpipe. He installs the blackwood pieces, one stock at a time, in the Gore-Tex. He slathers the rings with almond oil until the blowpipe fits into its hole. The drone stocks take a little longer and he has to add more oil. The material is much lighter than the sheepskin and he can't imagine how it will hold air under pressure. The bag comes with twine for tying the chanter stock and the instructions say to tape the edges of the holes. When it is finished, it looks like a green monster with stout black legs. He's glad he bought the bag cover. At least he won't have to look at the ugly green plastic. No one who wasn't a piper would have an inkling that the thing was a bagpipe at this stage.

Setting the new plastic drone reeds is easier than the old canes. Adjustment goes smoothly except that he has to apply waxed hemp to the base of all of them. He pushes them into the holes in the drones and tries them, one by one, guiding the drone reeds into his mouth until they almost touch the back of his throat. The bass is the longest and he fights to avoid gagging, but the sound is good. After he slips everything into the new bag cover, he twists all the parts into the stocks; the drones, the blowpipe, and the plastic chanter with the new reed. Tying the cords holding the drones together takes longer than he thinks but the drones look beautiful when he finally attaches them to each other with the black silk. Black silk. The silver on the drones catches the sun from the window, the ivory glows from the blackwood background. Beautiful. Better than they ever looked.

He slips his thumbs into the waist of his jeans as he moves around the table, observing the bagpipes first from one side, then the other. He moves his hand to touch the bass drone, just holds it there, feeling the warmth of the blackwood, the cold of the silver and the ivory, the plush pile of the velvet bag, but then he gets to the plastic chanter. It's too smooth, too temperate, but he'll get another one. A blackwood Naill. *This one will do for now,* he thinks as he carries the instrument, its parts now together, out of the cabin toward the woods.

"I'm going to tune out here," he says to Elaine. "It may take me some time."

She waves from her crouched position in the herb bed. Peter follows the path that leads to the Underwood cottage, being careful not to knock the pipes with tree branches. When he enters the Crossing, he slows and looks for a good spot. He places the drones on his shoulder and walks around the clearing a few times. When he was a teenager he used to play his pipes here and Old Man Farley hollered that the sound was enough to kill a moose but he always stood at the edge of the clearing tapping his foot.

The ground is soggy and he feels the water begin to seep through his boots and socks. The drones feel awkward so he walks around again, tries different positions on his shoulder, adjusts the drones, stands with his back to the entrance path. His teeth find the worn groove in the mouthpiece and clamp down on it, while his fingers find the holes on the slippery plastic pipe chanter. He fills the bag, surprised that it is easy, and presses with his arm, releases the pressure and strikes the side of the bag sharply. The drones sound with a roar and his E blats in tune with nothing. He plays a low A, then a C. His fingers find the drones one by one and twist them into tune. They slide up and down smoothly with the new waxed hemp. When everything is playing A together he stops. His mouth feels a bit numb and his arm is shaking.

He hikes the bag around to a more comfortable position. It's harder to hold than his old one when it's deflated. He slowly blows his warm air into the bag and strikes his hand on the side. The drones all come in together, the low A of the two tenors, the lower A of the bass, before he sounds his chanter. The sound is glorious. He plays the first few measures of a familiar tuning phrase before he goes into a slow march. One foot after the other, he circles the Crossing walking in time with the tune, his feet soaking up water in the swampy areas and squishing through the high ground, around and around until he has repeated the tune three times. Time to show Elaine.

"Elaine," he calls from the edge of the woods.

"I heard you. Now I want to see you and hear you," she says. Seamus whines from his position near the compost pile. "Play a dance tune."

He strikes in and sounds his E. "My Home." He's always loved the tune played up-tempo and it's a hornpipe. He plays it faster than usual and fumbles in the second measure. She begins to dance on the repeat of the first part, a waltz, her red dress flying out behind her. She hugs Azelin tight during the twirls and her bare feet scatter damp soil around her as she dances a few steps through the newly planted carrots. He repeats the whole tune because to stop would mean the end of her dancing.

He goes directly into "The Skye Boat Song," and she doesn't miss a beat. Her face is radiant. She dances toward him and he feels that he must continue playing. *Over twenty years,* he thinks. The blessed instrument at the bottom of his dark trunk. He walks toward her, playing the last few measures, stops, allowing the blowpipe to fall from his lips. Her arms reach for him. The bagpipes and the child are between them but they touch, their hands on each other's bodies, only T-shirts between hands and skin.

"Wonderful," she says into his ear. "It's just wonderful, but Seamus howled the whole time."

"Oh, and I thought he was deaf." His lips skim across her hair as he speaks.

The sound of a car in the drive breaks the moment, propels them apart, and they stand side by side at the edge of the garden, he with his pipes, she with her baby, watching the familiar blue sedan wind its way down the driveway.

C H A P T E R   2 1

*O*liver Sinclair is alone today. Instead of the black shoes, he wears beige canvas shoes with white athletic socks but he doesn't look terribly athletic. Peter is surprised to see him in shorts and a T-shirt, surprised that he has forgotten to wear his suit. The air is warm enough for shorts but Oliver seems cold; he hunches over, clutches at himself, reaches through the car window for his windbreaker which he slips on as he walks toward them.

Peter backs up holding his bagpipes. Elaine and Azelin need some room but he decides not to leave them totally alone. He places the pipes on the shady end of the picnic table and putters, picks things up, puts things down, moves tools from one pile to the other.

"Azelin?" Oliver says. He steps close to Elaine but Peter sees that he is merely looking at the baby.

"Do you like the name?" she asks.

"I've never heard it before. Why did you name her Azelin?"

"Because she is beautiful and because she's alive."

Oliver clearly is confused but doesn't press the issue of the name. He doesn't touch Elaine but he asks to hold the baby. Elaine picks her out of the sling and places her in Oliver's arms. She looks empty without

Azelin. She wraps her arms around her flattened belly. Peter wants to say "Be careful of the baby," but it isn't his place and he moves bales of straw from one side of the barnyard to the other and back again.

"She's lovely," Oliver says. "Are you feeling well?"

"Yes, thank you."

Christ, they sound like acquaintances at a cocktail party. Peter expects him to ask if she would like an olive sandwich or a lemon tart.

"I'm sorry, Elaine." He reaches out to touch the spot below her right eye, high on her cheek, but she steps back and his finger hovers in midair, touching nothing. "I was upset. I didn't mean to hurt you."

"I know. Do you have it? The journal?"

"No. I don't."

"Please send it," she says.

"Does she smile yet?" Oliver asks.

"Not really. Just little indigestion smiles."

"Does she sleep in the night?"

"Yes, except for when she nurses."

"Have you been here long enough?"

"What?"

"I mean, are you planning to come home or are you going to stay here with him? With your lover?"

Peter's hands clench into hard fists but it's not his place to interfere unless Elaine asks him to.

"That's not fair," she says, reaching for Azelin. He steps back, holding the baby close to his chest.

"I deserve to know when you are coming home."

"I need a little more time. Please pass her to me. She's waking up. She'll be scared."

"You're to come home with me. Remember Jezebel. Remember the Bible. He passes the crying infant to Elaine. 'Let wives be in subjection to their husbands as to the Lord because a husband is head of his wife.'

Ephesians 5:22," he says. "You forget easily the teachings of the Lord. If you don't come with me, Azelin will miss you."

"I need to sort things out. Please. Give me a couple of weeks to sort out my life. I will meet with Brother Eldridge. Then we can talk."

"Elaine," he says, stepping back, folding his arms across his chest. "If you won't come, I'll have to take the baby alone. Many men wouldn't even take you back after what you've done."

"What? What have I done?" Elaine's voice scares the baby. She pulls up her T-shirt and puts Azelin on her breast. Peter feels uneasy that Oliver should see that, Elaine's nakedness.

"This," he says, sweeping his arms around to include the cabin, the barn, and Peter. "What do you think? He might even have AIDS. Fornication. Adultery. Disobedience. Everything."

"We're not sleeping together," she says.

"Oh, sure. I'm not leaving here without that baby."

"That baby?" Elaine begins to pace. She glances at Peter but it isn't clear if she wants help. "No. You're not taking Azelin. You don't know anything about me. You don't even know why I'm here."

"No. I guess I don't. But I do know that I'm entitled to my own child. And I do know that you are not going to keep her here with that man. I apologized. That should be enough. What else is there?"

The corners of Oliver's mouth build up with froth as he speaks. He reaches for Elaine's arm, grabbing it just above her elbow.

" 'In this way husbands ought to be loving their wives as their own bodies,' " Elaine says. " 'He who loves his wife loves himself.' "

"What is this? A Bible verse competition?" Peter says. "Take your hand off her."

Peter is surprised when Oliver drops his hand from her and steps back. In his mind he picks up the pipes, the ancient instrument of war, and scares the living bejesus out of the bastard, because he doesn't think it is over. He knows that he wouldn't win in a fight. Oliver is strong.

Young. His bare legs, browned from his mother's genes, are thick, full of muscle; his hands although uncallused and smooth, are large and beefy.

"I will help you through this. Me. Not him. It's my baby—or is it?"

His fist, Peter knows, would snap a jaw, bruise a cheek.

"Give me a few minutes to pack. I'll need to finish feeding her and change her diaper, get her things together."

"Hey. What?" Peter moves toward her.

"It's all right, Peter. Don't worry. You stay here. I won't be long."

Peter thinks his head will explode. He stands immobilized by his own fright. He tears himself away from his piece of ground and steps in her direction. She puts up her arm. "No, Peter. I have to do this. Please wait."

"Well. I guess you'll have to find another woman," Oliver says. Peter ignores him because responding would be pointless. "I'm sorry for saying that. But she's my wife. I love her. I want her back. I miss her singing."

It can't be over. The thing with Elaine. She can't just leave with Azelin, go with this man. Go away from him. From Dora.

"Hurry up," Oliver says to Elaine as she opens the door to the cabin. "I don't have much time."

Peter tries to think fast. If he had a phone, he'd call someone. Dora? The police? Brendan? If he hits the guy, Oliver will hit back, hard. Elaine said "Wait, don't worry." How can he not worry?

"You play those things?" Oliver says, walking over to the bagpipes on the picnic table.

"Don't touch them," Peter hears himself say. "They're very delicate."

"Hey, how do you define a gentleman?"

Peter doesn't answer. He tries to keep his eye on the cabin door while watching Oliver's hands.

"Someone who knows how to play bagpipes but doesn't." Oliver laughs with a kind of nervous snort. "Someone at work told me that. But I've never seen them up close."

Peter watches as Oliver's light brown fingers pick at the fringe on the black velvet bag.

"I said don't touch them."

"I'd like to hear something. How about 'Amazing Grace,' or 'Scotland the Brave.' "

"No." Peter pushes past the man and scoops up the pipes, cradles them in his arms like he would Azelin.

"A little touchy, aren't you?" Oliver says.

Peter catches movement at the front door of the cabin. He was distracted. He didn't see the door open. Elaine stands on the landing, door closed behind her, holding his twenty-gauge against her shoulder like he taught her to. Oliver follows Peter's gaze toward the cabin, toward Elaine.

"Elaine," Oliver shouts. "What are you doing? Put that thing down. You don't know how to use it. You'll hurt yourself."

"I do know how to use it. And I will. Now get off Peter's property. I told you I need a couple of weeks and I'm going to take a couple of weeks. If you don't leave now, it'll make my decision easier." She sights the shotgun on Oliver. He steps away from Peter toward his car, out of the path of the double barrel.

"Put the gun down. I should have brought Brother Eldridge with me. You'd never point a gun at a brother."

"A brother would never force me to. I have no choice. You're not taking Azelin and I'm not ready to go."

They both shout as if they need to speak over a droning noise, some background din like heavy machinery.

"Put it down. Now. Obey me. 'If you see any oppression of the one of little means and the violent taking away of judgment—' "

"Git," she says, like she would to a stray dog. "Go on. Git."

Oliver steps toward her until he has gone halfway up the path. She follows his movement with the shotgun.

"Put it down, Elaine, it's all right," Peter says. "No one's going to take Azelin. I'll shoot the bugger myself if it comes to that." He still cradles the pipes, afraid to put them down, afraid to take his eyes off Elaine.

"I'm going to walk slowly toward you. Now put that thing down." Oliver points his finger, jabs it at her, and begins his advance.

"I don't want to shoot you. But I will," she says.

"Don't be stupid. Get the baby. Now. Right now."

The shot sounds like tree branches cracking, like the ice going out of Great Pond, like thunder. The dirt in front of Oliver sprays up from the path onto bushes, onto the woodpile, onto his clean shorts.

"If you come closer, I will have no choice." She adjusts the stock of the gun against her shoulder.

"Jesus," Oliver says, but he keeps coming. "You almost hit me. Goddammit, Elaine, cut that out."

He is two cabin-lengths away from the landing when the shot hits him. He falls into the path, clasping his leg.

"Oh, my God," she says. She leans the shotgun against the rail of the landing. "Is he moving? My God. I shot him."

"Just his foot, I think," says Peter, placing his pipes back on the table and running to the fallen Oliver.

"Get away from me," Oliver says as Peter tries to examine him. "Get away from me. You're all lunatics. Nut cases. You haven't seen the last of me." He struggles to his feet. One thin line of blood oozes from the fleshy part of his shin straight down into his white athletic sock. Oliver bends to examine himself.

"I'm sorry, Oliver," she says. "I had no choice. No one takes a woman's baby from her without a fight. I didn't mean to hurt you. I had no choice."

Elaine doesn't budge from the landing as Peter approaches Oliver again. The massive fist, the one Peter was afraid of, shoots out toward him, pushing into his shoulder, sending Peter to the ground. "Get away, you bastard." Oliver pulls a white handkerchief from the pocket of his windbreaker and wipes the line of blood from the sock up to the source. "This is going to need a doctor. Shot's still in there." After he ties the handkerchief around his calf, he turns from the cabin, from Elaine, from his baby, Azelin, and drags his left foot back down the path toward his blue sedan.

As Peter struggles to get up, Oliver raises his arm at him. "Don't," is all he says. "Don't."

Peter thinks Oliver is sobbing, but his face is turned away. His head bobs into his hands all the way to the car. It takes a long time because of the shot in his leg.

"You'll be sorry you did this," Oliver yells without turning around, at the door of the car.

"Do you want me to shoot you higher?"

"My God, Elaine. You're crazy. You could have killed me."

"No, Oliver. I didn't want to kill you. Just stop you. Two weeks," Elaine calls. "Two weeks and we'll talk. I have nothing to say until then."

He doesn't turn but Peter knows Oliver hears her. Her voice is strong and clear and the background din has disappeared. The still air of approaching evening carries her voice like a bird on the wing, "Two weeks. Two weeks."

The sound of his engine starting carries, too. Oliver doesn't look back. Just tears away up the driveway.

Peter waits until he can no longer hear the sound before he approaches her. This time, the baby and the pipes are no longer between them and he holds her close to him, feels her thin body trembling against his, strokes her corn-silk hair, until she is still.

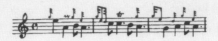

CHAPTER 22

Peter thinks that this might be their last night together because surely
Oliver will bring the police. You just can't shoot people without recrim-
ination. After supper, Elaine rocks and sings about black sheep and holes
in the buckets to Azelin until the baby falls asleep in the crook of her
arm. She doesn't waken when Elaine lowers her into Peter's old newspaper basket which has been turned into a bassinet.

The mood feels a bit like the night his father left for Germany to fight
Nazis. Peter was only a toddler then but the evening is one of his earliest
memories. Quiet hung over the kitchen table like a chandelier as they ate
macaroni and cheese with tuna fish and mushrooms. His mother baked a
chocolate cake with *come home soon* written across the top with white icing. Ironic. *Come home soon.* After supper they all sat in absolute silence
until Peter fell asleep. Never had a chance to say anything to his father.
He was gone the next morning. Gone for three years.

"Elaine," Peter says, breaking the silence.

"Yes," she says, turning toward him. "Yes, we have to talk."

"I can't believe you shot the guy."

"It was crazy, wasn't it?"

"Yes. Crazy."

"He'll be back, you know."

"Yes. He'll be back. But you don't have to go with him. There are laws."

"There are laws against shooting people."

"But—self-defense. He was on my property without permission and he threatened you."

"Threatened to take his own child."

They don't even hear the car, only the knocking. "Christ, they're here already. Sit there. I'll answer it."

"I'm Carl Eldridge," the familiar pudgy guy with the too-small suit says before Peter even gets the door open all the way. The man is alone, his gray station wagon left running in the yard. "I don't want to intrude but I need to speak with Elaine." He doesn't wait for an invitation but goes to her, bends, kisses her cheek, as if she was his friend. "Is there somewhere we could talk? Privately?" he says to Elaine.

"We can speak in front of Peter. He is not my lover. He is my friend."

"It doesn't look very good, you two living in the same cabin like this."

"Peter is helping me sort through some things."

"That's why we have elders. We are here to help you. You don't need to go to worldly people."

Peter wonders if he should offer tea or coffee. He doesn't want to leave them alone in the cabin but feels awkward standing by the stove watching them talk.

"I've seen Oliver. He says you shot him."

"Yes."

"Has he done something? Has he mistreated you? There is help if you have a problem. You know that. But you can't go shooting people."

"The last time I asked for help, you said I deserved it," Elaine says.

"You heard what you wanted to hear," he says.

"Two weeks. I asked him to give me two weeks. That's all."

"You know Jehovah says wives must obey their husbands. Do you have a Bible here? Husbands must be loving but wives must be obedient. That's the law of Jehovah."

"Please. Let me be. You've got to give me time."

"Oliver is willing to give you some time. We'll come two weeks from tomorrow to talk. We are all praying for you, praying that you find the truth. But the truth must be the real truth. John 8:32 says 'And you will know the truth and the truth will set you free.' "

"Thank you, Brother Eldridge," she says. "Thank you for your understanding and your prayers. Would you like to see the baby?" He nods. "She's sleeping."

Brother Eldridge searches Peter's face for permission to go deeper into the cabin and Peter nods.

"She's lovely," he says. "Looks like Oliver." Peter thinks he honestly wants to help Elaine, but that he vehemently will demand her obedience. "Two weeks." He turns to leave. "Good-bye." He nods at Peter, stares at his boots, his jeans with the gap at the knee, his scruffy hair. "It's important for the children to have a strong family."

"Good-bye," Peter says, opening the door for him.

Peter watches as the man, who looks a little like Tweedle Dum, steps down the path, avoiding stones with his silver-toed cowboy boots, watches him until his car disappears through the trees.

"Everything's all right now," she says.

"No. It's different. It's not all right. There are things between us. We're not just a typical American couple with baby and dog and little garden out back. We're not a family." Peter walks around the table, feels his pocket for his Luckies, pumps water into his coffee mug, drinks it down, cold against his palate. *The truth will set you free. Free.* What the hell is the truth? Whose truth is right? Free from what? Free from your own feats? "The dollhouse. I want to tell you about the dollhouse," he says, turning toward her.

"You don't need to."

"Yes. I do. Come."

He lifts the corner of the towel, nudges the books out of the way, exposes the entire front of the house. He feels as if he has been stripped naked in front of his class, his recurring dream every night before a competition, a small dirty boy, nothing on but socks, standing in front of his whole class, the teacher instructing. *There's his ugly belly button, his flabby bum, his scrawny neck, his withered dick. What do you think, class?*

But Elaine doesn't say those things. She holds his arm, leans her head on his shoulder. He can't speak. Leslie, Sarah, Nathaniel. He hasn't shown them to anyone. Ever.

"They're your family, aren't they, Peter?"

He nods.

"You loved them very much."

He nods again.

"I'm sorry I didn't wait for you to show me. I was curious. I had no right."

"It's just that having you see them changes everything. They're no longer my secret."

"Tell me about them."

"This is Leslie." Peter wants to speak to Leslie, tell her he's sorry about the intrusion, that he loves her. He can't look at Elaine, like a boy who has stolen from the five-and-ten. He picks up the Leslie doll, shows her to Elaine but wants to hide her, fears he has gone too far and can't back out. "This is Sarah. Nathaniel." He leaves them in their places. It is too awkward to hold them up, like some kind of lunatic show and tell. "They give me comfort." He has said all he can say.

"Shall we cover it up or leave it open?" she says as he turns away.

"Oh." He places Leslie back in the chair by the kitchen table. "I'd like to leave it open."

Peter staggers over to his bed. His head pounds and he thinks he might throw up. He collapses on top of his futon, his head in the pillow.

His face presses into the flannel pillowcase, presses until the pillow covers his ears, until he can't see the daylight. Her hands touch the back of his head where it is pounding, just touch with her palms, and he feels her heat. The side of the futon sinks as she sits beside him, hip against hip. *Elaine, Elaine, Elaine,* over and over in his hot pounding head. The heat spreads down the back of his neck as her hands smooth his hair. *Turn to her, turn to her,* a voice tells him. It is a voice he hasn't heard for years. Not since Leslie. Not since Leslie put her hands on him, trailed her fingers down the length of his back. *Hi, Les. Yes, I won. I miss you too. I ate with Colin and went to bed early. See you soon. Love you.* The last words. He can hear himself speaking into the black hotel phone. He has heard them every day for years. The last words.

"Elaine." He speaks into the pillow, muffled, lost in the white feathers inside the cover.

Turn to her. Turn to Elaine. Tell her something. Tell her she can stay. Tell her she doesn't have to go back.

She nudges him to turn his head, pushes with warm fingers until he turns to her. She bends over him, covers his face with her hair. She is so close he can smell her. Not soap or perfume but the tangible odor of skin and breast milk. He will remember that smell as long as he lives.

"I know you miss them," she says. He inhales her warm breath, catches her exhalation with his mouth, pulls it into his lungs.

"Elaine." He wants to say crazy things like *I love you,* and *Please, let me touch your bare skin, your breasts, between your legs.* The heat radiates down his back toward his pelvis until the pulse from his groin swells at the mattress, before he turns toward her.

She lies with him, pulls her legs up onto the bed, stretches out the length of it. She strokes his forehead and he is afraid to touch her. He has forgotten how to touch a woman. He realizes he is shivering and she is caring for him as if he were a baby, not a grown man who loves her. He cups her face in his palms, her skin stark white against his weathered hands. Her mouth opens and closes but he can't hear her voice over the pounding in his own head. *Shut up,* he screams at the demons in his head, *Shut up so I can hear her words.*

Suddenly she is gone from him, walking to the baby in the magazine basket. She lifts Azelin up to her exposed breast. Her mouth still moves as if she is saying words to him but the roaring in his head continues until she settles herself into the rocking chair.

To see what he could see, and all that he could see,
and all that he could see, was the other side of the
mountain . . .

Peter aches to cover his penis with his hand but she will see him. He turns his face back into the pillow, turns his body to cover his hardness.

Elaine rocks and sings. Peter struggles with himself. When she leaves he will be alone and he is afraid of that. It is getting dark outside and he needs to get up to light the lamps. He hears Elaine change Azelin from one breast to the other. She doesn't know. She doesn't know how he feels about her.

"Thank you for trusting me enough to show the dollhouse," she says. "I won't intrude. But if you want to talk about them, I'll listen."

He can't speak yet. The pounding inside his head is too recently gone and he is afraid to speak, to bring it back. The light in the cabin is dimming and the breeze from the open windows cools his hot skin. He can't stay on the bed. He wills his feet to the floor, wills his body upright, wills his throbbing groin to shrink. The gaping openness of the dollhouse startles him until he remembers what he did.

"I'll light the lamps," he says. "It's cooling off, too."

Only two of the lamps are filled with kerosene but that is enough to bring a warm glow to the walls of the cabin. He shuts the windows except for a small crack in the front one. Seamus's bowl is still full from the previous day but he tops it off with a cup of fresh dog food and the remains of the chicken soup.

Elaine carries the basket with sleeping Azelin over to the side of her bed. "I'm going to the outhouse. She shouldn't waken."

After she leaves, Peter approaches the dollhouse. "Les, I'm sorry." Then he isn't sure why he is sorry. For exposing her to Elaine? For letting her burn in the fire? For loving someone else? He raises his finger to touch the doll but hesitates. He feels foolish. He wishes Nathaniel would find the goddamn sneaker. And when was Sarah going to outgrow stuffed animals? For Christ's sake, she was almost a teenager.

On the way to bed he stops by the basket. Azelin's mouth sucks at the air, the corners of her tiny mouth pulsing her lips tight. Black hair sticks to her forehead in ringlets. He brushes it back from her dark eyes before he goes to his futon.

After Elaine returns from the outhouse, after she has blown out the lamps, after she has undressed for bed in the half light, they lie in the still cabin, still, except for the peepers. Peter hears her move her bare feet on the clean sheet, hears Azelin sucking, hears the old dog scratch, but then nothing again but the sound of thousands of peepers.

"It was my fault, you know. She told me there was a frayed wire. I said I'd fix it after the competition season." He speaks quietly. Matter of factly. "My fault."

"Do they know it was a wire?"

"No. But it must have been. I was always too busy. She called me that night, before the fire started. Or perhaps it was already in the walls, burning wires, melting the plastic around the wires, baking the plaster. *Hello,* I said. I remember the black plastic of the hotel phone. She told me about Nathaniel finally swimming from the float to shore and how proud he was. I told her that I ate dinner with Colin and went to bed early. But I don't remember what I had for supper. I don't remember where we went."

"Can you ask Colin? If it's important, ask him."

"I haven't talked to him in years. Not since he visited the hospital after the fire without my permission. Tried to get me to play. Held the pipes up to my mouth, placed the bag under my arm. *You can't quit. You are the best. You have too much talent to quit.* I told him to get the fuck away from the hospital and never bother me again. He never did."

"Have you thought about trying to find him?"

"No."

"Maybe you could. It's easier today than it used to be."

"He's still in the bagpipe circle. He was damn good. But, no. No. I don't think so. It's too late for that."

"It's never too late."

"Good night, Elaine."

"Peter . . ."

"Tomorrow. We'll talk tomorrow."

CHAPTER 23

They don't talk the next day, or the next. Not about Colin or Leslie, at least. The dollhouse stays open and while Elaine is in the outhouse or the garden he moves the dolls up to bed and down to the kitchen for breakfast. When they wash dishes together or weed the lettuce, Peter maneuvers himself to touch her. Just light brushes or taps that might be called an accident, or just a casual touch while working. When she takes her bath out by the barn, he holds Azelin, trying to position himself in the cabin so he can see her without intruding on her privacy. There is no word from Oliver except a letter two days after Brother Eldridge's visit that says he will respect her wishes for two weeks. Then they will talk. Elaine doesn't show him the letter but he reads it while she picks asparagus one evening. *Dearest Elaine,* the letter starts. Peter thinks that touching the letter and unfolding it would not be right so he reads as far as he can while it is in its position, stuck in the pocket of Azelin's diaper bag.

There are three days left for Elaine to make her decision but Peter doesn't know what she has decided, or that she has even thought about it. Sometimes at night, he still hears her praying from her bed, mumbling softly to herself, saying *Jehovah God*, both names together, just like that. Like calling someone *Peter Pete*, or *William Bill*.

He plays the bagpipes every day and his lip is coming back. The reed he bought at the music store, the one that was a little soft and mushy, is now much too easy for him and he writes on the grocery list, *hard pipe-chanter reed,* so that he won't forget next time he goes to town. He plays reels and jigs, strathspeys and marches, even slow marches, but he hasn't yet played a piobaireachd on the pipes. A couple of neighbors drive down the hill to ask what is going on. They want to hear "Amazing Grace." He plays it for them. But no one asks for a piobaireachd. That's what Colin would do. He'd want a lament, for sure, and Peter wouldn't be able to play it. Wouldn't even be able to play past the ground. He plays the ground of a couple of gathering piobaireachds on his practice chanter and feels all right about it. But he's not ready to play one all the way through.

Peter's head leans on Ruby's soft flank while his hands squeeze with alternate rhythm at her full teats. Milking is a good time to think about things like Elaine, Oliver, Azelin, bagpipes. No one talks to you and nothing interferes. There is only the sound of the milk squirting hard against the side of the stainless-steel pail. He thinks about tomorrow and the island shearing. Usually he waits until June but this year everything seems ahead of the usual schedule and they decided to shear a week earlier. He's been shearing his island flock for years but this year will be different. Elaine is planning to go with them. There'll be three boats plus the empty skiff filled on the way back with freshly shorn fleeces that Peter will tow behind his boat.

If someone asks him what the highlight of his year was he will answer, *shearing day,* not Christmas or solstice or birthday. Shearing day is the one time when he feels comfortable around other people, experiences a sense of camaraderie that otherwise is totally absent from his life.

Ruby kicks at the side of the near-full bucket. "Oh, no, you don't," Peter says. "Keep that foot right there with the rest of them." She settles down and Peter returns his head to her flank. The smell reminds him a little of Elaine and he thinks it must be the milk.

Shearing day preparations have already begun at Dora's. Elaine is there now helping bake trays of lasagna, at least three rhubarb pies, fresh bread. Folks who come to help expect a good meal and they always get it. Some goddamn photographer from *National Geographic* called Dora's, wanting to come out, but he was on his own. Seems that every year they have some media person—television, newspaper, college student—doing a thesis on rural culture.

Peter strips the soft teats. They hang like empty balloons from her udder. "Come on, Dizzy, come in with your mom. You can have your fill for the night." They still separate the two during the day to give Ruby's bag time to fill up. They've had enough milk to make cheese for themselves and a little for Dora.

Seamus waits for him at the entrance to the barn because Peter always pours him a small bowl of milk. Today, the dog just sniffs the milk and turns away. He follows the pail up the path to the cabin. "In you go, old thing," Peter says. With his free hand, he lifts Seamus's rear end into the cabin. Peter pours some milk over the food left in the dog dish from yesterday. He can't remember when he last put in fresh food. The dog just nibbles occasionally from the top of the mound. If he doesn't eat by tonight, he'll have to dump it and wash out the bowl. Maybe get some new kind of food from the grocery. He'd even tried some fresh rabbit meat last week but ended up throwing most of it out.

He pours the milk through the filter into the stainless-steel can on the counter. Half a gallon. Not bad, considering Dizzy takes so much. He'll have to start lowering the can into the root cellar because even the nights are getting warm and the milk spoils quickly.

Elaine said she would be back before dark. He lights one of the lamps just to set on the table, be lit when she arrives, just in case she is late. He wanted to be able to spend some time with the dollhouse today but the time got all used up on other things. It took him all afternoon to gather his shearing equipment together. Old pants, bags for the fleeces, tags and pens to mark the bags, shears, blades, blood-stop, odds and ends. The generator is in Dora's shed and he hopes it will be in running shape. He has bought fresh gasoline for that.

The dollhouse looks shabby. Peter wipes his finger along the kitchen floor and holds it up. Dust. Leslie's hair is coming off on one side and he's meant to glue it back. He pulls up a chair and brings the dolls to his lap. All the dolls. He tidies the rooms, straightens the stuffed animals and rearranges the furniture in the living room. The children's rooms always look neat and ready for them. He tucks them into their beds.

"It's been a hard spring," he says. "I've been thinking about the phone call. Remember? The last one? At the hotel?" He holds Leslie to his chest. "I don't remember where Colin and I had dinner. Do you? Did I tell you?" He knows she won't answer but sometimes when he talks the answers come to him as if she responds. *Hello,* he had said.

Hi, darling, Leslie said. *Did you win?*

Hi, Les. Yes, I won.

I miss you.

I miss you, too.

Where'd you have supper?

I ate with Colin and went to bed early.

Oh, that's nice. See you soon. Love you.

See you soon. Love you.

The dialogue has played in his head every day for years so what the fuck is wrong now? Something sounds wrong. Did he forget some of it? Something he said to her? Something she said to him? He wishes he'd written it down because it was important to be exactly correct. There was something about Nathaniel at the swimming pool and a message about the car needing a valve job but that wasn't important. The rest was what he wanted to remember. Each word exactly as it was said. It was the last time they spoke.

"Les, I'm sorry about the electricity. I should have fixed the wire. Did that start the fire?" he says aloud.

He hears the telephone bell ringing. One long low ring. Not like phones today. Seven rings before he picks it up. *Went to bed early,* he hears himself say. And whatever happened to that girl, Kate? Why didn't she go with them for dinner? He remembers asking her. Then what happened?

"Les. I'm forgetting. Sometimes I can't remember the smell of your mouth. I've forgotten how your voice sounded. *Where'd you have supper?* How did that sound? I can't remember."

Peter kisses the doll's forehead and settles her into bed with Sarah, pushes them close together, moves Leslie's arm until it hugs Sarah tight, pulls the covers up to their chins.

"There. You won't be alone."

It is Peter who feels lonely now. The old dog lifts his head and groans. "Seamus, you old dog, you are a sorry sight." Peter pats himself on the thigh. "Here, boy," he says. Seamus puts his head back down on the floor.

"All right then, I'll come down there." Peter's got a touch of arthritis in his hips and hopes Elaine won't be back when he struggles to get to his feet. He stretches his legs out in front of him and pulls Seamus's head to his lap. The fur is no longer soft. It is patchy and coarse. He'll have to start putting bacon grease into the food. Peter's fingers stroke behind the ears, down the neck. Seamus emits a low growl. Most of the hair around his muzzle is gray. Even the black fur of his coat is full of gray hairs. Peter is surprised at all the gray.

"You like Elaine, don't you, boy?" He strokes the old dog behind the ears. "Sheep . . . Rabbit . . . Wood . . . Fetch." There is no response from the dog. None of the old words makes any difference. His eyes are glazed with a gray film but Peter looks past the film to find the old

sparkle. "It's not so bad, dying. You're old. Just close your eyes, relax."
Peter lowers the head to the floor and struggles to his feet. "How about
a special treat," he says. "Chicken. Your favorite."

Peter hauls on the iron ring attached to the trap door. He loves the
root cellar, its cool earthy air, the shelves lined with canning jars, mostly
empty this time of year. There are two jars of chicken left. Peter takes
one for the dog. As he lowers the trap door, Seamus lifts his head, cocks
his ear. "Look, boy. Chicken."

Peter washes the dog dish, scraping away the bits of dried leftover
food and spoons the entire jar of chicken into the bowl. It happens while
he stands holding the bowl, ready to place it on the floor. Happens right
there in front of him. The dog sniffs at the chicken, lays his head back
down on the floor with a groan. The last groan continues a horribly long
time, too long for a mere groan, continues until the life is gone from
him, until his head rolls off to the side the way dead things do.

Peter lowers himself again and sits for a long time with his hand on
the dog's head, stroking the fur behind the long ears, until the flesh
underneath the fur cools. The weight of the dog's head on his thigh
puzzles him until he comprehends that Seamus will never again fetch
the wood for his stove. "Dog, bring the wood," he says in a whisper.
"Bring the wood."

When Elaine arrives back from Dora's with Azelin, Peter is still on
the floor, Seamus's head on his lap.

"What are you doing?" she says.

"Dog." He can't say the rest. Not yet. But she understands.

"Oh. Seamus." Elaine kneels with Azelin close to her chest, kneels
and brushes her lips across the face of the dead dog. She kisses Peter
on the top of the head. "I'm sorry," she says.

Peter wants to nestle his head in her breast, nurse from her, feel her
bare arms around his shoulders. But he can't do that. And he feels very
alone.

"He had a decent life. He was old," he says.

"Shall we bury him tonight or do you want to wait until tomorrow?"

"We can't tomorrow. We have to leave first thing for the island. It'll have to be tonight."

"I'll help you."

The digging is easy. Peter chooses a spot between the compost and the barn. Three feet down is plenty to avoid any plowing or garden work. The sun is glowing red by the time the hole is finished. Elaine offers to help carry him but Peter wants to do it himself. The dead dog is heavier than the living one and Peter struggles to keep his legs from collapsing on the path down the hole. He means to lower the body into the hole but it slips and lands hard, smacking the compact ground.

"One more thing," he says to Elaine.

He chooses birch because that was the dog's favorite. A perfect birch log with no knots or branches. Smooth white unbroken paper bark, perfect for a dog's mouth, especially an old dog. This time he's careful to lay the log beside the body, careful not to drop it. When he begins to shovel, some of the dirt falls on the dog's still-open eye. Peter drops the shovel and runs into the barn. He rummages through a bin of old grain bags until he finds a burlap sweet-feed bag: smell like molasses, no holes, no stains. He lays it on the dog's head to keep the dirt from going in his eyes and continues to fill the hole. There is a mound left when he is finished and he stamps on it until it is ground level.

He expects Elaine to say some prayer over the grave when he is finished. There should be something said. But neither speaks. Azelin snorts in her sleep.

"It's getting dark," he says. "Let's go in."

The cabin is illuminated only by the one lamp which throws shadows on the back walls. The eerie quiet as they sit at the table is broken only by occasional mouth noises from Azelin.

"Play something," Elaine says.

Peter doesn't speak but as if in slow motion, stands, walks to the shelf, picks up the chanter.

"I'm going to play you something you probably haven't ever heard. It's called *pee-broch*, but spelled an ungodly complicated way. A Gaelic word. *Piobaireachd.* Ancient classical bagpipe music. It can't be played on any other instrument. This one is by one of the MacCrimmons. They were hereditary pipers to the MacLeods in the sixteenth and seventeenth century." Peter's voice is low like the light in the room. Reverence for old Dog. "I'll only play the ground. I used to play piobaireachd in competition years ago, before the fire."

The piece begins high, too high for anyone to sing. His fingers remember the notes and move limberly from one to the other, performing the grace notes perfectly. As he plays, the tune of the ground comes to him easily. He closes his eyes because it becomes too much to include the outside world in his lament. The closing measure comes before he is ready for it, the Bs, that last long and lonely B.

" 'Lament for the Children,' " he says when it is finished. "Patrick Mor MacCrimmon. That's just the first movement. The ground. The rest builds on that."

"Will you play the rest of it?"

"Not yet. Someday I'll play it on the pipes for you. I'm not quite ready yet."

Elaine rustles around the kitchen, pumping water, putting things away, while Peter opens the old musty trunk. At the bottom, past the clothes, past his kilt, past Leslie's flute, flat on the bottom of the trunk, is a stack of books and papers, bound with a heavy cord. He pulls it out and cuts the cord on the kitchen table. He leafs through the stack until he comes to a battered softcovered book. *Composition Paper,* it says on the front, his name printed neatly underneath. At the back are a few blank pages.

The jar of pens and pencils on the counter contains one lone pencil with a broken point. Peter shaves the end with the blade of his jackknife until the point is sharp. He sets up the piece on the lined paper. It will be four four. Directly over the first line, he writes "ground." At the top of the page, he writes, "Azelin's Lullaby," in block letters. The notes are in his head, have been there for several days, now playing faster than he can write them down with the pencil. He allows the music to get ahead and then pulls it back to the beginning. It's kind of like fishing, he thinks, let the fish pull the hook enough to get it interested, then pull gently, keep tension on the line, wait, reel in. The measures build up. The first part is repeated. He draws in the heavy line perpendicular to the bar lines with two dots in front of it at the end of the first line. The second part is two lines, no repeat, and it's high, like Elaine's voice, like the song of a thrush.

Three lines of ground. A new piobaireachd. The variations will be technical work. Assigning movements to the notes of the ground. Busy work. But the ground. He goes over the measures to make sure the timing is correct, that he has all the notes accounted for. Elaine goes to say goodnight to Dizzy and visit the outhouse. When he is alone, he begins to sing the piobaireachd from the sheet music in front of him. It is Elaine's voice. He sings it again, filling in a few grace notes, changing the time on one of the quarter notes to a half and stealing its worth from another note. His fingers find E but he can't close his eyes because he needs to read the notes. The repeat of the first part sounds slightly awkward and will need a few changes but the second part swells and grows until the resolution concludes the movement.

When Elaine comes back, he waits until she tends to Azelin, brushes her teeth, sinks into the rocker. "I've written a tune," he says.

"A tune? You mean you've just written it? Just now? Will you play it for me?"

"Yes. But I've been hearing it in the woods for days. It comes from the trees and the wind. After shearing day, I'll play it," he says.

Peter picks up the pencil again, changes the last two notes of the first measure, and writes directly under *Azelin's Lullaby* the words *For Elaine, May 28.*

CHAPTER 24

*P*eter is out of bed before there is any sign of sun in the morning sky. Instead of lighting the lamps he uses the flashlight as he gathers his shearing tools and organizes himself for the day ahead. A green plastic fishtote leans by the door and he begins to place things in it. A bottle of last year's blueberry wine for celebration at Dora's after shearing, his bag of tools, two boxes of Oreos, oil for the shears, a sharpening file, dry socks, bandana for his hair. He won't make coffee this morning. They'll stop at the store on the way and get coffee to go.

"We leave at seven," he says.

Elaine moans in return, turns over in the bed. Peter looks for faithful old Seamus before he remembers the night before. Remembers what happened. By the time he heads to the outhouse and the barn, the rising sun provides a warm glow over everything he can see. He feeds Alice, who hasn't kicked yet, and Ruby. Everybody goes out today, even Dizzy, who will stay with Ruby because no one will want to milk a goat after a day of shearing. He feeds and waters the chickens but he'll have to collect eggs later. It's too early for them to have laid.

In the outhouse, he drops his stiff shearing pants to the floor and sits down on the wooden seat. New catalogs fill the magazine rack. In front of the catalogs is an *Awake* magazine. One of those Jehovah's Witness things. Peter thumbs through it. Pictures of a variety of people, all smiling, plucking fruit from trees. He reads the back. "If You Could Live Forever, Would You Choose To?"

"Fuck, no," he says. Sitting in some nursing home for a thousand years, trapped in a wheelchair. But the people in the pictures aren't in wheelchairs. They're running and laughing. *"Live Forever in Paradise. Young and Healthy." That sounds even worse.*

Peter tucks the magazine at the back of the stack. Johnny's Seed catalog in front is covered with tomatoes, all colors and sizes. He pulls it out of the rack, exposing *The Voice.*

"Where the hell did this come from?" he says aloud. He hasn't seen *The Voice* since before the fire. Used to come every month full of news from the bagpipe circuit but after the fire, they piled up with the other publications until finally his mother canceled it along with *National Geographic* and *Gourmet.*

The address on the back is the music store in town. Curtis Music. Elaine must have picked it up on a trip to town with Dora. The front page covers upcoming highland games. He begins from back to front. Lists of up-and-coming bagpipe competitions, a discussion of the new plastic drone reeds, the merits of Gore-Tex bags. The list of judges for Maxville lists a familiar name. Colin Robertson. Old pipers. They never get out of it. Colin. Got to be his Colin. He leafs through to see if there are any pictures. A couple of group shots of open winners. Nothing of judges. Colin Robertson of Toronto, Canada. Got to be his Colin.

He reads through the newsletter until his ass is numb and his legs begin to shake. Before he goes, he replaces the *Awake* just in behind *The Voice.* He pulls up the stiff shearing pants, wishes he'd worn underwear today but realizes he doesn't have any. The scratchy material is going to rub against him all day. He snaps the suspenders onto the loose waistband. He thinks he might wear a pair of shorts underneath.

By seven o'clock, he has packed the back of the truck with the overflowing fishtote and the rest of the odds and ends he might need for the day. He's told Elaine to make sure she brings plenty of warm clothes and a change or two for Azelin. Brendan has loaned them a baby life preserver that just fits. Peter's never seen one so small. Brendan said he had it for one of his kids. They are all grown up now, but he keeps things like that around just in case. Peter piles the burlap grain bags on top of everything and starts the truck.

"Time to go," he hollers up to the cabin. Elaine carries Azelin down the path and buckles her into the car seat between them in the truck. The drive to Dora's doesn't take more than ten minutes and there are already cars in the yard when they arrive. A couple of cars have small skiffs tied to the roofs. They gather in Dora's kitchen.

Every surface is covered with some kind of food: pans of lasagna, jars of pickles, bread, pies. Margaret helps Dora arrange the food, their stooped bodies performing a kind of elderly pas de deux around the table.

"Oh, you're here, are you?" Dora says. Peter bends and kisses her cheek. "Well, kissing me, is he? That's something."

"Looks like you got everything under control," he says. "Who's sorting?"

"Susanne, the girl who helped us with the birthing, she's been learning to sort. I figured after the gathering, Elaine can help too. She knows enough about fleece to bag."

A couple of strangers hover by the kitchen door, young folks wearing proper L. L. Bean clothing for a job like this. "Joshua," the man says, sticking out his hand to Peter.

"Mary Jane," the woman says.

Peter nods. They look nice enough. "You two will gather along with Elaine and me. We'll go over everything once we get out there. You'll split up in the boats. Josh, you go in Dora's boat."

"It's Joshua."

"Well, whatever. The girl goes with Cecilia. Where the hell is Cecilia?"

"Looking for me?" she says from the doorway.

Peter swears she's grown another foot since last shearing day. She towers over everyone in the kitchen and her hands are the size of pies. The Passamaquoddy in her looks is stronger than the Irish from her dad. Her black hair is pulled back with a bandana or it would hang down over her face, covering the scar on her chin. Everyone said her Da smacked her around, especially after her mother died.

"You all set with your shearing gear?" he asks her.

"Yeah, and I got a bunch of new blades if you need any. Forgot my blood-stop, though. If I cut one bad, I'll holler."

"One more's coming," Dora says. "Margaret says she's going to stay here. She's afraid she'll be a burden. Shelley from next door is coming to help with the food. She's good in a boat."

"Here she is," says Josh.

"She can go with Mary Jane and Cecilia. I want Cecilia rowing," Peter says. He recognizes Shelley from Dora's. She helped cut up the deer meat the previous fall. He thinks she's the one whose husband caught his foot in a rope coil and went down with his trap a couple of years ago.

"Hi, Peter. I guess I'm helping out this year. Always wanted to come out for shearing. Me and everyone else, I guess," she says.

"What's the story with that *National Geo* feller?" he asks the crowd.

"He's coming out with some writer. They're already down on the dock. Got one of them blow-up boats. They're down there blowing it up with a contraption runs off their car cigarette lighter."

Cigarette. Shit. He's forgotten to have his smoke and he sure couldn't have it now. Not with those women after him. Dora would belt him on the head if he lit up in front of her. He'll have to wait till later.

The caravan of skiffs sets off from the dock. Peter's boat has a small outboard secured to the stern, just enough horse to tow the fleece boat behind. It's almost empty now but on the way back it will be piled with thirty bags of fleece. Well, actually, twenty-nine. He notices it has a few odds and ends stacked between the seats; a couple of fancy backpacks, probably from the new couple, the empty burlap sacks, water jugs.

Elaine sits holding Azelin in the middle seat. Peter remembers when not too many years ago, Dog sat up in the bow like a mate on watch. Peter asks Elaine to wear her life jacket. "Don't know when something might happen," he says to her. Tiny Azelin has her royal blue doll-sized life jacket buckled around her chest, hiding everything but her face.

He doesn't like the noise of the outboard but towing the fleece boat using oars would be nigh to impossible. It's the only time he puts the outboard on unless he absolutely has to go out in bad weather. Elaine faces the island. Peter watches her back, her hair hanging in one thick braid past her shoulder blades. Her legs straddle the seat, allowing her to turn back to him to ask a question or show him something she discovers. They scream back and forth over the roar of the small motor, pointing and gesturing to make up for the lack of hearing.

The other boats bob up and down in the small swells. The air is crisp, clear, with no bad weather predicted. Of course, on the coast of Maine, you never know about the weather. The small caps break on the bows of the skiffs behind him. The rowers all make headway, some of the boats low in the water, especially Cecilia's, because of the generator. But she is strong, arms more muscular than anyone on his crew team back in Connecticut. Mary Jane sits on the bow of Cecilia's skiff with her feet dangling in the cold ocean water. Peter gestures to her to pull them up. Christ, she's so stupid, she doesn't know how much she's adding to the drag of the boat. If she acts like a nincompoop out on the island, he'll make her sit in the hut with Shelley. No room for poor judgment out there.

The water becomes shallow enough for him to see the seaweed bottom, although even at low tide there isn't any spot in the channel that

is shallow enough for his outboard to touch bottom. He knows these
waters like the back of his hand. He cuts the motor and flips it up just
before the bow touches the stony beach, allowing the skiff to glide to
shore. The only sheep in sight is the ram who munches on seaweed at
the water's edge a little further down the beach.

"Wait, Elaine. I'll put it up a bit before you get out."

She is busy extracting Azelin, who begins to scream, from the fandangled life preserver with its straps and buckles. The boat is heavy but
Peter manages to haul it up just enough for Elaine to step out on dry
land. After he unties the fleece boat painter from the stern of the skiff
and hands it to Elaine to hold, he runs with the little boat up the beach
all the way to the line of trees. Next is the fleece boat which is old wood
and much heavier to haul over the stones. He's glad he put on his shorts
under the stiff pants because even with them on, he is getting chafed by
the rough material.

As soon as the other boats arrive on the shore, the organizational
efforts of Dora take over. Everyone, including the *National Geo* men,
know what to do, what is expected of them. Peter wonders when they
had the lecture. Did he miss something? Cecilia and Josh haul the generator over to the holding pen while the others carry food and drinks
up to the small hut in the center of the island. The *National Geo* men
try to help Dora and are assailed with swear words they probably didn't
even know. After that they stay out of the way, asking polite questions
of Josh and Mary Jane, who know nothing.

Soon, Shelley is serving up fresh coffee and baskets of cinnamon
sugar–coated doughnuts. Peter runs up to the hut at the call because he
forgot to stop at the store on the way over. The mug warms his hand
and he blows the steam up into his face. The first sip burns his tongue
and he soothes it with a doughnut.

"Damn good doughnuts, Shelley," he says. "Who's been coaching
you?"

Shelley slaps her ample hips, throws her head back with a laugh. A young Dora. And almost as good a cook as Margaret. Peter wonders how she gets the old woodstove going and has coffee within twenty minutes of landing. Already the old pine table in the hut is camouflaged with a yellow print cloth. Pies and salads cover one end and the lasagna ringed with pickles and platters of bread weigh down the other.

"Doughnuts now. Cookies at nine. Lunch at eleven. That's it," Shelley says, and everyone believes her.

Josh arrives to report that all the equipment including the generator is in position and the pen area is ready for shearing. The group follows Peter to the holding pen, except for Shelley, who stays guarding the food. Peter barks orders about securing the top rail of the algae-splattered fencing and shoring up the sides of the chute. "If one goes through, they all go through." Most of the people have heard that before, except for Josh and Mary Jane, and, of course, the magazine guys, who snap their cameras too close and continue to ask Josh about how it's done.

Cecilia takes over the lecture about rounding them up, how it's important to keep low, to move slow, to make a thorough sweep of the entire island, to funnel them directly into the chute on the first try because after that they get skittish. This is one of the smaller islands he and Cecilia will shear together; his is always the first one they do. She's good. Strong, adept, fast. But she's ugly. Her scarred chin juts out so far past her face that Peter wonders how she chews her food. There isn't any fat on her anywhere but her thighs are the size of two of his.

Dora goes to the shore and sits on the side of one of the skiffs to wait for the sheep. She knows she is too old for the gather. She hasn't asked about Dog and Peter feels a need to tell her before they start. He follows her to the boat.

"The old dog," he begins. "He died last night. Just gave up. His time, I guess."

"Oh. Poor old thing," Her deep rheumy eyes become wetter than usual, blink deep in their sockets. She's probably thinking she'll be next.

Peter does something he's never done. He embraces the old woman, holding her snug in his arms and his eyes tear up over the old dog, too. She seems surprised at the embrace but nestles into him, brings her arms around his filthy shearing shirt. He hears a small moan, feels it in his hands coming from her back.

"We'll miss him, won't we?" he says. Not a question, really. "I buried him out by the barn. Do you think I should get a pup?"

"A pup?" She breaks from him. "A pup? Have you ever had a pup?"

"No. All my dogs came from the pound."

"They chew everything, shoes, table legs, and they piss all over the floor. Yes, get a pup. One of them border collie dogs. Help you with the sheep."

"Let's talk about it," he says as he turns to go back to the pen.

The gatherers are ready, all equipped with long sticks. Even Elaine stands quietly by the side of the chute, a three-foot length of driftwood in her hand. Azelin is quiet, snugged against her breast by the baby carrier. All of them except Dora and Cecilia will spread out around the island and gather the sheep toward the chute. Cecilia will be ready to open and close gates and keep them from veering away at the last minute. Dora will talk to the gulls, think about the wool that's coming, figure out who to ask about pups for Peter. Peter knows her. He sees her mouth moving from his place on the small hillock. Talking to the gulls.

The L. L. Bean folks start off too fast and Peter hollers at them to crouch and slow down. Luck is with them today. The sheep are all together except for the ram. Peter detours around the peninsula and herds him into the circle of ewes and lambs. The flock rises as if one sheep and moves slowly toward the other end of the island, the chute end. Peter gets a whiff of coffee while he crouches against a boulder. The new folks have got the idea now and crouch and sway just like pros. Elaine whacks her stick on the ground when an errant ewe tries to break from the flock. The ewe turns back into the circle and moves with the rest.

"Slow down," Cecilia says. They all hear her and crouch. Elaine moves in slow motion out to the side to cover the southern getaway point. The camera guy hangs out at the pen and Dora yells at him. "Sheep ain't going in the pen with you standing there," she says.

"They're going in," Peter hears. He's not sure who says it. Once one sheep goes through, the others follow, even the ram. Three lambs are left outside but they won't be a problem unless the mothers try to leap the fence. The fence is too high for all but the very craziest to attempt.

"Got them," he says. "Close the gate."

They trot through the chute toward the pen. When they are all in the pen, Cecilia shuts the gate. "I count twenty-nine including the ram, excluding the lambs. That it?"

"Yes."

"Shouldn't take us too long to do them. Somebody start that generator," she says. She barks instructions to the gatherers-turned-catchers. Josh and Mary Jane will catch. "Have you done this before?"

"We practiced at Woodcock Farm. They showed us how to hold them and move them around," Josh says.

Dora spreads tarps out on the beach. There is no sign of Shelley coming to help sort. Peter thinks it will be Dora and Elaine. Cecilia already grips a ewe between her legs, sets it on its rump, and begins the first blow across the belly, the sound of the shears droning in the background. She throws the belly wool into a heap over the fence. The next few blows shear the head and begin down the side. The dirty ringlets fall off the skin, leaving a stark-white eight-inch layer of fuzz, next year's tips. He takes the black, she the white. Keeps the integrity of the fleece that way. They peel the layers onto the tarps, one sheep at a time, borrow each other's Marvel Mystery Oil when the shears begin to run hot. The fleece goes to Dora and Elaine, who toss dungy globs and short scraps into an old burlap bag which they'll take back to the mainland to make manure tea for their gardens. The rest is labeled after it is rolled and pushed into the burlap grain bags. They'll weigh it after they get back to the mainland. They get top dollar for the strong island fleece, absent of any hay chaff or barn debris.

Josh and Mary Jane ruin their new clothes but keep going. They're out of breath and Mary Jane takes a rest while Josh does both the black and the white. The ram catches a foot in Josh's new pants and even Dora looks up at the sound of the rip. Peter's boots and pants are covered with urine and shit and oil. He has to use the blood-stop only once when he cuts the groin of one of the ewes a little too close. It bleeds like a faucet for a minute and he thinks he might have hit an artery but the flow ceases when he pours the powder onto the slice.

After a few hours of intense work, there are only a few lambs left in the pen. Cecilia opens the gate and shoos them out. They all help get the last few fleeces into bags before they head up to the hut. Shelley has a steaming bowl of hot water on the ground just outside the hut door and a clean towel laid on the stump next to a bar of soap. Even Margaret never had that. Peter rubs the soap over his sticky palms until the lanolin is scrubbed off, until his fingers no longer stick together. They all wash their hands except for Cecilia. He can't tell when she's washed last, but it's been a long time.

The lasagna steams on the table next to a pile of plates, napkins, and forks. The green Jell-O mold appears to contain fruit salad from a can. The red Jell-O mold is full of white things: coconut, miniature marshmallows, and pears. An institutional-size stainless-steel bowl of baby salad greens takes up the entire center of the table, the top sprinkled with sliced radishes, fresh herbs, spring flower blossoms. Peter begins with pie. He is the head shearer and owner of the flock which entitles him to do anything he damn well pleases. He heaps two large slices of rhubarb pie onto his daisy-printed paper plate and digs in with the white plastic fork. It is tart enough to pucker up the pope and that's the way he likes it.

"Great pie," he says to Shelley, who appears to be waiting for a comment from him. As soon as he speaks, she relaxes, lowers her shoulders, stops staring at his fork.

"Dig in," she says.

Cecilia eats the most. Shelley brings out the third lasagna and slices the fourth loaf of bread. Peter's been counting. He knows there's one more pie hidden in the bottom of the food crate but he doesn't mention it.

"Beautiful clip," Dora says. "Those kids did all right."

"Yes, they did." He sees Mary Jane looking his way. "Both of them did a fine job," he says loud enough to spread through the hut.

There isn't really enough room for everyone to be inside at once so they take turns coming in to get food and going out to eat it. Elaine is like a child at play. Her laugh becomes more like Dora's full belly laugh every day. She wears her child like one would a piece of clothing and they romp in the meadow like lambs. The ewes have brought their babies to the far end of the island away from the shearing party but a few lambs, curious about the newcomers, venture to the edge of the bush line.

"That the last pie?" he says to Shelley.

"Yup," she says.

"Thought there might be one more. Thought you said *four*."

"Peter, you're like a food-smelling dog, one of them bloodhounds," she says.

Peter brings his fourth piece of rhubarb pie out to the meadow in his hand. He and Elaine sit on a dry hillock, their backs to the hut and the beach while Peter finishes his pie. He wipes his hand on the grass.

"The newsletter in the outhouse. Thank you," he says.

"I'm so happy here. I've decided that I'm never going back to the city, or even some town. I've always hated living in Bedford. I'm a country person."

"I read the *Awake* magazine, too."

"You did? What did you think?"

"A bunch of crap," he says. "Total crap."

She laughs. "I'll leave some more. Read them and if you want to talk about them, I'd love to."

"I'll give that some thought," he says.

"Thank you for everything," she says. "Especially for leaving me alone. For letting me work out my thoughts without adding your two cents."

She sounds like she's leaving. *Thanks for everything and good-bye,* he thinks. "I've enjoyed the company," he says. Her old denim dress is hiked up above her knees and he sees that she has freckles on her legs. He's never noticed that before, even when she had shorts on. Their shoulders are almost touching. He kisses the top of her head, right at the place where her hair parts. It smells of rosemary from the shampoo she uses when she washes her hair in the sink. Her head leans on him and she begins to hum. Something familiar, he thinks.

Tender shepherd, tender shepherd
Watches over all her sheep
One say your pray'rs and two close your eyes and
Three safe and happily fall asleep.

"Do you know it?" she asks.

"Yes, I think so."

Tender shepherd, tender shepherd
You forgot to count your sheep

One in the meadow, two in the garden
Three in the nursery fast asleep.

"It's from *Peter Pan*," she says.

"Yes, I've heard it. But never as beautiful."

"I need to decide what to do."

"Yes."

"I know that I want us to remain friends. We can do that, can't we?"

"Yes," he says, but he isn't sure he believes it. What if she goes far away? What if he never sees Azelin again? What if she moves back in with that Oliver? "You can stay if you want. I can build onto the cabin." He can't believe he's said it. His eyes are closed and he imagines Elaine in his bed, a larger bed, sensing when she is ready to turn over and turning with her, sleeping with his arm draped over her shoulder, his penis pressed against her warm back. "Please stay."

"There's a lot to consider. My religion. I love my religion and need to go back to it. I want to talk to the elders."

"Just know that you have a place."

She kneels, adjusting Azelin's hat before she rises to her feet. The dress falls to her ankles, hiding the freckled legs. "Come on."

He's glad she's turned to join the others before he struggles to his feet. He's lost his ability to make believe it doesn't hurt. His hips and ankles are stiff for the first few steps. Shearing is a young person's job, he thinks. Maybe next year he'll have to find another shearer as good as Cecilia.

After they load the generator into Dora's boat, the rest goes quickly. They push the boats to the water line, which is closer now because the tide is full. Shelley has packed the few leftovers and food containers into baskets which Joshua tucks under seats. The wool bags are tossed into the empty skiff and shoved in the bow and under the gunwales. All twenty-nine bags fit into the old tub. Peter ties the painter onto the stern of his skiff. The magazine guys shove off first with much praise. The tall, skinny one says "Wow" one too many times while the pudgy guy rows better than Peter expects. Elaine sits in the middle seat with Azelin trussed into her flotation device while Peter pushes off. He wears big rubber boots and can wade out without getting wet. It's kind of tricky making sure the lines from the fleece boat don't get caught in the motor as he shoves off.

He pulls the starter cord. It catches the second time and they begin to *put* across to Dora's. It's midafternoon and there's a thick unexpected bank of fog that begins to obliterate the far shore. Nothing on the radio about fog. The air is suddenly cool on his bare arms and he reaches for his sweatshirt. In the distance he hears a larger motor coming out of the fog. Elaine faces full forward, an armful of royal blue, craning to see Dora's house. The other boats bob along behind them. It will be fine. There's never anything in this channel. Too narrow for most boats, big boats anyway. And besides, the lobsters haven't come in shore yet and the tourists are still in Philadelphia.

The drone of a far engine approaches through the fog bank. Loud voices yell above the din. Sounds like a bunch of drunks. Peter flicks on his flashlight and waves it at the noise but he knows it isn't dark enough for them to see it. He doesn't know which way to turn the motor, doesn't know where the boat attached to the loud engine is going to spring out of the fog.

CHAPTER 25

The lobster boat hits them before Peter has a chance even to register the sight of it. Hits them just off the bow of his small boat. He doesn't even have time to think about bracing himself, holding on to the gunwales, protecting Elaine or Azelin. The first thing Peter knows is the slap of the water against his face. The cold seeps through his clothes, fills his rubber boots, before he begins to move his arms and legs to keep afloat. Then he feels the strike of the fleece boat against his cheek and hears the noise of the lobster boat almost drowning out the small sound of his outboard. Elaine and Azelin must be still in the boat. The fog surrounds him like a down comforter, settles in around his face until his own hands, when he waves to show where he is, are all that he is able to see. The noise of the lobster boat engine hums in the water as he calls out, hums louder than his shouting can transcend. He treads water, feeling the weight of the sheep-shearing pants pulling on him.

"Elaine," he calls.

He hears the small motor of his skiff pass by at the right, feels the wake of the skiff pulling the sheep boat, then hears Elaine's voice. "Azelin," she says.

Azelin. Why is she calling Azelin? The baby isn't in the cold water.

No. The baby is not in the cold water. "Azelin," he says, first in one direction, then in the other. His clothes are soaked through and weighing him down. His arms and legs barely move against the cold water which laps at his mouth. The boots have got to come off. *When you fall in cold water, always take your boots off.* He tries to push off his heavy rubber boots with his feet, like he would on dry land, but they stick. He takes a breath and lowers his head down to his boots, struggles to pull them off with his stiff hands. It takes five dives before he finally pulls the waterlogged rubber boots from his frozen feet, allowing them to sink to the bottom. His mind tries to keep up with the noise of the boats and the yelling of Elaine but the cold fuzzes up his head. *Only one thing at a time.* His arms slip under the suspenders holding up his shearing pants and he thinks they will just drop off, float away from him. The baggy pants hug his wet body, making it almost impossible for him to kick his feet. He's got to get them off. He dives again and tugs the stiff material until the waist of the pants is down to his knees. Then his feet kick at the material until the pants are free from his body.

With his limbs free, he treads water, struggling to keep his face above the white chops. He sees nothing but gray water in all directions. Gray water that blends into gray fog.

The large engine cuts. Just stops as if someone turned it off. The outboard still hums in the distance, changing position back and forth. "Elaine," he calls out into the fog.

Voices emerge out of the haze. "Here, Peter, over here," and "I think I see him," and the last, the worst, Elaine's voice, "Azelin," long long long and high, like the moan of a seal. "Aaaazzeelin." Elaine must still be in the boat. But Azelin? Where the fuck is she? Peter kicks and swims in one direction, toward the *put put* of the outboard. The noise edges closer to him and he waves his arms. "Here, Elaine. Cut the engine. Cut the engine." A tiny infant, no matter how large the life preserver is, can't survive the whack of a propeller blade. "Cut the engine."

There is silence, suddenly. Beside him is Dora's boat. "Azelin," he says.

"I don't know," says Dora, her face monstrously misshapen, older than death.

"Elaine." He yells as loud as he is able from his position in the frigid salt water.

"Elaine," says Dora. "Elaine. Elaine." Loud. Shouted into the fog.

Then, Elaine's exquisite voice, haunting and terrified. "She's gone. She's in the water."

"Sing," Peter says. "Everyone sing and form a circle. Elaine, there's an oar under the seat. Sing and listen." A swell from the skiff slaps his face hard, sending salty water rushing into his nose and mouth. He coughs the water out of his chest. "Sing. That way you'll all know where everyone else is."

The singing begins from Dora. *"Well, it rained all night the day I left."*

From the left of him, *"The weather it was dry."* It is the new man, Joshua, singing strong. From the right, *"The sun so hot I froze to death, Susanna don't you cry."*

"Tighten the circle. Watch for the baby. Royal blue," he says. The sense of the boats surrounding him allows him to organize his mind, think about what to do, imagine what might happen.

"Oh Susanna, oh don't you cry for me, for I come from Alabama with my banjo on my knee."

"Stop," yells Dora. "Listen."

The boats are close, circled around Peter and a bobbing infant that no one can yet see. She's got to be here. "Come in closer, slowly, watch for her in the water." There is no baby sound. Peter swims back and forth within the circle of boats watching for a royal blue life jacket bobbing in the water.

"Everybody all right over there?"

"Yeah, looks like we might have hit somebody."

"Holy shit."

"I told you fuckers we'd get in trouble."

It's kids, Peter thinks. Goddamn kids drunk out in a boat. His legs no longer feel the cold and he forces them to kick.

"Get in the boat, Peter."

"Shut up," he says, paddling around and around within the circumference. Then he sees her. Only a few feet away. "Here she is," he yells at the fog. His arms and legs move in slow motion, pushing at the water, until his stiff hands reach out to the royal blue life jacket. Azelin is tucked securely inside, belts holding her upright in the frigid water of Stanley Strait.

Oh, please God, oh, please. The baby bobs away from his stiff fingers and for a moment he has lost her in the fog. He's afraid to find her, afraid to find a dead child, afraid to lose her. She reappears just behind the next wave, her hat gone, her fine curls now stuck in straight streaks to her head. His hand touches her face while the other hand lifts at the cold wet package. She doesn't cry. He pinches her cheek. She doesn't cry. Her skin feels like rubber when he wraps his fingers around the small arm sticking through the hole in the jacket. A rubber doll. A little rubber doll.

Joshua's boat lolls next to them now, four hands extended toward him for the baby.

"Pass her up," they say in unison like a choir. "Pass her up."

He can't let Elaine see her like this. Cold. Lifeless. His hair drips on Azelin's still face and she doesn't flinch. Her eyes are open, staring at his chest.

"Come on, pass her up here, Peter. Pass her up."

He feels a hand on his shoulder, grasping his collar. He has no choice, no choice at all. She is heavy, hard to lift past the surface of the water, but the hands grab for her life jacket and he pushes, pushes toward them, feels her leave his grasp. There are more hands for him.

They lift him into the boat. Peter's legs don't help at all and it takes too long, too much hauling, yelling, grasping for hands, kicking feet against the gunwales. "Azelin," he says. Joshua holds her. She is out of the life preserver but doesn't cry. She doesn't make any noise.

"She's dead. Oh, God, she isn't moving. Oh my God," Joshua says.

In the distance, Elaine paddles Peter's skiff and the towed fleece boat toward them. He hears her frantic questions. "Do you have her? Is she all right? Answer me."

The drunks on the lobster boat won't shut up. "What's going on? Anybody hurt? Sorry about that." And then laughter. Laughter.

"Oh, God," Elaine says. "I let her go. I just opened my arms and gave her to the ocean."

A cold body isn't dead until it is warm and dead. Warm and dead. Warm and dead. He falls onto the boat floor, yanking the wet clothes off his body. The shirt, socks, boots, shorts. "Give me some clothes," he says. Warm dry clothes. Mary Jane opens her pack and begins to rummage around. "Clothes. Off your back. Now." She pulls off her sweater.

"Oh, my God, the baby's dead," Joshua says again.

"Shut up and hold her. Talk to her. Get her wet clothes off. Hold her close to you. Hurry up."

Peter wriggles his bare wet skin into the wool sweater. Mary Jane continues to undress. Her socks. Her shirt. Until she is in underpants. The *dip dip* of the paddle nears. When Peter takes the baby from Joshua, she is naked, cold, blue-lipped. He shoves the beloved Azelin under the sweater, slap onto his bare chest. "More clothes," he says. Joshua pulls off his own windbreaker and helps Peter's arms into it, zips it up the front. Mary Jane shoves heavy wool socks onto his blue feet. Cecilia's boat pulls up alongside just as the fog begins to dissipate. Peter shifts in the seat, moves back and forth, breathes fast, holds the cold baby close to his skin. Cecilia throws her sweater over to Joshua who presses it against Peter's chest.

"Jesus, is it moving?"

"Hey, anyone hurt over there?"

"Peter, is she all right? She's moving isn't she? She has to be. She's been spared by Jehovah."

Peter sees her boat. She sits on the bow seat, digging at the salt water with her paddle, the fleece boat still in tow. "Come on, baby, warm up," he says down into the sweater.

Clothes come flying into the boat from Dora and even from the two *National Geographic* men. The drunks from the lobster boat toss down an old wool blanket full of moth holes stinking like stale beer. Soon almost every one around is half naked except for Peter and Azelin. Azelin, still cold in his arms, on his bare chest under the sweaters, makes no noise. Elaine's boat is at the gunwales now and Joshua grabs her painter and helps her into their boat.

"Keep low," he instructs.

She doesn't pull the baby from his chest, she slides her hands, warmed by her own belly, up under the sweaters to touch her child. She presses herself against Peter to help with the warmth. "My God, she's stone cold."

"Don't move her. Don't jerk. A cold body isn't dead until it's warm and dead."

Elaine breaths into the top of the sweaters, pushing the warm air from her lungs into the baby cocoon, her hands still touching the chilled quiet child.

"Please, God, let her breathe. Let her live," Peter says.

"Azelin, it's Mama," Elaine says into the sweaters.

"Here, help me take her out with the clothes around her. She's got to get breathing. You can keep exhaling warm breath around her."

Mary Jane and Joshua help pull the whole package of sweaters and blankets with Azelin at the core off Peter's chest. Peter lays her on a seat and tells Elaine to keep her body steady. He strains to remember infant CPR. *Are you okay?* The rescuer is supposed to ask the victim,

Are you okay? She isn't okay. She isn't breathing and her skin is blue. He pulls aside the sweaters to look at the skin on her chest and abdomen. Waxy. Mottled. She is like cold rubber. Shout for help. No point. Who does he shout to? He lowers his mouth to hers before he remembers the airway. *Tilt the head,* he remembers. His index finger looks large, out of place, on Azelin's chin but he tilts her stone-cold head back and listens for breathing. He leans toward her face, covers her wee mouth and nose with his sealed lips and puffs into her lungs twice. *Just a little, just a little.*

"Not dead until it's warm and dead," someone says.

"Her chest moved." It is Joshua's voice. Peter can't tell them that it is because he has breathed his own breath into her lungs.

He continues puffing into her, trying not to focus on the coldness of her face under his lips. One minute. He stops. His fingers rest on the flesh of her inner arm and he counts way past twenty before he thinks he feels a faint pulse. He breathes again, blotting out the quiet grieving of Elaine and the hushed speculations of the others. The mottled chest rises with his breath. He feels it against his beard. Again he checks for a pulse. The counting is interminable until he reaches twenty-two and he is sure this time.

"I have a pulse," he yells before he places his mouth on hers.

He's not sure how long he breathes for her before his lips feel the intake of air past them, just before he lowers them onto her face. Then the cool exhalation from her. He doesn't dare expect another breath, but it comes, and another. Small short breaths without his help.

"Don't stop," Elaine says. "Keep breathing for her."

"I don't need to. She's breathing."

"Hey, we called the cops. I can't tell you how sorry we are." The faceless voices emerge from the fog, shouting apologies. Apologies for what? Being drunk. Plowing the boat into their defenseless skiff?

"She's breathing on her own. Let's get her on my chest again. Slowly."

It's Joshua and Mary Jane who do the work, somehow maneuver her onto Peter's still bare chest, surround them both again with the sweaters and blankets.

Elaine shoves her hand up into the sweater, being careful not to jerk or move the baby. The cold baby slowly takes on his body temperature and once he thinks he detects movement. The rise and fall of her chest is barely detectable but he knows it's there. Enough movement to feel it on his chest. Through the dispersing fog, blue and red lights flash in Dora's driveway.

"Row," he says. "Row."

It takes under five minutes for the inexperienced Joshua to row to Dora's dock. Two men and a woman wait with a rolling stretcher, ambulance flashing red, police flashing blue.

"Elaine, you've got to take your hand out now," he says.

Joshua and Mary Jane steady him as he stands and grips the edge of the dock. He's done this hundreds of times but now he forgets how to move his limbs. The men on the dock rush forward and pull him up because he can't take his arms from Azelin. Azelin. Sarah. Nathaniel. And Leslie, Leslie. Why wasn't he with Leslie when she died?

"Not dead until she's warm and dead," he says. "Infant. Three weeks old. Hypothermia. I thought I felt some movement. She's barely breathing."

"Look, bud, we're going to take everything off at once, all the sweaters, and the baby. Just relax your limbs. Let us do the work." They are fast. They know what they're doing. Don't they? They don't seem to notice that some of the people are half naked. "The mother here?"

"Yes, right here."

"Get the baby in the ambulance. That's the best place to check her out."

Everything is fast. No time to think what to do. The police hand out blankets. The air is balmy but the fog has dampened the little clothing that people have left on. Peter can't see past the emergency workers.

He recognizes one of the men from the local town meeting. He thinks he is a doctor. He strains to hear some kind of baby noise, not necessarily crying but a whimper or something.

"Looks like a blown lung," the woman says. "Get the oxygen on her."

When he changes his position, he sees them place a clear mask over her face, soft like a pillow. They wrap her in what looks like tin foil. He can't see any movement. Blown lung? Did he do something wrong? Did he remember to blow just a little bit? Did he blow a cupful of air into something the size of a large grape?

"Look, fella, there's a helicopter on the way. They're coming from Eastern Maine and want directions to land in that field."

Peter takes the phone and barks out the location of Dora's pasture to the voice on the other end. The next twenty minutes fill with directions from the medical people and background murmurings from the sheep-shearing crew and prayers to Jehovah God. Prayers that plead and then demand.

The noise of the helicopter blots out any conversation. He feels the air from the chopper blades across his face until everything is silent.

"The mother can come in the copter," the man says.

"You guys got a fourteen-gauge needle? We got a blown lung here. Air in the pleura."

"Was it me? Did I do it?" he asks.

"Yes, bud, you did it. But you also got her breathing. We can fix the torn lining."

Until the helicopter leaves with Azelin and Elaine, Peter shivers in the background, trying to understand all the words that fly back and forth.

"We're going to Eastern Maine. You can get there in an hour and a half, driving fast," says the medic from the copter. "We're going to do everything we can. She's got a good chance."

Elaine looks like a frightened child climbing through the opening with help from the pilot. He tries to remember how much gas he has in the truck. The blades cause a whoosh of noise and wind and then it is hovering over Dora's pasture, turning toward Bangor.

"Dora, give me some clothes. Just something I can wear to the hospital. Quick."

She is quick. She flings a sweater, her garden overalls, T-shirt, flings them out to Peter. He steps into the pants on the way to the truck, shoves his arms into the T-shirt and sweater. There is silence in Dora's yard except for the start of the lobster boat engine. It's Brendan's boat. His kid driving it. The police will find him.

The truck bounces through the potholes in the driveway and turns out onto the main road. Azelin, Leslie, Sarah, Nathaniel. Did what he could. Did what he could.

The ring of the phone startles him, makes him swerve into the opposite lane.

Hello, he said.

Hi, darling, Leslie said. *Did you win?*

Hi, Les. Yes, I won.

I miss you.

I miss you, too.

Where'd you have supper?

I ate with Colin and went to bed early.

Oh, that's nice. See you soon. Love you.

See you soon. Love you.

He sees his hand gripping the receiver of the hotel phone. He turns away from it, silent now, finished with talking to Leslie, turns to someone warm in the bed. *Went to bed early, love you.*

Was that your wife?

Yes.

Who the fuck was that? Something he made up. He pulls the truck over to the side because he can't drive any more, not even to the hospital, not even to Elaine. *Love you. See you soon.*

Yes, it was my wife. He doesn't want to remember what happened after that. He doesn't want to remember that he slung his arm around her and fucked her again. He doesn't want to remember that he liked it, that he thought he might see her at the next games. Kate. Her skin, milky under his fingers, freckles covering her arms, dotting her breasts.

He was with her when the call came. *Is this Peter MacQueen? There's someone in the lobby who needs to speak with you. He will be right up.* Peter has always remembered that part. But not the part about jerking Kate out of the bed, throwing her clothes at her, telling her to hurry up and get out, that someone was coming up. *I'll call you later,* he says to her incessant questions. *Just go. Get out. I'll call you later.*

Peter taps his shirt pocket for a cigarette before he remembers he has Dora's sweater on and that Azelin is frozen. He opens the glove compartment. A new package of Luckies. He uses the cigarette lighter on the truck dash and inhales the first drag deep into his lungs.

Mr. MacQueen. It was a policeman in plainclothes with a social worker, he found out later. He can't remember if he got rid of Kate or not. She must have gone out the door. He never saw her again, just that one note after the funeral. No wonder the note was strange. *Mr. MacQueen, may we come in and sit down?* Only one chair in the room. Peter and the social worker sat on the bed, the smell of sex everywhere. *There's no easy way to tell someone this.*

He sobs into the steering wheel, the cigarette ash burning into his fingers. Kate? She was nothing. Nothing. "Leslie, she was nothing," he says aloud. No. Don't lie again. She was something. She was naked, in his bed, she kissed him. He kissed her back, everywhere, shoved his dick right up inside her. And liked it.

Azelin. He has to get to Azelin. His hands are wet from the crying, the steering wheel moist and slippery. "I'm sorry, Les," he says.

You've paid enough, Peter. It is his own brain talking to him. *Enough.*

She never knew of the lie. Did she? It was the first time he'd done anything like that. Would he have done it again? He doesn't know. He shakes his head, wondering where all the tears are coming from, how there could be any left to come out. "I was a different man then," he says. "Creative, joyful, dishonest." What the fuck did he want to be? He feels for a few minutes that he could choose what he wants to be. He can't imagine lying to Elaine. He can't imagine lying to Leslie. How the hell could he have said, *I ate with Colin and went to bed early.* That was a goddamn lie. The last words he said to her were goddamn lies. No. The last words. The very last words. *See you soon. Love you.* Those words were true. He did love her. He will always love her. But *see you soon.* He never saw her again alive. He saw her. Blackened, shrunken. Eyes exploded. Christ. He saw her sooner than he thought he would. And the children. He couldn't look at them. His dad held him up while he squeezed his eyelids shut, turned his blank face toward the small charred bodies, and nodded to the authorities. Police, maybe, or medical examiners. He told them he had a right to see his children. And then he couldn't look at them.

It was over. They were dead. His family wasn't in the dollhouse. They were only in his memories. Those stupid dolls were only that. Dolls. Children's dolls, for kids who are learning to become grownups. Azelin. She has to be alive. He turns the key in the ignition and it spews out loud, grating machine noises. He pulls out onto the highway and turns on his emergency flashing lights. This is an emergency. An emergency. He wipes his face with the back of his hand, gets the blur out of his eyes, presses down on the accelerator. The police car from Dora's passes him, turns on the blinking blue light, gestures out the window for Peter to follow.

C H A P T E R 2 6

They won't let him into the room. "Only the parents," the nurse says. "Are you a relative?"

"Yes," Peter says. "An uncle."

"Name please."

"Just say Uncle Peter."

"I'll tell the mother you're here."

He wishes he believed in God. Then it would be easy. "Put everything in Jehovah's hands," Elaine said last week. "God will take care of us if we let him." The metal seats lined up against the chartreuse wall feel cold even through his clothes. He is still wearing Mary Jane's wool socks, Dora's overalls, and someone else's boots.

The hospital smells evil but he doesn't like breathing through his mouth. At least if he breathes through his nose, the hairs filter out some of the contaminants if not the stink. Urine, cleaning fluids, vomit. Smells of the sick and dying.

On the floor around his chair, bits of grit, hay, garden dirt accumulate in piles and he feels foreign in the stinking sterile hall. His leg jiggles up and down. He can't stop unless he crosses his calf over his knee. More debris falls off the boot onto the pile on the floor.

"Peter MacQueen?" the nurse says.

He stands up so abruptly that he feels lightheaded, leans on the back of the chair.

"Yes. I'm Peter," he says, although he isn't positive that is true. It doesn't sound quite correct, maybe a lie.

"You may come in. Mrs. Sinclair is asking for you."

Mrs. Sinclair? Elaine. No one he knows uses Missus or Mister but this is a hospital, not the real world, not rural Maine, not Black Harbor. This is Bangor. Men and women in white suits and green pajamas scurry around and Peter thinks the baby must be dead. There is no crying. Only the sound of Elaine's voice.

We'll rock on the water
I'll cradle you deep

When she takes a breath, he hears the drone of the machines before her voice drowns it out again.

And hold you while angels
Sing you to sleep.

A clear tube snakes out from Azelin's nose toward the noisy machine. Her body is covered with a plastic canopy but he clearly sees the IV protruding from her scalp and another line attaching her chest to a high-pitched beeping device.

"She's sedated but the nurse said to sing if I wanted to. I think she hears me. Look," she says, pointing to the heart monitor's peaks and valleys, squiggly lines that wave up and down in rhythm to the plum-sized heart. "Look. They're strong and regular. They've got her on a respirator to help with breathing. They say the lung will heal itself."

Elaine continues the verses of the lullaby, soft and low by the crib. She nods to him as she sings, the silent language of someone who believes in God. The nurses and doctors give quiet orders to each other in a vernacular that Peter doesn't understand.

Will they stop him if he reaches out his hands to lift the still baby? If only he had fixed the wiring, at least taped those bare wires together to prevent the sparks, he'd have grandchildren. If only he'd refused to take the baby out in the boat. How stupid. He blew too hard. Blew a cupful of air into a thumb-sized lung and exploded the paper walls. Went out to dinner with Colin and went to bed early. He struggles to organize his thoughts but Leslie and Elaine and Nathaniel and Azelin and Sarah blend into each other so that he no longer knows their individual faces. Peter wants to believe in God. How do you get to believe? I believe. I believe. He repeats inside himself the words that will make him be able to pray.

Elaine brushes her fingers on his arm, on the side of his cheek, and the touched places sting from the heat of contact. Her face is not the face of a parent who has lost a child. He knows what those faces are like. He looked at his own face in the mirror, trying to find a sense of himself hidden behind a shroud of sadness for years after the fire. The woman, Elaine, has no shroud. He isn't sure if he has spoken to her but he knows his mouth will crack if he moves it. She must sense that because her finger draws a searing line toward the corner of his lip where the moisture freezes into rigid crystals and he feels her heat begin to thaw the ice. Her smooth skin traces the edge of his upper lip and around the lower before she speaks.

"Azelin," she says. "Saved twice."

"The lung," he says. His mouth says the words in slow motion, but finds that Elaine understands him. "Is the lung working?"

"They're watching her very closely. Her heart could stop. And they aren't sure about brain damage."

Peter searches the slight hump under the tinfoil blanket for proof of life, a foot kicking out or head rolling to one side. The stiff airway that they forced down into her lungs at the helicopter has been removed, replaced with the thin clear tubing. White, dots of pink on her cheek-bones. No blue.

"Come over to her," Elaine says.

The medical personnel come and go thinking about God knows what. Their date for dinner, their vacation plans, the infant tossed out of the seagoing skiff into the frigid brine. They swerve out of Peter's way as he nears the plexiglass crib. There is no skin except her face available to touch. It is all covered with blankets or tinfoil.

"Azelin?" Yes. It's Azelin.

"Azelin. You must live. You must. You see, I lost my own children and when I pray, God is going to listen to me, by God."

Elaine stands next to him, rests her hand on top of the blanket.

"You saved her, Peter. They said that your breath saved her."

"But I blew the lung."

"The lung is all right. You got her oxygen circulating."

Peter reaches around Elaine and pulls her to him. He knows she'll stay with him. Her hair smells like lily of the valley as he slides his palm down the length of it. She makes small lurches against his chest. She is crying, sags against him, trusts him to hold her. His eyes close as he breathes in the scent of her, holds her tight against him.

"I called Oliver," she says softly at his ear. "I had to. He's her father. He's coming. Be here soon."

"Elaine. You and Azelin. We'll build an addition, rig up a bathroom. Please. Please." He lowers his mouth down to Elaine's face, brushes his thawed lips on her ear, her chin, the corner of her smile, as close to her mouth as he can. His hands slide to Elaine's cheeks, cradle her delicate face and only then does he open his eyes. He kisses her closed eyelids, follows a lone tear down her face until he kisses her warm open mouth. He knew the inside of her would taste like summer flowers, like apple blossoms and lilacs, like white clover, like nectar of angels. He knows she will stay with him. There is plenty of space at the back of the cabin to build another room, even two if she likes, and a room for Azelin when she gets a little older. The heat of his body against her breasts, her shoulders, the thighs of her jeans, dampens his borrowed clothes where they touch each other. Peter gives himself to her, allows his stiff bones and muscle to melt into hers, turn soft. With one hand he touches the plexiglass of the cradle, to be a family, to be part of a family.

"I've been thinking about a new dog. Maybe even a puppy. Anything you like. Children should have dogs, don't you think?"

In the background, he hears the silent caregivers whispering long medical words, feels the brush of their uniforms when they pass. He holds Elaine and keeps his finger on the baby's bed, imagines the three of them, a family, related, the family that lives in the cabin, you know, the family that has the horse, Alice, and the goat, Ruby. *Remember? She came to him during the ice storm. They say she left her husband. Peter is the father now. My, oh my, isn't he a good father.*

He notices the absence of the high-pitched beeps just before the chirping alarm and his body stiffens.

"Code."

Hands push at him, push him away from the crib.

"Code."

The uniformed workers line the perimeter of the baby bed, no longer speaking in hushed tones but yelling orders. A green-pajamaed woman wheels a cart to the bed and the rest step aside.

Hands blur pulling out tubes, hooking up the new machine, pulling down the blankets. A man in teddy bear clothes breathes for her with a plastic football bag. Azelin lies still and white against the blue sheet like a birch against the sky of winter. The woman holds up two very small paddles with hearts painted on them.

"Charge."

"All clear." They step back in a chorus.

"Rhythm."

Azelin leaps from the blue for a second before she falls back down.

"Do we have a pulse?"

"Yes, we have a pulse."

"All right. Good."

They all know what to do. The man continues breathing with the plastic bag, the others watch the monitor, the woman with the paddles stands ready.

Peter hangs onto Elaine and leans against the outside wall of the room, hangs on to keep her away from the bed to give the nurses space.

"You'll have to step out into the hall," the woman in green pajamas says to them. Then, as if understanding their pain, she pats Elaine's arm. "It won't be long. This is an experienced team. I'll keep you informed."

Peter wants to stride up to the bed, part the hovering health professionals, force Azelin to keep breathing, but he did that before and blew a lung.

"What is happening? What the fuck is happening?"

"Come, Peter, let them do their job," Elaine says.

"The hell I will," he says.

A man from the hall steps in placing a firm hand on Peter's shoulder, turns it to steer him out of the room.

"No. I stay. And the mother stays. We won't be in the way. This is our child and we love her."

The medical team continues to work on Azelin, orders now calm, composed. "Let them stay," a man who stands at the head of the bed like God says in a quiet voice. "The child's heart is strong. We need to watch her very carefully for a few days, but I think she's going to pull through."

Peter realizes the man cares about Azelin, but doesn't even know her name. Cares about her because he cares for all children who are in danger of dying, not because he knows Azelin.

"Thank you," Peter says.

Elaine slumps against Peter. He strokes her hair and guides her to a metal chair by the door. She watches as the caregivers leave the bedside, one by one, until there is only the woman in the green pajamas, watching the monitor and the baby. As if pulled by a cord, Elaine moves toward the bed. Peter follows, steadying her. The round wet circles on her sweater grow larger as she stands at the side of the bed.

"Oh, Mrs. Sinclair. I'm sorry no one has attended you. Come, let me help you pump your breasts. They must be sore. When she's off the respirator, she'll want to nurse," the woman says.

"Will you stay with her?" Elaine asks him.

"Of course. Go," he says.

Another woman comes into the room to watch. Peter studies the machines, their bleeps and zigzaggy lines. They look even, rhythmical—heartbeats from a baby with a future.

"Your baby?"

"Well, yes, in a way."

The woman doesn't respond but smiles as if she knows what that means. Peter drags a heavy metal chair up to the side of the bed to watch. His eyes scrutinize the mound covered with tin foil attached to machines and bottles of liquid, waiting for movement, waiting for a sign. Azelin's face is hazy under the plastic hood but he notices her eyes blink and he leans forward to see better. Her mouth purses and sucks air, searching for something more substantial.

"We're easing off the sedative. She'll gradually become more alert, practice her sucking."

"Yes, baby, you practice, keep searching," he says.

"She's looking good," says the woman. "Her color's back already."

"She's going to live, isn't she?"

"Yes, I think so. It's in God's hands." the woman says. "It's a miracle she survived that frigid water."

"The mother is very religious," he says, matter-of-factly, as if that is the reason for the survival. "Do you pray?" he asks.

"What?"

"Pray, you know, to God."

"Sometimes, if I have a problem. Not down on my knees like the movies. It's just kind of a chat to a higher being." The woman fusses with the tin foil before she begins touching Azelin, touching her like a healer would. Her large hand envelops the baby's skull and stays longer than a casual touch, moves to grasp the small hands and the feet as if to impart her own warmth to the infant. Peter hesitates to interrupt and waits until the nurse turns to adjust the IV before he speaks.

"I don't believe in God but I feel like I ought to be doing something."

"Yeah, I know what you mean. Try talking to her."

"Who? Azelin?"

"Why not? She's the one who's sick."

The woman, maybe to give him privacy, fusses for a moment at the tubes and instruments before she turns toward the monitor and settles into watching, leaving him alone with the baby and his own meditation. The baby's head moves to the side and a limb juts out from underneath the foil, stretches her toes and he is now sure it is Azelin. She has the wee second toe, the one Elaine kisses.

"Spared by Jehovah. Come on then, live up to your name." Her black mass of hair, her father's hair, sticks to her head from the sweat.

"How about a song then?" He hums the old Gaelic song that Elaine sang the night she told him of her miscarriage. The words are just beyond his reach but the tune is there, like thousands of tunes in his head. Like laments, retreats, marches, lullabies, piobaireachds. "Did you like that? When you are a little older, we'll go for a ride behind old Alice in the cart. This summer, maybe. Mama will hold you on her lap and we'll ride around the old wood's roads." That's the first time he has thought of Elaine as *Mama*, and for some reason the thought is frightening. "And the old dog died, you know, the one Mama calls *Seamus*." He leans forward, his arms on the bed, hands touching the foil. "We're going to get another dog. A puppy, I think. Would you like a puppy?" Yes. She looks at his mouth, listens to his words. It's getting through.

Better than praying to God. The machine blips continue, regular peaks and valleys, light beams dancing on the screen.

Peter reaches out and touches the tip of the tiny toe, imagines Elaine's lips there.

Elaine's voice permeates the silence, disturbs the cadence of the heart monitor. "She's got good color and they're cutting down on the sedatives," she says.

"What in God's name were you doing with her out on the ocean in a boat? She's not even a month old," Oliver says from just outside the room.

"It was an accident," she says. "A terrible, terrible accident."

CHAPTER 27

*P*eter tries to make himself small in the baby's alcove so he can't hear them talking but he's not willing to leave the room. He drags the metal chair back over to the wall, leaving the area in front of Azelin's bed open. He picks up an old *People* magazine, holds it too close to his face to read, and turns his body away from them toward the chartreuse wall. They, Elaine and Oliver, hold hands and utter words Peter cannot understand. He thinks they are praying to Jehovah. He tries not to stare at their hands. His position makes it difficult but he peeks through the crook of his arm. Their hands hold each other loosely, his brown fingers caress the white skin of her knuckles, follow the blue of her veins, the pulse of her heart, and Peter curls his body tighter, turns until he cannot possibly see.

The voices continue just loud enough for Peter to catch a few words; "God," "heal," "obey." He wishes Elaine would sing to Azelin instead of mumble incantations to invisible beings. It is almost morning and time for singing, like the thrushes, the warblers. Morning is a time for singing.

He reminds himself to be patient with her, allow her time to work through her relationship with Oliver. After all, Oliver is the father and has a right to be concerned.

Light from the narrow window creeps into the hospital room. Peter sees Oliver pass a small black book fastened by a silver lock to Elaine. He sees her accept it, tuck it into her bag, hears her say "Thank you." As if receiving a signal from the rising sun, Elaine's voice sings softly, *"Bheir me o, horo van-oh, Bheir me o, horo van-ee, Bheir me o, o hooro ho,"* as Oliver advances toward the isolette. Peter wishes she would stop singing because Oliver is listening. He wonders how many times Oliver has heard her sing that song.

Oliver bends toward the baby. Peter leans forward to watch. Elaine ceases her song.

"Her toe," he says. "Elaine, she has the same toe as mine. My toe."

Peter turns away, back to the *People* magazine, something about the Academy Awards. He doesn't want to see any more but can't get himself to leave the room. Oliver nods to Peter when he leaves the baby's side. No smile. He thinks of the riding crop in Elaine's mother's closet and thinks that there might be one in Oliver's closet, too. They will have to bring in the police if Oliver causes problems, get a court order to keep him away. He knows a lawyer in town who handles separations and divorces.

"I'll be back at two with Brother Eldridge. We'll talk then. We can work this out," he says to Elaine before he disappears through the main room and walks straight down the hall with no observable limp.

Peter struggles to remember which of Oliver's legs she shot. "Let's go and get some breakfast. Coffee, anyway," Peter says.

"Go ahead," the nurse says. "Azelin's coming along just fine. Go. Get something to eat. You'll need it for your milk."

There is no sign of Oliver in the hall as they head toward the cafeteria. The smells of urine and vomit and pine cleaner combine in a repugnant stink which follows them down the elevator and hovers over them as they stand in line for bagels and coffee. Elaine orders tea but changes her mind at the last minute and asks for coffee. They sit over in the corner away from the chatter of medical people and worried relatives. Stares follow them until Peter stares back, hard. It's because of their borrowed clothes or maybe their age difference or Elaine's ivory hair. Peter doesn't belong here with people in dress shoes and suits and mainstream American ethics. He misses Alice and Ruby. Most of all, he misses the old dog.

"Will Cecilia feed the animals this morning too?" Elaine asks.

"She's going to stay there until I get back. Nice of her."

"Yes."

"I've got a friend, a lawyer. Well, she's not really a friend but she did some work for me a couple of years ago. She handles divorce cases. And separations. Do you think we should call her?"

"I'm so confused." Her milk-white hands slide across the red-checked plastic tablecloth, opening toward him. His hands are too rough for hers but he places them on her palms like an offering. "I've been happy with you. I'll always be grateful."

"I don't want gratitude. I want you and Azelin. You belong at the cabin. You are part of my life. My family."

"We're going to talk this afternoon. We have to talk alone. Oliver, the elder, and me."

"You'll talk about the fist? The bruise?"

"Everything."

"I suppose he's entitled to see the baby."

"Peter, I cherish what we've been to each other. I don't know what will happen. I've got to throw my troubles to Jehovah. I know you don't believe in all that but I do. Do you understand that?"

"Yes," he says, although he isn't sure he's telling the truth.

"I'm not going back to Bedford. I never wanted to live there but was afraid to speak up. This time I will. Goats, a garden. That's what I want."

"The puppy. What kind should we get? All the children need a dog."

"Wait. Please wait until after our talk. I've got to trust in God and in myself."

"What the fuck does God know about us?" He sips too fast. His tongue and throat burn from the heat of the black coffee.

"He knows. He will tell me what I need to do."

"I love you. I haven't said that word in many years. I didn't think I would ever say it again."

"I know you do. I feel it. And I know you love Azelin, too. We have something that few couples have. Respect. Love. Friendship. I'll always treasure that."

Peter knows he is squeezing her hands too tight. He eases off, relaxes, fights back the rising anger at her God and her louse of a husband. "Please. Please don't go back to him. Azelin needs a father. I can be her father."

"You will always be part of her life. You've got to trust me. I need to go in the direction God guides me."

"The puppy. The addition. The pipes. My old friends. What about them? I can't do those things without you."

Her laugh is like the song of spring birds. "Don't be silly," she says. "You can do anything." She pulls her hand away to take a bite of the cold bagel and sip her hot coffee. "I've got to do what I think is right for Azelin and me and you and Oliver, and I don't know what that is yet."

"I know. I have to go home to check on things. I'll be back tonight. Call Dora if there's any change. She can drive over and tell me." He kisses the back of her milky hand, follows the veins to the platinum band around her finger. "Don't let him call you names. Please don't let him hurt you," he says.

He smokes three Luckies on the way back to the cabin. The smell of the smoke makes him nauseated until he pulls over to open the window on the passenger side. Traffic is sparse in the early hour and he makes it home before eight thirty.

"You make out all right?" he asks Cecilia in the barnyard.

"Fine. Slept like a log. How's the baby?"

"Coming along. I think they'll release her in a couple of days. Her heart stopped once. That happens in infant hypothermia. That's why they have to keep a close eye on her. They're easing her off sedatives and the respirator today."

"Christ, that was crazy out there. The damn drunks. The cops took them off. Boat belonged to the father of one of the kids. The dad was ballistic over the whole thing."

"How's the clip look?"

"Beautiful. The best ever. I gave my bill to Dora. We're scheduled to shear Gooseberry Isle day after tomorrow. Is that still on?"

"Yes. For now, anyway. Come on in. I'll make some coffee," he says.

"Too late. There's a pot on the stove. Just need to heat it up."

Peter watches her prance up the steps to the cabin. Like a giant. Arms big enough to hug a sheep. Skin even darker on her arms than the rest of her. Ugly mug of a face. If it weren't for the scar running down from her ear to her chin, she'd be tolerable. But she's the first person he's invited into his cabin in over twenty years.

"Alice is some wicked nasty," she says, opening the door. "Kicked her blooming stall at six this morning. I thought the end of the world was coming." The smell of coffee fills the cabin and cinnamon buns spill from an open Dunkin' Donuts box on the table. "Made them myself," she says, laughing. She slides him one, scattering icing and crumbs over the entire top of the table. He pours coffee into two mugs.

"Take anything in your coffee?"

"Nope. That white stuff ruins the taste."

"You're a helluva cook. Where'd you get the recipe?"

"Up to Tuttle's Store. They buy 'em from the doughnut place in

Ellsworth. I eat them every morning. Had some in the car. Say, do you play them doodlezaks? That's German for bagpipes. Read it in a joke somewhere."

"Just started playing again. I used to play a lot."

"I'd love to hear you. Them bands play at the Eastport Fourth of July parade every year. Five or six bands from all over. Canada, Ellsworth, just everywhere. I always cheer loud when I see them coming."

Cecilia's face is large, like a frying pan. Her ears look like someone stuck them on as an afterthought. But her eyes are kind and her voice is lusty. He's never noticed that before and she's been shearing with him for at least five years.

"Love the dollhouse. You play with that?" she asks.

"It's mine. It was my daughter's. I don't really play with it. What do you do after shearing?"

"Gardens. I work for other folks and tend my own after that. They got me designing flower beds and planting vegetables. Just about everything that grows in dirt. Notice you got a nice garden started."

"Yep. Thanks for helping me out. I'm all set now. Going back tonight but I can do chores myself."

"Sure. It was fun. I've been thinking about getting a goat. My Da used to have one. She followed me all over. That's where I learned to milk. He kicked her around so much, she got some internal bleeding and died. We had to eat her. Shit. That made me gag. Eating my own pet like that."

"Maybe you'll come for supper some night. Elaine and the baby should be back in a couple of days. It would be fun. I'll call you."

"Sure. She seems like a nice lady. Never saw such white skin and that hair is something else. Seems kind of frail but she certainly got into the work on the island."

"She loves the garden and the goats. She's stronger than she looks."

"She your woman? Your baby?"

"It's a long story. Good story for supper conversation."

"Sure. It's always a long story. So you gonna invite me over so's I can hear it?"

"I'll call you."

"I gotta be at Wyman's by ten. Planting some roses today. I told them they'd never make it through these Maine winters. Told them to plant Rugosas. But, no, they want new fandangled hybrids. It's their money."

"I make some mean doughnuts myself. Bear grease. It's the best for deep frying. You could give me your recipe and I'll make them. You could come over for breakfast. Elaine makes good coffee."

"Sure."

"Thanks again," he says as she grabs the remaining cinnamon buns, tosses him one, and barrel-asses through the door.

The rest of the day is like a slow motion movie. He weeds the lettuce, plants a few peppers and eggplant, takes Dizzy for a walk through the woods to the Underwood house, picks up his chanter about seven times, puts it down about seven times without playing it. The clock seems to hover around two for a long time before it resumes its ticking and he wonders about the meeting.

Don't let him call you bad names. Don't let him use the riding crop. The image of his fair Elaine, flinching from the lashes of her mother's crop on her bare white legs. He imagines welts on her thighs, her calves, her feet. If Oliver hurts her, Peter will punch his mouth until there are no teeth left.

He dumps the evening milk because the cans are full from the previous milkings. He forgets to collect the eggs and remembers on the highway halfway back to Bangor. They'll probably still be all right tomorrow. It hasn't been very hot. The radio has nothing but news and top forty. News. People killing other people. He turns the dial to the top forty before he lights a cigarette. He's going to try to quit again. Maybe try that patch Brendan told him about. But he loves his Luckies.

He pats his shirt pocket, feels comforted by the feel of the full package against his palm.

Apple blossoms fall like weightless hail as he passes the large orchard on the left side of Route 1. The ground is covered with petals, soft and fragrant like snowflakes that decompose into the grass, enrich the soil underneath. He breathes deep to fill his lungs with the scent of blossoms, to save it up for the hospital corridor, to push away the smell of sickness and death. Lilac flower buds swell on hedges along the highway, any spot that ever supported a farmhouse. Purple, mauve, white cover the bushes that will soon take over the blooming from the apple blossoms.

The news at six interrupts the tail end of the number three song on the hit parade just as he enters Bangor city limits. Frost tonight. "Cover all your tender plants," the voice on the radio says, as if that included the entire state of Maine. Should be the last frost of the year. His cabin on the small knoll in Black Harbor rarely gets hit by frost after the middle of May, especially at the side of the barn where the peppers and eggplant grow. He even has some apricots on the tree this year, first ever. Had something to do with the ice storm, Dora said. The worse the winter, the more chance of having apricots, as long as we didn't get a late frost.

He pats his jeans pocket to make sure the bank book is still there. If Elaine doesn't have insurance, the fire account has plenty to pay for Azelin. He hasn't touched the money and according to bank statements, it has grown steadily over the years. Stuart Smoke Alarm Systems had paid without any court action, just stepped up and volunteered. "Out-of-court settlement," they called it. There was some talk about malfunctioning alarms. The whole thing was a little vague. His mother said they were trying to save their skins, so he took the money, shoved it into the bank. "For your children?" the teller had asked. He wanted to say *In exchange for my children,* but he didn't respond at all. Why else would a young man deposit so much money in a long-term account? Old age? Children's college? Calamity?

The hospital looks the same as it did that morning. He parks the truck near the entrance and steps into a puddle created by an afternoon shower. The nurses nod as he walks past the station as if he had been coming here for years. The hush of the morning is replaced by the clanging of dinner trays and silverware and the blasting of dissonant television sets. From the main intensive care room, he sees that the bed is empty, the IV stand gone, the heart monitor dark. Around the corner, nestled in a rocking chair, sits Elaine, her breast in Azelin's mouth.

"Look. She's nursing. Strong, too."

"Can you come home now?" he asks.

"They want to keep her a couple more nights, just to check everything, make sure she is back in balance."

Peter pretends the rocking chair is painted green with a white pillow hand-crocheted by his mother on the seat. He pretends, as he drags the metal chair toward her, that it is his red high-back chair and that underneath them is that root cellar, shelves lined with pickle jars and jam. He can't ask about the meeting. He can't. He waits.

"Peter," she says, rocking gently. She fingers Azelin's feet, strokes her long toes, hesitates at the short one. "I'm going back with Oliver."

"No. I can't."

"What?"

"I can't."

"You can't what?"

"I can't stand it."

"We had a good talk. I was wrong, too. Wrong to lie about the blood. We've both been dishonest with each other. We want to try it for Azelin. Brother Eldridge and the other elders will help with counseling. Both of us need to work at it. He's a good man, Peter. He admits he's been unfair, hasn't listened to me, but I've lied to him. We're both at fault. We're going to work on it."

"No," he says into his hands, down into his lap.

"Oliver agreed to move to the country. The other side of Bangor. A place where I can have sheep and a garden. He won't hurt me. He won't hurt the baby."

He can't look at her but he watches her white ankle moving with each rock of the chair. "The riding crop," he says.

"What?"

"The riding crop." That's all he can say. It makes no sense.

"That's my mother. She had the riding crop. Not Oliver. Oliver doesn't have a riding crop."

"I'll miss you," he says. "I'll miss you both." He can't lift his head. He tries but it seems stuck to the palms of his hands.

Azelin's Lullaby

For Elaine, May 28

C H A P T E R   2 8

The brush mound flames up each time Peter throws on a new branch, mostly birch branches, because the birches received major damage in the ice storm. They bent to the frozen ground and stayed that way even when the ice melted, as if their tips were glued to the earth. A few of the younger ones unfurled themselves. Broken branches littered the yard and edges of the pasture and it has taken almost a week to collect them in a pile. Alice pulled some in the wagon but most had to be dragged by hand over rocks and through gates.

The flames crackle after he throws on a fir bough which broke from the old tree by the barn. He thinks about the dog when he resumes with the birch, some chunks just right for *Get the wood.*

He barely hears the car enter the yard because of the popping of the fire. It is Elaine, come to remove the things accumulated during her stay with him. Baby furniture, diapers, clothes, her drop spindle and fleece, the ripped denim dress. Oliver waits in the car while she comes in with the baby. She kisses Peter on the cheek when he gives her the box containing the new spinning wheel he's bought for her. "For old times' sake," he says. "I'll help you out with it." When he asks to hold

Azelin, Elaine smiles and passes her over, the rosebud mouth spitting drool down her chin.

They say their good-byes in the cabin before they go out, an embrace unlike the last one, an embrace with an imaginary sheet of plywood between them. He pats her shoulder, kisses her hair, breathes in the smell of Azelin's mouth.

"Good-bye," he says.

"Good-bye. Thank you."

They don't say they'll see each other again soon, but Peter knows that they will. He has to let her go. He wants her to be happy and maybe she can be. The image of the riding crop fades a bit when she describes the small farmhouse near Waterville that Oliver has agreed to look at. The urge to pull out the plywood, press her body into his, almost over-powers him but he pats her hair again and kisses Azelin's forehead.

"Be happy," he says.

"Yes," she says. And they go out to the waiting car carrying the spin-ning wheel and the baby. Peter and Oliver don't speak, even when Peter opens the car door to jockey the box onto the floor or when he helps settle Azelin into her car seat. They nod politely like courtly adversaries. Elaine breaks away to go to Dizzy while Peter stands by the car holding the open door. He notices that Mr. Oliver Sinclair wears sneakers.

He doesn't wait until they are out of sight but busies himself in the barn, shoveling goatshit from the stall floor into the wagon. When the noise of the engine is gone, he plods back to the cabin, leaving the pitchfork sticking up from the smelly load on the wagon bed. The crab-apple by the landing drops petals onto the walkway like a flower girl and the smell of the blossoms mingles with the opening lilacs on the other side of the steps. The heady fragrance makes him dizzy and he holds the railing until the feeling passes. On the way into the cabin, he breaks off a few branches of lilacs and one of the flowering crab to put on the table. He'll use that old glass milkbottle of his mother's.

He plucks the stainless-steel pail off the nail in the wall. *It's a little early to milk,* he thinks. He slips off his sweatshirt because the evening air feels balmy. The noise of the peepers fills the air around the cabin as he heads toward the barn. He'll milk before he goes back to the brush pile.

"Come on, Ruby," he says.

Ruby trots up to the gate and follows the pail into the milking stanchion. She loves her sweet feed and gobbles it quickly. Peter pulls up the three-legged stool close to her flank and positions the pail under her. The warmth from her teats loosens his stiff joints. The first squirts go onto the floor behind her. The next hit the side of the pail and drip down to the bottom. The rhythm is easy, fluid, as he squeezes the white frothy milk into the pail. He touches his forehead on her flank close enough that he hears gurgles from her stomach as he milks. The sound of the streams hitting the pail become less metallic and more melodious as the pail fills. After he strips the teats and removes the bucket, he leads her back into the paddock with Dizzy who's glad to see her and sucks at the empty teats, back and forth, the sound of the sucking over-powering even the music of the peepers.

Back in the cabin, he pours the steaming white milk through the filter into the clean milk pail and lowers it into the cellar through the trap door. The cabin looks bare without diapers hanging from nails and Elaine's clothes piled next to her bed.

When he checks the brushfire again, the flames have died down to smoking embers but ignite as soon as he throws on more birch. The white bark peels and blackens before flame tongues lick at the paper white shreds, devour them in a poof. He piles more brush on the heap, throwing logs thick enough for the woodstove off to the right. The heart of the fire glows blue-red and if the sun weren't beginning to set, he would try to burn the entire pile. Then, as if the idea just occurred to him, as if he hadn't considered it before, Peter reels away from the fire toward the cabin.

The dollhouse sticks to the shelf when he pries it with his fingers. He locates a screwdriver in the junk drawer and shoves the tip into the crack between the shelf and the bottom of the house. He pries all along the shelf until the house is free. It has been many years since he placed it in that spot and some of the shelf paint has adhered to the bottom of the dollhouse. It is much heavier than it looks and he struggles to keep it level on his way over to the kitchen table. The light is better there.

They are in the living room. Leslie stands by the kitchen door, coffee cup in her hand, and the children sit together on the couch. Sarah's leg is slung over the arm and Nathaniel's feet are propped on the table, one sneaker still missing. Peter goes back to the junk drawer and empties the contents on the counter. An item at a time, he brushes them back into the drawer until he finds the sneaker. It is the size of Azelin's toe and light as cattail down. He works the boydoll's left foot into the sneaker until it seats itself.

He pulls the girldoll's leg down off the arm of the couch and stands back. They were lovely. His children were the most beautiful children. The Leslie-doll's coffee cup falls to the floor as he touches it. He brings the doll to him and holds it up to his face, just holds it there, doesn't talk or cry or anything like that. Before he places it in the bed, he smooths his side and turns back the covers. He's lost the nightgown so it will have to go to bed in street clothes. He curls the doll's legs up and lays it on its side. That's the way the real Leslie always slept, too.

Carrying it out the door of the cabin is awkward but he turns sideways and squeaks by the jamb. The flames ask for the house, shoot out toward it as Peter stands by the pile. It flies easily from his hands into the center of the flames. They're only dolls. He believes that. This is only a dollhouse full of furniture and dolls, a dollhouse that has outlived its usefulness. "I ate with Colin and went to bed early, see you soon. Love you," he says aloud.

Although the sky darkens, Peter remains by the fire until the embers merely glow red. He sprinkles fallen blossoms onto the hot ashes and they sizzle when they land. Tomorrow he'll put everything in the new compost behind the barn. He could use more phosphorus in the garden. The full moon rises, crisping the air, and he wishes he had his sweatshirt on. He wonders if they might indeed have a frost. It takes him half an hour to prop up a makeshift greenhouse around the peppers, tomatoes, and eggplants before he goes in.

He finishes off the rest of the Oreos with a glass of Ruby's milk after he lights the lamps and tidies up the sink. The empty spot on the shelf glares out for filling so he brings some of the books down from a higher shelf; Eliot's early poems, Emily Dickinson's *Complete Works,* a first edition Allen Ginsberg. From the trunk, he removes a stack of music that fills the remaining space. Leslie's flute clatters to the bottom of the trunk. He wraps it in the blue towel to keep it from denting. He's been playing his pipes almost every day now and they sound solid, melodic. The drones tune beautifully and he appreciates the new Gore-Tex bag. Now he blows warm air through the blowpipe until the reeds almost sound and strikes the side of the bag with his hand, bringing in the drones. He barely has to tune them, only a slight adjustment to the bass. He plays his tuning phrase a few times until all the reeds sound aligned and begins the tune. "Lament for the Children," piobaireachd by Patrick Mor MacCrimmon. The sound bounces off the cabin walls. The tune is too fast. He slows it down, backs off just a bit, tries to see the children, feel the lament. He slips into all the variations; variation one, variation two, the taorluath, doubling, crunluath, doubling, and only fumbles once during the crunluath variation. His mouth aches and he moves his lips to stop the cramping.

By the time he finishes, the sky is lit only by the full moon and the faint glow from the fire. The cabin is dark. He fumbles with the matches to light the lamp on the table. He doesn't have to look far for the music. The glow of the wick reflects on a sheet of paper stuck under a pile of books. He pulls it out. *"Azelin's Lullaby," For Elaine, May 28.* He's never played it on the pipes, or the chanter, only sung it that one time. Pio-

baireachd for a baby. The first E sounds high, like Elaine's voice. Piobaireachd can find the soul, seek it out, dig for it, crack open any shield.
The drones keep the chanter grounded, prevent the note from taking
off into the universe, from leaping toward God. The drones, steady and
low, allow a mere human the privilege of seeing the heavens.

The variations build and build on the ground until he reaches the
final doubling, until he can barely blow another note. "Azelin's Lullaby."
He wonders how Colin will like it. "Azelin's Lullaby," by Peter
MacQueen.

When he is finished, he carefully pulls the blowpipe out of the stock
and places the protector over the soaking reed. He blows out the lamp.
It is quiet. He misses the sounds of Elaine and Azelin stirring and the
old dog shifting position. He pulls off his boots and socks, tossing them
into the corner. His T-shirt, damp from the night air and from playing
so long, follows. He unsnaps his jeans, allowing them to fall to his ankles.
He steps out of them and walks toward his old bed. A slant of light
from the moon falls on the floor by his bare feet.

When he pulls the covers down, he smells her and it is difficult.
After he lowers himself onto the mattress and pulls the blanket over his
body, he closes his eyes, imagines her lying on the sheets. His hand finds
a comfortable place over his genitals. In the dark of his mind he listens
to the cabin and hears his own heartbeat, the pulse in his chest, in his
groin, in his head. He hears a cabin full of sound. He hears the tune of
the piobaireachd, the staccato of breaking ice, the song of thrushes, the
rhythm of thaw, the beat of his soul. He hears the steady exhalation of
his warm breath in four-four time until he loses track of even the cadence
of his own heart.

A CERTAIN SLANT OF LIGHT
CYNTHIA THAYER

Discussion Questions:

1. What kind of role does religion play in the novel? What about faith, in any form? How has the characters' faith and religion changed over the course of the story? Is there one message to be gained about faith or religion from the novel?

2. Compare and contrast the images of pregnancy and birth with those of aging and death in the novel. How does the author use such images to tell or enhance her narrative?

3. How important to the story is the novel's setting: the landscape, the weather, the wilderness, the water? How does the author make use of these physical details?

4. What is the role of music and song in the book?

5. What is the nature of guilt and responsibility, according to Peter? According to Elaine? Should either of them feel responsibility for their personal tragedies?

6. Peter has held onto his daughter's dollhouse as an embodiment of his grief over the fire. What role do such objects play in the cycle of grieving and healing, in the novel and in life? Was his decision to burn the dollhouse a method of moving on, or a form of celebration? Does his grieving seem self-indulgent? Healthy? Understandable?

7. Discuss the role of fate in Peter and Elaine's lives, before their meeting and after.

8. If you were the author of *A Certain Slant of Light*, would you change the end of the novel in any way?

9. Why do you think Elaine makes the decision that she does about her marriage?

Also look for other reading group guides, including
Strong for Potatoes by Cynthia Thayer, at www.stmartins.com

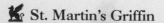 St. Martin's Griffin